Dark Hunter's Prey

THE CHILDREN OF THE GODS
BOOK FIFTY-SEVEN

I. T. LUCAS

Published by Evening Star Press

EveningStarPress.com

ISBN-13: 978-1-957139-08-1

Orion

❦

"**D**on't worry." Alena put her hand on Orion's cheek. "Kian is not going to pull the big brother routine on you." She smiled. "He can't because I'm older, but he's no doubt going to warn you again to keep me safe, or else."

"Your brother doesn't intimidate me." He planted a chaste kiss on her cheek. "Enjoy your shopping spree with Amanda, and don't worry about me. I'll be fine."

Alena needed new clothes for their trip to Lugu Lake, and Amanda had insisted on accompanying her and providing stylistic expertise.

"I'd rather spend more time with you." Alena wound her arms around his neck and pulled him down for a proper kiss.

They were standing in front of the office building in full view of everyone who cared to look their way, especially

Kian, whose office windows faced the village square, but if Alena wanted a kiss, Orion wasn't going to deny her.

They'd spent another incredible night of passion together, and parting ways was doing unexpected things to his gut, but maybe his unease had more to do with the journal tucked inside his pocket than being separated from Alena for a few hours.

When her phone rang, she reluctantly let go of him. "I'd better go. Amanda is waiting for me in the parking garage."

"Have fun."

"You too." She smiled before pivoting on her heel and heading toward the glass pavilion.

As he watched her walk away from him, he tried to focus on the gentle sway of her hips, the casual confidence of her gait, the thick blond braid swinging from side to side with each step, and not on the tightening sensation in his chest that grew worse along with the distance between them.

Alena was spectacular, and for some reason, she found him worthy as a potential mate. Hopefully, their trip to China would solidify her decision and not weaken it. They'd known each other for all of four days, and thinking about forever was premature, but he couldn't help it. He was consumed by her, utterly enamored and helpless to resist.

Orion patted the pocket containing his father's journal, unease churning in his gut. He hadn't expected it to be so difficult to hand it over, and he had to remind himself that he was doing it for Alena.

The journal was a bribe, a show of goodwill that had convinced Kian to let him accompany his sister to China.

Besides, Orion wasn't giving the original up, only a copy of it. The journal traveled with him wherever he went, safely tucked away in his carry-on luggage, but the truth was that he should have made a copy years ago and kept the original in a safe.

Perhaps it hadn't occurred to him before because theft hadn't been a consideration. After all, the journal wasn't valuable to anyone but him. Still, he should have considered that accidents happen, and it could get damaged or lost.

Since stealing it from the god nearly four decades ago, Orion had only parted with it once when he'd given it to a linguist to translate.

Back then though, separation anxiety hadn't been an issue because he hadn't formed an attachment to the manuscript yet. In the beginning, it had only been a means to an end, providing him with clues about Toven's lovers, which in turn could potentially lead him to discover more of Toven's children.

In time, however, the journal had become so much more to him.

Looking at his father's sketches and neat handwriting, he felt grounded, connected to the god—the father whom he'd only gotten to know through those handwritten pages—a father who didn't want anything to do with him.

Orion wished things could have been different between them, but all he had of his father was the damn journal, and despite the resentment he felt for having been so rudely and unequivocally dismissed, it was important to him.

It had provided solace when things spiraled out of control, the way they had after Geraldine's near-fatal accident, and it kept the ennui at bay when life felt pointless and everything seemed meaningless.

Flipping through the pages, looking at the lovingly sketched portraits of his father's beautiful lovers, Orion would imagine the kind of children those women might have brought into the world—half-brothers and sisters to him and Geraldine with whom he could connect. And sometimes, he would pick up the journal to remind himself not to become like his father—an emotionally-bankrupt empty shell.

Although given how meticulously Toven had been recording details about his former lovers, or at least those who'd left an impression on him, immortalizing them in his journals, the guy wasn't as dead on the inside as he'd wanted Orion to believe he was.

The jerk had claimed to have lost the ability to care about anyone and anything, but those lovely drawings and poetic descriptions belied the stony cold manner in which the god had treated Orion.

It made the rejection worse.

A lifeless sociopath couldn't have filled pages upon pages of numerous journals with portraits of beautiful young women, capturing with his pencil their unique characters as well as their outer beauty.

Perhaps Toven had a preference for the company of females?

Orion could understand if the god had grown disillusioned with the males of all species—human, immortal, and god alike—but still retained some fondness for the females. If Toven's gripe with the various sentient inhabitants of the earth was their bloodthirstiness and cruelty, then females were far less prone to these afflictions than males.

Would his father have reacted differently if he'd encountered Geraldine on a Parisian street instead of him?

Perhaps the god wouldn't have dismissed a daughter. Perhaps he wouldn't have told her to get lost and that he never wanted to see her again.

But Toven hadn't known about Geraldine. The god had been convinced that he was infertile, and coming face to face with his doppelgänger had been a shocker.

Maybe later, he'd regretted throwing Orion out? Or maybe Toven was so consumed with self-loathing that he couldn't stand the sight of a son who looked exactly like him?

What if his father had come to regret not knowing whether he had any other offspring?

According to Alena, most gods were lucky to produce one or two children, so it was possible that throughout Toven's very long life, he had fathered only two.

Alena, his lovely, beautiful Alena, was over two thousand years old, and unlike other immortal females, she'd been miraculously fertile. Curiously though, all of her thirteen children had been born during the first five centuries of her life. And it wasn't as if she'd been abstaining since.

What if Toven had experienced the same spikes and dips in his fertility? What if he had fathered many children thousands of years ago and then none until Orion and Geraldine?

Perhaps Alena would be the same? What if she was capable of having more children?

Orion certainly hoped so, provided that they were his.

Before being captured by the clan and learning the particulars of immortal fertility, he'd given up hope of ever becoming a father, but now that he knew that fatherhood was still a possibility, he was once again allowing himself to yearn for a child of his own, provided that Alena was the mother.

Ugly jealousy clouding his reasoning, he resented those thirteen human males who'd fathered her children, and he felt guilty for it. He should regard them as sperm donors, but that wouldn't be true. Alena had told him that she felt grateful to those males for the gift of motherhood and for contributing their genetic material to make each of her children a unique individual. She attributed her children's good qualities to the upstanding human males she'd chosen to father them.

He should be glad that her experiences had been positive, and he was, but he was also insanely jealous, not only of those who had fathered her children, but of every male who had ever laid hands on her, and there had been many.

Damn, he shouldn't feel so possessive of her—he had no right. Hell, he'd known her for all of four days, but in that short time she'd become indispensable to him.

Too indispensable.

What if things didn't work out between them?

How could he go on without her?

He couldn't, and getting aggravated thinking of all the males she'd been with as he was heading into her brother's office was the last thing he should be doing.

Kian was super protective of his sisters, and if Orion let the less than perfect side of him show, the guy might decide to retract his approval and forbid him from accompanying Alena to China.

Hell, getting Kian's permission to go with her on that trip was why Orion was standing in front of the office building with the journal in his pocket, and he should get on with it.

He'd wasted enough time on what ifs. Sharing the journal with the clan was the right thing to do regardless of creating goodwill between him and the brother of the woman he wanted. The clan would put it to good use, possibly helping him locate Toven and perhaps additional siblings who would enrich his and Geraldine's lives.

Alena

As Onidu helped the heavily pregnant Amanda step out of the limousine, Alena was reminded of the less than fabulous moments of her pregnancies. She'd loved the feeling of a life growing inside of her, and she'd cherished every moment of the journey, but some moments had been better than others, and feeling like a bipedal whale had not been among her fondest memories. Neither had been the frequent visits to the bathroom, especially since toilets back then had not been the porcelain thrones of today.

"It's so nice of your friend to open her boutique for us an hour early." She followed Amanda to the front door.

Her sister chuckled. "For me, Joann would open it in the middle of the night and on her birthday, and not because I thralled her to do so. She knows that I'll make it worth her while." She rang the doorbell.

"Don't count on me filling Joann's coffers. I'm not going to buy that many outfits. You'll need to get some as well."

"No way." Amanda patted her big belly. "I'm not getting anything new until I can fit into size six again."

Alena patted her arm. "Don't be silly. You never wear anything more than a couple of times anyway, and by the time you get your pre-pregnancy figure back, you'll have grown tired of those 'enormous' size eight outfits and will buy new ones."

"Good point." Amanda rang the doorbell. "That's odd. I've never had to ring twice before."

The door banged open, and a tall, leggy blonde with an apologetic expression on her perfectly made-up face walked out. "I'm so sorry for keeping you waiting. I was upstairs unpacking a new delivery, and my hair got tangled in one of the plastic ties." She gently embraced Amanda and then turned to Alena. "You must be Amanda's sister, but you two look nothing alike. You're both gorgeous, of course, just in different ways." She paused her rushed monologue to take a breath. "You must forgive my blabbering. After hearing so much about you, I'm just so excited to finally meet you. I'm Joann." She offered Alena her hand.

"I hope you heard good things." Alena cast Amanda a sidelong glance. "What stories have you spun about me?"

Her sister waved a dismissive hand and pushed past Joann into the boutique. "I told my dear friend that you need an entire new wardrobe for a romantic vacation to a lake located high up in the mountains of China. I checked, and it gets really cold there at night. In fact, the temperature drops to near freezing this time of year, so regular Southern California attire won't do."

"Don't worry." Joann put three of her expertly manicured fingers on Alena's arm. "I've made a few emergency phone calls to colleagues of mine who offer exclusive designer attire for colder climates, and I had everything you need delivered. One of those shipments was what I was busy unpacking when you rang the doorbell."

Alena could just imagine the price tag that came with such a bespoke service. She had plenty of money, but she didn't like frivolous spending. A donation to a worthy cause would make her much happier than wasting a small fortune on a fancy new wardrobe.

Her sister, however, didn't have such qualms. Donating her designer outfits after she'd gotten tired of them was what Amanda considered to be a worthy charitable contribution.

"What about Amanda?" Alena asked. "Did you prepare a selection for her as well?"

"Of course." Joann smirked. "I wouldn't neglect my best customer." She glanced at Amanda, who was pressing the heels of her palms into the small of her back. "Let's get you ladies comfortable." The boutique owner motioned for them to sit down on the two white chaises. "Coffee? Tea?"

"Coffee," Amanda said.

"Tea for me, thank you." Alena forced a polite smile.

When the woman strutted away on her four-inch heels, she pinned her sister with a hard look. "Yesterday, you said that I needed a few key items. From what Joann said, it sounded like I will leave with truckloads of new outfits."

Amanda chuckled. "Only a couple of truckloads, darling. No need to be so dramatic."

"I'm not the dramatic one in the family," Alena murmured under her breath.

"I heard that." Amanda leaned back and lifted her legs onto the chaise. "Don't be such a mood spoiler, Alena. Not everything in your life needs to be about service to the clan. You deserve some pampering, and you can afford to be frivolous for a change."

There was some truth in her sister's words.

Alena would probably end up buying too many outfits that she would never get to wear after the vacation was over, but if it made her sister happy, she could live with that.

Amanda was putting up her usual façade of a spoiled rich princess and pretending that everything was okay, but Alena didn't buy the act. She knew that her sister was terrified of becoming a mother again.

Talking about her fears with Vanessa would have bene-fitted Amanda, but since she was refusing to admit them even to herself, shopping therapy would have to suffice.

"After we are done here, do you think you'll have enough energy left for a little more store hopping?"

Amanda's eyes sparkled. "What else do you need to get?"

"I need to buy clothes for Orion. I've seen what he has in his suitcase, and there is nothing in there warm enough for Lugu Lake's cold nights. He also doesn't have anything that's suitable for a visit to an archeological dig. At the very least, he needs hiking shoes and a warm coat."

"Do you know his size?"

Alena arched a brow. "Intimately."

Her sister laughed. "I meant shoe size. How intimate did you get with his feet?"

Leaning forward, Alena whispered conspiratorially, "He has the sexiest feet ever. Am I weird to find a male's feet so attractive?"

"Not at all, darling." Amanda pushed up against the chaise arm and tried to cross her arms over her belly. "I think Dalhu's feet are very sexy, and I also buy him clothes and shoes, but that's because he hates shopping. Orion seems like a stylish guy, though, who doesn't need help in that department. Besides, you've known him for four days. Isn't that too soon to start dressing him up? If you ask me, that's more intimate than sex."

Well, for immortals, it might be.

Alena shrugged. "I don't feel as if only a few days have passed since we met. I feel like we belong together, and since we do, I need to take care of my man." She smiled apologetically. "Still, I don't want to appear too pushy or presumptuous, and I don't want him to think that I'm mothering him, but he needs clothing for the trip, and he doesn't have time to get it himself. He's meeting with Kian to talk about Toven's journal and to devise a strategy to find him. It might take all day, and we are leaving early tomorrow."

Amanda's expression turned serious. "I hope that Orion feels the same, and if he wants a life with you, he needs to accept you for who you are, and you are a mother at heart. You need to take care of others. If he can't deal with that, then he's not the one for you."

Eleanor

"I'm worried." Emmett got to his feet and walked over to the suite's balcony. "We've left Leon and Anastasia to run Safe Haven without giving them proper training." He turned around and looked at Peter. "Can you call your former partner and check how they are doing?"

"I can do better than that." Peter pulled out his phone. "We can have a video chat with Leon and Anastasia, and you can ask them anything you want."

"I'd appreciate that."

So far, Eleanor's fears about Peter and Emmett being at each other's throats hadn't been realized. On the flight over, the two had been civil to each other, but that was probably because they'd each gotten their own little pod in the business class section of the cabin and had slept on the red eye from Oregon to West Virginia.

Sharing a two-bedroom suite didn't seem to be a problem either.

"It's nine o'clock in the morning in Safe Haven," she said. "Leon and Ana are having breakfast right now. Are you sure it's a good time to call them?"

"It's the perfect time," Emmett said. "If they are in the dining room with Riley and her cohorts, it's even better. I want Riley to know that I'm checking up on her."

"Leon can handle Riley," Peter said.

"He doesn't know her," Emmett countered. "She seems agreeable and effusive, but she is cunning and manipulative. She'll have him wrapped around her little finger without him being any the wiser."

Peter shook his head. "Anastasia knows her well, and she's a smart girl. Riley won't be able to manipulate her."

"Anastasia didn't spend all that long in Safe Haven, and she wasn't in management." Emmett let out a long-suffering breath. "She was a maid, for heaven's sake. She barely interacted with Riley."

"We need to get ready." Eleanor rose to her feet. "The funeral is at three o'clock, and it's half an hour's drive."

"What about the call?" Emmett asked.

"Safe Haven survived without you for months, and it will survive a couple more weeks."

She didn't add that if he was that worried, he should have stayed behind instead of twisting Kian's arm to let him join the mission. Not that she minded. It was good to have him with her.

"We have plenty of time." Peter ignored her and placed the call.

"Good morning," Leon answered. "How was your flight?"

"Great. We flew business, and we had those seats that turn into beds, so we slept like the dead. Listen, Emmett is worried that he left you without proper instructions. Can you tell him to relax?" Peter switched the phone to a video call and positioned it so Leon and Ana could see Emmett.

"Don't worry, Emmett," Anastasia said. "Safe Haven runs like a well-oiled machine. As long as nothing unexpected happens, everyone knows how to do their jobs. All that Leon and I have to do until you come back is supervise and handle the unexpected. What could possibly happen over the next week or two?"

"A lot," Emmett said. "But you are right about everyone knowing their jobs." He puffed out his chest. "The standard operating procedures I put down are so clear that a trained monkey could follow them and do a great job."

"Then you shouldn't worry." Eleanor clapped him on the back. "I'm going to get dressed."

"Good luck," Anastasia said. "Leon and I are keeping our fingers crossed for you."

"Thank you."

A lot was riding on her today, and Eleanor would be lying if she claimed that she wasn't nervous.

Roberts's widow was hosting a late luncheon after the funeral, which would provide the perfect setup for what Eleanor needed to do. All the trainees were attending, as well as the higher-ups who would decide the paranormal program's future.

Convincing the bosses to let her take over the program shouldn't be too difficult, even without the use of compulsion. With the fake doctorate the clan had arranged for her, she had the right credentials, and as someone who had been instrumental in finding talent for the program, she was also the best candidate to run it after its two founders had died.

Her second task was to check which of the trainees were unhappy and wanted to leave the program, so she could recruit them for a different kind of job and offer them a new life. The third was to find someone who worked in the Echelon system and compel them to supply the clan with the information they needed.

Kian wanted access to what the spying system was collecting about mentions of paranormal abilities. He also wanted her to give the person a list of Kra-ell words. If spoken or written over communications lines that weren't as secure as the clan's system, they would get flagged, and the clan would be able to find the source.

All three tasks were super important, and it made her feel good that she'd been entrusted with them. Did it mean that Kian no longer regarded her as an outsider?

Eleanor wasn't sure about that.

Perhaps Kian trusted her, which in itself was a huge achievement, but he still didn't think of her as a clan member. He'd accepted her proposal to run Safe Haven alongside Emmett too easily. Was it because he was glad of the opportunity to get rid of her?

Kian

"Good morning." Kian motioned for Orion to take a seat at the conference table next to Onegus.

"Good morning." The guy smiled tightly.

The journal he was holding with a white-knuckled grip was bound in brown leather, with the date of January 1929 embossed on its spine and no end date. If that thing contained all of Toven's lovers for over half a century, then the god either wasn't very active sexually or recorded just a small fraction of the women he'd been with.

"Do you mind if I take a look?" Kian extended his hand. "Or do you prefer for me to wait until the copy is ready?"

With an effort, Orion released his death grip on the thing and handed it to Kian. "Be careful with it. Some of the pages are loose."

"Of course."

Following Syssi's advice, Kian tried to put himself in the guy's shoes. It was a hack she'd suggested to help him develop empathy, but so far it had been only marginally useful. Often, Kian found himself feeling ambivalent about things that meant a lot to others and vice versa.

When he tried to imagine how he would have felt if that leather-bound five-by-eight journal was all he had from his father, Kian realized that it would have held no sentimental value for him.

He'd never been overly curious about the human who'd fathered him. His mother had told him fantastic stories about the Scottish warrior who'd sired him, but Kian regarded them more as fanciful tales than an accurate description of the man.

Besides, he wasn't a sentimental guy, especially with regard to mementos.

Still, out of respect for Orion he handled the journal with care, gently flipping the pages and admiring the beautifully crafted sketches. He didn't know much about art, but the portraits were pleasing to the eye and seemed to have been drawn with a fondness for the subjects.

"Toven is talented." He handed the journal back. "But then he had thousands of years to hone his skill." Kian chuckled. "That being said, I doubt I would have graduated from drawing stick figures even after a thousand years of daily effort. I just don't have the eye or the inclination for artistic expression."

As the door opened and Shai entered with a cardboard tray of coffees, Orion snatched the journal off the table and put it in his lap.

"Good morning, Shai." He gave the guy a smile. "Is one of those for me?"

"Naturally." Shai handed each one of them a paper cup filled to the brim with the aromatic dark-roast brew from the café. "Tell me when you're ready, and I'll show you how to operate the scanner."

"Where is it?" Orion glanced at Kian's desk, his eyes passing over the device without recognizing it for what it was.

Shai pointed to the scanner. "It's the thing that looks like a desk lamp. You put the book open on the tray, and it scans both pages. It's just as time-consuming as with a traditional scanner, but the way it's designed makes the copying gentler on the original. You don't have to flatten it because the software compensates for the curvature and flattens the image. It's not perfect, but it's good enough for what we need."

"I'll start on it right away." Orion pushed to his feet. "Can you show me how to operate it?"

"Drink your coffee first," Kian said. "Copying the manuscript will take you several hours, so you'd better get caffeinated before you start."

Orion nodded. "I'll just put the journal next to the device, so it's safe. I don't want it anywhere near food or liquids."

When he returned to the conference table, Kian put his coffee cup down and leaned back. "By the way, do you have the original translation with you? It could save Edna a lot of time."

"I don't." Orion removed the lid from the paper cup and took a sip. "By now, I know everything written in it by heart, so I no longer need it. Besides, I like the idea of a fresh set of eyes tackling the translation. I don't know how good the original was, and Edna might do a better job. Perhaps she will uncover new hints that had been lost in the original translation."

"Good point," Kian agreed.

"I have a question," Shai said. "Do you happen to remember some of the titles of Toven's novels?"

Orion shook his head. "I don't. Why?"

"You were correct in your assumption that an author's anonymous work can be identified by his writing style. If we can find even one book written by Toven, we might be able to find others, and if he used traditional publishers to sell his novels, we could get them to reveal information about him. Even if they never met him in person, they must have paid him, and money leaves a trail."

covering the entire wall of windows behind Kian's desk and darkening the office. A moment later, a bespectacled guy popped up on the screen, occupying most of its area.

"Good morning, Kian. To what do I owe the pleasure of this call?"

"I'm here with Orion, Onegus, and Shai, and we have some AI-related questions for you." Kian pressed another button on the remote, and a camera descended from the ceiling, its lens rotating until it was trained on the conference table. "Can you see us?"

"Yes." William smiled. "It's my pleasure to finally meet you, Orion. After the meeting, come over to my lab. I have a clan phone ready for you."

"Right," Kian said. "I forgot to mention that. Our phones work all over the world and are secure. All communications with clan members are to be made from that phone."

"Thank you." Orion inclined his head. "A smartphone was one of the innovations I adapted to very quickly and now can't live without. I didn't expect its lack to make me so uncomfortable."

"It's easy to get used to good things," Kian said. "And it's always difficult to go back to the way things were before."

"How true," William said. "So, what did you want to ask me?"

After Kian explained the problem in a few words, William turned to someone else who was not in the camera's view. "What do you think, Roni?"

As his nephew rolled his chair over so they could see him, Orion smiled and waved. "I didn't know that you and William shared an office."

"I have my own," Roni said. "But I like working with William. Two brilliant minds are better than one. As for your question, I think that with some tweaking by our very talented William, the software will detect style even in a translated text, provided that the sample is big enough. How long is Toven's journal?"

"Not that long," Orion said. "No more than twenty thousand words, if that."

"It might be enough, but I would have preferred a larger sample."

Kian frowned. "No offense, Roni, but you're a hacker. What do you know about literature and style?"

Roni grinned. "I don't need to know anything about literature. The same software that can analyze the writing style of novels can analyze computer code. Not many people realize that, but coding is a form of expression and it's not anonymous. How do you think hackers are exposed? Plagiarism is not exclusive to creation in human languages. Code gets plagiarized as well. To prove that plagiarism has occurred, researchers create abstract syntax trees that show the code's structure, the same way it would have been done with any human language." He chuckled. "Or immortal, for that matter. But in order for the algorithm to learn Toven's style, it needs a large sample—at least one full-length book."

That explanation had flown over Orion's head, but he understood enough to figure out how Roni's hacking related to Toven's writing. The other thing he realized was that it was imperative for him to remember at least one of the many titles he'd seen scattered around Toven's townhouse nearly four decades ago.

"Can immortals undergo hypnosis?" he asked. "What I saw in Toven's place should be in my head, recorded in my subconscious, but I need someone to help me retrieve it. I heard that hypnotists can do that."

"Maybe the Clan Mother could thrall you," Onegus suggested. "Thralling shares many attributes with hypnotizing."

Kian nodded. "It's worth a try. I'll give her a call to see when she's available."

Annani

"Master Kian and Master Orion." Oridu bowed. "The Clan Mother is expecting you."

As they entered the living room, Orion inclined his head. "Good morning, Clan Mother. Thank you for agreeing to see us."

Sitting on the couch, Annani gave her son and her adopted nephew a welcoming smile. "Good morning to you too. You were lucky to catch me between appointments. Unfortunately, I cannot spare more than half an hour, so we need to do this quickly."

"This is important, Mother." Kian leaned to kiss her cheek.

It was indeed important, but not for the reason they were there. Orion had just handed Annani the perfect excuse to test her powers on him, and she was sure Kian was not only aware of that but had planned for it.

If she could retrieve Orion's submerged memories, she could also do much more.

Orion nodded. "Half an hour should suffice. I only need to remember the title of one book, and I'm sure that I have it stored in my subconscious mind."

"Come." She patted the seat next to her. "Sit with me."

As Orion sat beside her on the couch, Kian walked to the other side of the room and sat on a barstool, probably so his presence would not affect her concentration.

"Give me your hands," she commanded Orion. When he tensed, she gave him a reassuring smile. "My thralling is not like Edna's probing. In fact, you will probably not feel it at all."

"I didn't mind Edna's probe." He shifted a little closer. "I don't have anything to hide from you or the rest of your clan. I'm just a little nervous."

Of course, he was.

It was not easy to submit one's mind to another's scrutiny, even if one had nothing to hide. Additionally, Orion might feel reluctant to show her his memories because the freshest ones included intimate moments with Alena.

Annani would have to be careful to avoid those, not just out of respect for her daughter's and her mate's privacy but because they were irrelevant to what she was after. The best way to prevent an accidental peek was to divert Orion's focus to the subject at hand.

"If you follow my guidance, this should not take long. Relax, close your eyes, and visualize Toven's townhouse. Start from the moment you entered."

Loosing a long breath, Orion relaxed his shoulders and closed his eyes. "I'm ready."

When she entered his mind with surprising ease, Annani wondered whether it would have been more difficult if he had resisted her.

She was ready to scan the room for book titles, but she had not prepared herself for the shock of seeing Toven through Orion's eyes.

He was not the same male she had known five millennia ago. His eyes were still his most striking feature, the intelligence palpable even through someone else's eyes, but the spark of interest that had shone so brightly before was gone.

Orion had been right about his father appearing emotionally numb.

As Annani's heart squeezed with sorrow, she refocused on the physical resemblance between father and son. They looked a lot alike, but as someone who had known Toven well, Annani could easily discern the differences.

Who was the more striking one, though?

Orion was more animated, bright eyed, but even though he was by no means simpleminded, he lacked his father's sharp intelligence, which had always been what had attracted Annani to Toven. However, looking at him through his son's eyes and with the perspective of age, she wondered whether Toven had always been somewhat cold, and she just had not been aware of that. The male was ruled by logic, not heart, and he had probably been that way even when she was a young girl.

"I see a title," she murmured. "It is written in Russian."

Orion's eyes popped open. "It says *An Angel in Moscow*."

"You can read Russian?" Kian asked.

"I do." Orion turned back to Annani. "Did you see any other titles?"

She shook her head. "That was the only one you noticed."

"Let me see if I can find it online." Kian pulled out his phone. "That's the precise translation? *An Angel in Moscow*?"

When Orion nodded, Kian typed on his screen. "Interesting." He frowned.

"What did you find?" Annani asked.

"Nothing that's related to Toven, but there is a book called *Angels over Moscow—Life, Death and Human Trafficking in Russia – A Memoir* that's written by an American doctor. I find it quite serendipitous."

"What makes you so sure that it wasn't written by Toven?" Orion asked.

"First of all, the writer is a female, and her name and photo are included in the article about the book.

Secondly, it's a memoir, not a novel." He kept reading for a couple of moments. "Although the way it's written, it could be a novel. After skimming through the excerpt, I'm actually intrigued, and I never read memoirs."

"What about the title I saw?" Orion asked.

"The search didn't reveal anything. Perhaps it was published only in Russia." He walked over to the couch and sat next to Orion. "Here." He handed him the phone. "Type the title in Russian."

"That's not going to be easy." Orion sighed. "I can speak and read it but not write in it."

"Take your time. We are not in a rush."

It took Orion a long time to type the three words in Russian, and when the search did not bring up any results, he looked disappointed. "What now?"

"Not everything is online." Kian took the phone from him and put it in his pocket. "We will have to search in Russian libraries." He chuckled. "I bet Turner has someone who can do that for us."

"Turner," Orion said. "I've heard that name mentioned before. Am I ever going to meet the guy?"

"I'm sure you will soon." Kian rose to his feet. "Turner is a great strategist, and I wouldn't be surprised if he comes up with a new angle that we haven't considered. But it will probably have to wait for after your vacation."

Kian

Now that Kian had proof that Annani could thrall Orion, he felt much better about Alena going with the guy to China. If he tried to compel Alena to do anything she didn't want to, Annani could override his compulsion. It didn't seem likely, and Kian wasn't really worried about Orion stepping out of line, but he wanted added protection for Alena nonetheless.

Since Lokan was joining their group at Lugu Lake, it was possible that he would be followed. It was highly unlikely, but Kian had no tolerance for risk where the Brotherhood was concerned. Then there were the Kraell, who had probably lived in the area thousands of years ago but were long gone by now. Still, on the remote chance that they were still there, he wasn't taking any chances where his sister was concerned.

If he could, he would send an entire contingent of Guardians with her, but she would never agree to that, so one Head Guardian and three compellers would have to do.

As Annani took another peek into Orion's memories of his encounter with Toven, Kian pulled out his phone and texted Arwel. *I need you to go to China after all, but not with Mey and Yamanu. I want you to accompany Alena and keep an eye on her. You can bring Jin along.*

Having his mate with him hadn't hindered Arwel's performance before, but Kian would have preferred that the Head Guardian's attention was fully on Alena and not split between her and his mate. On the other hand, having him join the expedition along with Jin would be a much easier sell than sending Arwel alone.

Alena and Jacki would be glad of the additional female company, so Alena wouldn't object.

Arwel's return text arrived a few moments later. *I spoke with Jin, and she's excited to go.*

Kian typed back. *I'm glad. Come over to Annani's place. I want her to transfer command of Oridu to you.*

When Annani let go of Orion's hands, her disappointed expression told Kian that she hadn't found any more titles hiding in the guy's subconscious.

"I'm sorry." Orion raked his fingers through his hair. "I wish I'd paid more attention and read the titles on the spines."

"It is what it is," Kian said. "Don't beat yourself up over it."

Orion nodded. "I keep thinking about other ways to find Toven. He said that he had a lot of gold, and that means that he had to store it somewhere and sell it from time to time to cover his expenses. Perhaps Roni can hack into the gold depositories."

"It's worth a try." Kian put his phone back in his pocket. "Arwel is coming over in a few minutes."

"What for?" Annani asked.

"I assigned him to the Mosuo trip, and I want you to transfer command of Oridu to him."

Annani arched a brow. "I planned on transferring command to Alena. Is there a specific reason you want Arwel to command the Odu?"

"Arwel is a Guardian. If the group is attacked, he would know how to defend them better than Alena would. Naturally, she will retain command of Ovidu, but I want Oridu at Arwel's disposal."

"Alena is not going to be happy about that." Annani cast a sidelong glance at Orion, who pretended as if the discussion had nothing to do with him. "You agreed that two Odus would suffice as her guard."

Kian shrugged. "I changed my mind. Besides, Arwel is bringing Jin along, and I'm sure Alena and Jacki will be glad to have her with them."

Annani smiled. "Clever, Kian."

"Is Kalugal's jet big enough for two more passengers?" Orion asked.

"It is. And before you ask, Kalugal knows better than to refuse my request to add additional security for my sister."

When a knock sounded at the door, Oridu rushed to open it for the Guardian. "Good morning, Master Arwel." He bowed. "Please, come in."

"Thank you." Arwel strode in. "Good morning, Clan Mother." He bowed to Annani. "Hello, Kian, Orion."

"Have we met?" The guy pushed to his feet and offered his hand to the Guardian.

"We haven't." The two shook hands. "But we are about to get very well acquainted over the next two weeks."

"I'm looking forward to it."

As Orion smiled, Kian wondered what Arwel's opinion of him was. The Guardian's empathic ability lent itself to character evaluation, but it wasn't always accurate.

Arwel had thought that Eleanor was evil when he'd first encountered her. She'd been filled with hate and resentment, but it hadn't corrupted her to the core. After having been shown kindness and acceptance, the woman had changed a lot. Her character was still abrasive, and she was extremely ambitious, but now she used those qualities for the clan and strived to prove herself.

Kian still didn't trust her a hundred percent, but if she managed to achieve all the objectives he'd tasked her with in West Virginia, he might have to get over the remaining vestiges of doubt and officially acknowledge her contribution to the clan with some kind of title or position.

He would need to give it some further thought or perhaps ask Syssi to come up with something appropriate.

"Oridu," Annani called him to her. "As we have discussed earlier, tomorrow you will join Alena and Orion on their trip to China, but there was a slight change of plans. Instead of obeying Alena's commands, you will obey Arwel's."

"As you wish, Clan Mother." Oridu bowed. "Should I obey both their commands or just Master Arwel's?"

Annani shifted her gaze to Kian. "I suggest both. Do you object?"

"What happens when their commands contradict each other? One has to be the primary and the other the secondary. I want Arwel to be the primary."

Annani didn't look happy, but she nodded nonetheless. "Very well." She turned to Oridu. "You are to obey both Mistress Alena and Master Arwel. But if their commands are contradicting, you should obey Master Arwel over Mistress Alena."

Emmett

E mmett sat on the bed in his and Eleanor's hotel bedroom and watched her pull on a pair of silky black nylons, shimmy into a tight black dress, and then push her feet into a pair of black pumps.

"You look good." He reached for her hand and pulled her into his lap. "Too good. Let me come with you, or I'll go crazy thinking about all those humans ogling what's mine."

"We've talked about that." She put her hand on his cheek and gave him a little peck on the lips. "Peter is coming as my date."

"He can come as your brother. I want to be your date for the funeral."

She rolled her eyes. "I can't show up with two guys. I'm not a family member, and I can't justify bringing additional guests who didn't know Elijah to the funeral."

"You can do whatever you want. You're a compeller, and so am I. Who is going to tell us that we can't be there?"

She furrowed her eyebrows. "You have a point. But there is no need for you to come. Actually, it's better that you don't. I'm going to lay on the charm and pretend to flirt with the big honchos that will decide the program's future, and I don't need you growling at every male I talk to."

"I'm not going to growl. Didn't I behave admirably so far? I'm playing nice with Peter despite the coveting looks he sends your way."

"You're imagining things. Peter has absolutely no romantic interest in me. In fact, I hope he will find a connection with one of the trainees. Naomi is pretty, but she's only twenty-one, so she might be too young for him. Abigail is not as good-looking, but she's thirty-two, and she's a healer—gentle, soft-spoken, and curvy—the opposite of me. I think she and Peter would be perfect for each other."

That eased some of the pressure in Emmett's chest, but he still didn't want her going without him. It wasn't about jealousy but about his need to protect her. Eleanor was a confident, strong female, and Peter was a good Guardian, but neither of them could match Emmett's compulsion ability or physical strength.

No one could protect Eleanor better than he.

"I'm glad that you're thinking about hooking Peter up with someone else, but he's not the reason I want to come with you. You're my mate, and I need to protect you. I can't do that from the hotel."

Her eyes softened. "I'm not walking into the lion's den. It's just a funeral with mostly old people attending. And as you said yourself, I'm a compeller. What could they possibly do to me?"

"Just let him come," Peter said from the other side of the door. "He's not going to stop begging, and he might crawl after you to the car, holding on to your ankles. I really don't want to see that."

"Fine." She let out a breath. "Do you have anything appropriate to wear?"

Emmett smiled triumphantly. "I came prepared."

"Of course, you did. You knew that you were going to win."

"I don't give up easily, and you love me because I'm tenacious." He tightened his arms around her and lifted his lips to hers.

Eleanor gave him another small peck. "I love you for many reasons, but we don't have time. If you want to come, you need to get dressed." She pushed on his chest. "Let me go."

"One more kiss, a proper one, and I will."

A loud groan sounded from the other side of the door. "You know that I can hear every word. This is not the village, and the soundproofing here sucks."

Emmett smirked. "I know."

Vrog

It was lunchtime at the café, Wendy's busiest time of the day, but instead of letting Vrog help, she'd told him to sit on a barstool, learn to use his new phone, and do what Kian had asked of him.

The device looked like an iPhone, or one of its Chinese-made clones, but it was much more sophisticated.

"Does William have my number?" he asked Wendy when she had a moment between taking orders from customers.

"He's the one who programmed your phone, so naturally, he has your number. Did you send the emails Kian asked you to?"

"Not yet. I'm still figuring out how to use this thing."

She rolled her eyes. "The same way as any other cellphone."

"Not exactly, but similar enough." He tapped on the icon that looked like an envelope, hoping it was an email service. "I got the email. I'm good."

She gave him a quick smile before turning to her next customer.

Kian wanted the team to stay at the school instead of a hotel, which made sense, since it would be more convenient and save them on travel time, but it would be difficult to explain to Doctor Wang and the rest of the school's faculty.

Vrog had never hosted guests at the school's staff quarters before.

Could he claim that they were all prospective teachers? He could make the principal forget that he'd ever seen Mey and Yamanu before, but that was never foolproof. Doctor Wang was a smart fellow, and his mind was not as easily manipulated as those of others. For it to hold it would have to get reinforced daily, and that was too much of a hassle. Vrog needed an excuse that retained the fake identities they'd provided to the principal before.

He could tell Doctor Wang that Mey and Yamanu were interested in purchasing the school, and that they wanted to experience it firsthand before making their decision. The poor guy might get distressed by the prospect of foreigners buying Vrog out, but he could reassure the principal that no staff members would be replaced following the change of ownership, so Wang should not worry about losing his job.

Not that he would ever sell the school, but it was a good story. Later, he would tell Wang that the deal fell through.

As before, Alfie, Jay, and Morris would pose as Yamanu and Mey's personal staff members, and naturally, they would need to stay close to their bosses, so accommodations had to be prepared for them as well.

"Vrog," Wendy whispered close to his ear. "Don't look now, but Dorothea is eyeing you, and I think she's about to come over and talk to you."

"Who is Dorothea?" he whispered back.

"To your left. The tall brunette with the waist-long hair."

That sounded promising. Tall brunettes were his preferred type.

Pretending to move the phone's screen out of the direct sun, he took a peek.

The female was indeed looking at him, but he wasn't sure if there was interest in her eyes or suspicion. So far, most of the looks he'd gotten were of the second kind, and she was too far away for him to detect her scent.

"I don't think she likes me very much," he whispered to Wendy. "She's just curious."

"That's a good start," she whispered back.

As he typed an email to Wang, Vrog kept checking on Dorothea out of the corner of his eye, but she never made it to the counter and eventually left with a friend.

Could she be his match? Had she come to the café to take a look at him?

He was still awaiting William's call, hoping that a match had been found for him. But if Dorothea was the one the software had matched him with, he knew she would decline to participate.

When his phone rang Vrog was so startled that he almost dropped it, and when he saw William's name as the caller, he almost dropped it again.

"Hello, William. Do you have good news for me?"

Wendy abandoned her customer and came over to listen.

"I do," William said. "The software found you a match, but the lady can't do it tonight."

"Did you tell her that I'm leaving tomorrow?"

"She was very sad to hear that, but she couldn't change her plans for today. She said she'd wait for you to return. I didn't tell her that you're probably not coming back. Should I?"

"No. I'll be back."

Vrog hadn't been sure before, but now that he had a confirmed match with a female who was willing to wait for him to return, he wasn't going to disappoint her.

"Does she know who I am?"

"It wasn't too difficult to guess. It's a small village. But I didn't confirm her suspicion. Fortunately, you are not the only one who's leaving tomorrow, so she can't know for sure. Kalugal is taking three of his men to China as well."

"Kian told me about the Mosuo trip. That's the reason my visit is ending too soon."

"I'm sorry about that," William said. "What should I tell the lady? Are you sure that you're coming back?"

"I am, but I don't know when that will be. It depends on Mey and how successful she is with finding echoes left by my people."

Eleanor

❦

E leanor surveyed the crowd gathered at the chapel in the funeral home. Up front, Roberts' widow was seated between her adult children, their spouses, and her grandchildren. Other family members filled the three rows behind her, and the rest were colleagues—past and present—everyone from the paranormal program, including the new doctor, the nurse, the other instructors, and the bosses, two of whom were in uniform and the other two in civilian attire.

So far, no one had asked why she'd brought two men with her, but then they'd arrived when nearly everyone was seated, so other than a few curious looks, no one had had a chance to ask her anything.

She'd approached Dora to offer her condolences, and the tears in her eyes had been genuine—not for Roberts, who'd been a prick, but for his widow, who'd lost a lifelong partner. Perhaps Elijah had been a good husband in his old age, but even if he hadn't, he and Dora had been together for decades, and his widow would miss him.

After wiping her tears and regaining her composure, Eleanor had located the members of the paranormal program and given them a genuine smile, but it hadn't been reciprocated.

They hadn't changed much since the last time she'd seen them. James had lost more hair, Mollie had gained a few pounds, Sofia had changed her hair color from mousy brown to fiery red, and Spencer had lost his baby face to a scruffy beard. The others hadn't changed at all. Naomi, Abigail, Jeremy, Andy, and Dylan looked the same as they had before, except for the hostile looks they were sending her way.

Without periodic reinforcements, her compulsion over them had worn off, and their true feelings for her had re-emerged.

Oh well, she could always compel them again, but she had no doubt that it would be more difficult this time. They were no longer the naive recruits she'd lured into the program with promises of earning big money by serving their country. Now they were jaded, suspicious, and not as easily impressed.

Once the service was over and everyone moved into the luncheon reception area, Eleanor found the one higher-up she knew. The colonel might not be the one making hiring decisions, but he could refer her to someone who was.

Leaving Peter and Emmett at the buffet, she walked over to the man. "Good afternoon, Colonel Crowley." She offered him her hand. "Do you remember me? I'm Eleanor Takala." She affected a charming smile. "I worked closely with Elijah and Edgar to create the paranormal program from its very inception."

"Of course, I remember you." He shook her hand. "Although I have to say that your sabbatical has done wonders for you. You look incredible, Eleanor."

"Thank you. I also used the time off to finish my doctorate." She leaned closer. "With that degree in my pocket, I'm the most qualified candidate to replace Roberts as the head of the paranormal program. I know the objectives, I know each one of its current members, and I'm available immediately. With me, the program will continue without a hitch. Not only that, but I'm also the only one who was able to recruit real talent. After I left, Elijah didn't add a single new paranormal. Without me, this program will die. You need me."

That speech should have been good enough even without the element of compulsion she'd added to it, but since she'd been as subtle as a bull in a china shop, Crowley might have been put off by her aggressiveness. The compulsion served to overcome any such personal misgivings, making it impossible for him to reject her offer out of hand.

Crowley regarded her for a long moment, his dark brown eyes boring into hers as if he was trying to see into her soul. "You've convinced me that you're the best candidate for the job, but I need to convince others. I know that you didn't leave the program voluntarily, and I need to know why Roberts kicked you out."

Grimacing, she cast a sidelong glance at the widow and then leaned even closer to the colonel. "It doesn't feel right to talk about it here. Can you walk outside with me for a moment?"

"No problem."

As he offered her his arm, she threaded hers through it and cast a quick look at Emmett, telling him with her eyes not to follow.

He didn't look happy but nodded and turned to Peter.

When the door closed behind them, Crowley pulled out a cigarette box. "This is a nasty habit, but it provides the excuse for much-needed breaks." He flipped the top open and offered it to her.

"No, thank you. I don't smoke."

"Will it bother you if I do?"

"Not at all." She smiled. "I didn't want to say anything next to Dora and her family, but Roberts and Edwards were a couple of philandering bastards. They both hit on me at one time or another, and they hit on the young recruits as well."

"Interesting. No complaints were filed."

First of all, that was a lie. None might have been filed recently, but there had been several in the distant past, and given that Crowley didn't seem shocked in the least meant that he was aware of that.

Bastard.

He was probably guilty of the same thing and didn't think it was a big deal. The good-old-boys covered up for each other.

Eleanor struck a pose and pinned him with a hard stare. "I know of several complaints that were filed a couple of decades ago when both Roberts and Edwards were a little younger and still using their station and influence to coerce subordinates into sexual situations they would have never agreed to otherwise. They also threatened anyone who might have dared to come forward, explicitly and implicitly. I was fired and denied access to the facility precisely for that reason, and frankly, I stayed silent out of fear for my life."

"Really?" He arched a brow and puffed on his cigarette. 'What made you come forward now?"

She smiled coldly. "They are both dead, and I doubt anyone else is motivated to go to such extremes to prevent this from getting out. I would rather not cause their widows additional grief, but I can easily collect a number of testimonials from their other victims. That's neither here nor there, though. You wanted to know why I was kicked out despite the exemplary service I provided, and now you know."

The colonel wasn't a stupid man, and she didn't need to spell out the threat for him to understand what would keep her quiet.

"I can't give you an answer on the spot. I will need to schedule an interview for you to present your qualifications. Also, we will need to run a new security check on you."

"Naturally." Roni had already taken care of that, and since her doctorate was from an online university, there was no one for the Feds to interview. The records would show her as attending online courses for the past six years and earning her doctorate a little over a month ago.

Annani

"Ronja." Annani opened her arms. "You look absolutely amazing." She hugged her friend and then smoothed her hands over the woman's defined biceps. "What a transformation."

Ronja looked at least ten years younger since the last time Annani had seen her, and if she did not know better, she would have thought that Ronja had transitioned.

"Thank you." Her friend smiled. "Merlin's health regimen works, and not just on me."

"I want to hear all about it." Annani took her hand and led her to the couch. "You look so much thinner and more toned. How long ago did you start exercising?"

"About six weeks ago. I didn't actually lose that much weight. Only seven pounds, but Merlin says that I lost much more than that, but the fat was replaced by muscles." She sighed. "I love the way I look, but I don't like how sore I am most days."

Annani frowned. "Is Merlin being too rough with you?"

Ronja tilted her head. "He has to be, or I wouldn't get out of bed in the morning. I hate running, and I hate lifting weights, and I hate swimming more than both. The only activity I kind of enjoy is bike riding."

Annani laughed. "I do not think we are talking about the same thing. I was referring to Merlin being sexually rough, not his training routine."

Ronja's cheeks reddened. "We haven't done that yet."

"Why not?"

"You know why." Ronja pushed a stray strand of hair behind her ear. "But I have to admit that I'm fighting a losing battle with my hormones." She smiled shyly. "Merlin is exercising alongside me, and his transformation is even more dramatic than mine." She laughed. "He was always handsome, but he has turned into an irresistible hunk, and the sly man knows it. He flexes his new muscles whenever I look at him and gives me those sexy looks that make my heart flutter."

"Only your heart?" Annani waggled her brows.

Ronja's blush deepened. "Among other things."

Annani was overjoyed to see her friend not only looking healthier and more beautiful but also happier. Merlin was good for her.

She patted Ronja's knee. "Well, you know what I think about your abstinence, so I am not going to repeat it. Tell me how Lisa is doing."

"She's wonderful. Out of solidarity with me, she joins us on our morning jogs and sometimes also the afternoon swims."

That was admirable, but it was also hindering romantic progress. Merlin could not put the moves on Ronja with Lisa around.

"You two should go on a vacation," Annani suggested. "Just you and Merlin."

"I can't." Ronja crossed her legs. "I can't leave Lisa alone."

"You could take her to Scotland, leave her with David and Sari, and tour the country with Merlin, but winter is not a good time to visit Scotland. The Highlands are cold even in the summer."

"I went to Scotland with my first husband. It's beautiful, even more so than Norway." She uncrossed her legs and leaned forward. "Speaking of vacations, though, I heard that Alena is joining Kalugal and Jacki on a trip to China. Are you going to be okay without her?"

"Of course," Annani said with more conviction than she felt. "I have you to keep me company while she is gone."

Ronja seemed taken aback. "I can't possibly take Alena's place. She's your heir, your second-in-command, so to speak. I'm just a simple woman."

Obviously, Ronja was not thinking about the next two weeks but more long-term. Was she afraid Annani would take her away from Merlin and Lisa?

Even if she was free to go, Ronja was no substitute for Alena.

"First of all, you are not simple, and secondly, no one can take Alena's place, and I am not looking to replace her. I just need a friend."

"I can do that. I hope." Ronja averted her eyes. "You are a goddess, Annani. And I'm just a simple mortal who has just a smidgen of your spark in me. I try not to think about your glowing skin and ignore the power you emit, but the truth is that next to you, I feel insignificant. I don't think that makes me a very good friend."

"Nonsense." Annani took Ronja's hand. "I know that I am a lot to take in, and we have not spent enough time together for you to get comfortable with me. But in our souls and hearts we are the same. We are both mothers, and we are both widows. We have experienced the same kinds of sorrows and the same kinds of joys, and since people are shaped by the sum of their experiences just as much as they are shaped by their genetics, you and I are more alike than you think."

Eleanor

"Let's make a toast." Eleanor raised her wine glass. "To Elijah Roberts, may he rest in peace."

As the paranormal program's members lifted their glasses, some repeated her words while others nodded in agreement.

Surprisingly, none had refused her invitation to a local bar after the service was over. She hadn't even had to resort to compulsion to get them to agree.

Unlike Jin and her cohorts, those who had stayed were not aware of Eleanor's real role in the program and had only remembered her as their recruiter—the one who supposedly had negotiated the extravagant pay for them. They might not like her as a person, but they were smart enough to realize that befriending her could benefit them.

"What now?" Mollie asked. "Are they going to end the program? My annual contract is about to end, and I have no idea what to do on the outside."

"You could start a psychic lost and found," Jeremy suggested. "Or help the police solve crimes."

Mollie's talent was post cognition, so Jeremy's ideas for her future employment weren't wrong, except for the fact that no one was hiring.

She snorted. "What would that pay? Not a quarter of a million a year, that's for sure."

"The program is not going anywhere," Eleanor said. "Not if I can help it. In fact, I'm working on a plan to move it out of the crypt you've been complaining about to a beautiful beachfront property in Oregon. I also plan to recruit new talent."

Jeremy eyed her from below his dark lashes. "How are you going to achieve all that?"

"First of all, I'm going to take over as the program's director, and then I'll offer the higher-ups a deal they can't refuse on the new location I've scouted for them."

"They have no use for us," Abigail said. "We are not worth the expense, and they are going to get rid of us soon."

Eleanor frowned. "Did someone tell you that?"

Abigail shrugged. "It's easy to deduce. Only James, Mollie, and Spencer were ever sent out on an assignment.

The rest of us are treated like lab rats. They just keep testing us."

"We are still learning," Sofia said. "My telekinesis has gotten better since I've started training."

"You can affect a dice or coin in motion," Dylan said. "Your talent is only useful in Vegas, but if you get caught, well, you know what happens to cheaters in casinos."

Abigail's comments gave Eleanor the opening she needed. "If I can get any of you out of your contracts, who would want to leave? Raise your hands if you do."

No one did.

"What if I can get you the same pay on the outside?"

This time everyone lifted their hands.

There was no way Kian would approve paying the nine remaining members of the program a quarter of a million each for doing basically nothing. He had no use for their talents, and he was only interested in them as potential Dormants. She had no doubt, though, that those who had the godly genes would trade the pay for immortality.

"I see. So you love the pay and hate your jobs."

"I hate living underground," Naomi said. "And I hate being treated like an experiment, which is what we are really here for. But my family and I need the money. I'm treating this as a necessary evil to secure a better future."

Spencer, who so far hadn't said anything, kept glancing between Eleanor, Emmett, and Peter. "You, your boyfriend, and your cousin all have spectacular auras. Are you on something?"

Eleanor tensed. "What do you mean? Like drugs?"

Spencer shrugged. "That's what it looks like to me."

"What you see," Emmett said. "Is the aura of enlightenment. All three of us have reached deep within and brought forth the best version of ourselves. With proper training, all of you can have auras that glow as brightly."

"How is enlightenment achieved?" Andy asked. "Through meditation?"

"Among many other techniques."

As Emmett launched into one of his sermons, Eleanor let out a relieved breath. Her mate was a masterful bullshitter, and right now, she was grateful for that talent. If not for him, she would have had to compel Spencer to keep his mouth shut about their glowing auras.

The troubling thing about that was that the kid could apparently identify immortals. If he turned into one himself, he would keep it to himself, and perhaps his ability could be used to the clan's benefit in some way.

It was a shame, though, that he couldn't detect Dormants by their auras. That would have been super useful.

Perhaps he could train himself to do that?

Obviously he couldn't do it now, or he would have noticed that the four trainees who'd escaped the program had auras different than regular humans. But perhaps he'd attributed it to their paranormal abilities?

Nah, then all of the program's members should have glowing auras, including Simmons, who had been a Dormant.

"I have a question for you, Spencer," she said when there was a momentary lull in Emmett's lecture. "Are the auras of people with paranormal talents different than of those without?"

"Every person's aura is different," he hedged.

"I know, but you noticed that my aura, as well as Peter's and Emmett's, shone brighter, and I wondered whether it was because of our enlightened state or because of our paranormal abilities."

Spencer's eyes widened. "You have a paranormal ability? You never told us about it." He looked at James, who was sitting to his right. "Did you know?"

The telepath shook his head. "She can be very persuasive. Maybe that's her talent."

He had no idea how close to the truth he was.

"That's right," Eleanor confirmed. "Emmett and Peter are both telepaths," she added before anyone had the chance to ask. "But not very strong ones."

That earned her a brow lift from Emmett. "I can be very persuasive as well."

"Yes, you can, dear." She patted his shoulder. "But back to the auras." She looked around the bar. "Are the auras of those seated around this table noticeably different than those of other people in the bar?"

Spencer looked around. "I really can't tell because they are all different. Only the three of you have brighter ones."

Eleanor wasn't ready to give up yet, but she couldn't keep leading the kid on without revealing too much. Perhaps she would get him alone some other time, tell him precisely what she was after, and then compel him to forget it.

Vlad

ᐕᗦ

Vlad carried a tray of freshly baked cupcakes to the living room and put it down on the table.

"They smell divine," Wendy's mother said. "Thank you."

"You're welcome." He sat down next to Vrog, who seemed to be uncomfortable with Margaret and Bowen for some reason.

Naturally Wendy had noticed and was trying to cover up for him by chatting up a storm. "Anyway, as I was telling Vrog, the Fates must have planned our journey all along. Otherwise, there is no way my mother and I would have ended up being rescued by the clan."

Margaret smiled at her mate. "I was rescued by Bowen, but only because I fell and broke my knee, and that happened only because the clan faked a fire in Safe Haven to rescue Eleanor and Peter. I didn't need rescuing."

"That's arguable," Bowen said. "Emmett compelled you to fear outsiders. You needed to be rescued from that."

Next to Vlad, Vrog groaned. "I must apologize for my tribesman's misuse of power. He shouldn't have held you against your will and prevented you from contacting Wendy."

So that was Vrog's problem. He felt guilty by association.

"I don't blame Emmett for that," Margaret said. "He thought that he was protecting me, and he was probably right. Roger, my ex-husband, was an abusive man, and Fates only know what he would have done to me if I showed up on his doorstep."

Bowen growled. "I should've killed the maggot a long time ago. The only reason he's still alive is that you don't allow it."

Margaret patted his knee. "He's not worth it. Besides, Vlad thralled him to never harm anyone again. Right, Vlad?"

He nodded. "Can we change the subject, please? This talk is upsetting Wendy."

It was upsetting him too.

"Yes, it is." Wendy backed him up. "Let's talk about cheerier things, like Vrog's match for the virtual adventure. William called earlier to tell him that he found a match, but the lady was unavailable to do it today, so it will have to wait for Vrog to return." She smiled triumphantly. "And that means that he's coming back after the team completes the assignment at his school."

"That's wonderful," Stella said. "I'm glad that you decided to return to us."

"It wasn't just because of that." Vrog leaned forward and snatched a cupcake off the tray, probably just to have something in his hands because he wasn't going to eat it. Grains and baked goods didn't agree with his digestion. "I haven't had enough time with my family." He looked at Wendy. "I hope it's okay with you if I come back here and stay a little longer?"

"You're always welcome here," Wendy said. "Our home is your home."

From the corner of his eye, Vlad saw Richard grimace, but he didn't say a thing, which was smart. Stella had been upset with him for the way he mercilessly teased Vrog, and he'd promised to curb his jabs at the guy.

Bowen grinned as he wrapped his arm around Margaret's shoulders. "You've changed so much since I first met you, Wendy. You're like a different person."

She blew him an air kiss. "Thanks in part to you. Your fatherly advice helped both Vlad and me. If not for you, we might have not ended up together."

"Love has a way of overcoming obstacles." He took Margaret's hand. "It might have taken you longer without my sage advice, but you would still have ended up together. The Fates wouldn't have allowed things to unfold any other way."

After casting Bowen a fond look, Margaret turned to Vrog. "Emmett told us that the Kra-ell revere the Mother of All Life, but he didn't elaborate. What does that entail? Do they have a shrine for her? Are there any special holidays to celebrate her?"

"There was no shrine, but there was an altar in Jade's house for the Mother. I don't know what the purebloods do with it other than consecrate vows and celebrate children's transition into adulthood. Those were the only two I took part in. On my thirteenth birthday, I got my first weapon. It was a hunting knife, which I used to cut off my hair for the first time ever and put the braid on the Mother's altar. Then I used it to make a cut in the palm of my hand and drip blood over the braid. After that, Jade ignited my tribute and chanted some ancient Kra-ell prayer that I didn't understand."

"We also have a rite of passage celebration for our boys at thirteen years of age," Bowen said. "But instead of making sacrifices, our boys challenge an older immortal to a fight, get bitten, and transition."

"Do you have another celebration upon completion of training?" Vrog asked.

"We don't. Did you?"

"The second time I was brought before the altar was upon the completion of my training to vow my eternal loyalty and servitude to Jade. I had to cut my palm again and drip blood into a chalice. This time, Jade cut her palm as well and combined her blood with mine. She again chanted something incomprehensible and set our combined blood offering on fire."

"Very voodoo-like," Stella said. "I wonder whether those were legitimate Kra-ell rituals, or did Jade invent them to scare the hybrid young men into serving her for as long as they lived."

Orion

"I don't like it that you're leaving so soon." Geraldine wiped tears from her eyes. "I've just found you, and we've gotten to spend so little time together."

Orion put a hand on her arm and smiled. "You've never lost me. You just didn't remember me."

When Geraldine had organized the goodbye dinner for their small family, Orion had expected her to be a little sad, but not the tears. Before, he'd had to thrall her every time they'd parted, and he saved himself the sorrow of seeing her cry. This time around no thralling was needed, and he was thankful that Geraldine had Shai and Cassandra to console her so he could feel less guilty about leaving.

"You know what I mean." Geraldine waved a hand. "Don't mind me. I'm really glad that you are going on a romantic getaway together with Alena and the other couples. I hope you have a wonderful time."

Orion wondered whether Kian might have agreed for Geraldine and Shai to join the expedition. Perhaps even Cassandra and Onegus. Could Kalugal's jet even accommodate so many passengers?

In either case it was too late to suggest that, and besides, Orion was a guest himself. For him to invite others to join would have been inappropriate.

"Thank you," Alena said. "We'll be back before you know it. Two weeks is nothing when you have eternity to look forward to."

"True." Geraldine forced a small smile. "Besides, Cassandra and I are going to be so busy that the time will fly. We have two houses to decorate, and we also need to convince Darlene to attempt transition."

"We are not going to try to convince her," Cassandra said. "We are only going to give her the option and explain the risks. I don't want to pressure Darlene to take a potentially deadly risk. I don't need that on my conscience."

Orion shook his head. "Wait until I come back. You need me to compel Darlene to keep what you tell her a secret. We agreed that thralling her to forget about her godly genes right after you tell her about them is a bad idea."

"I agree," Onegus said. "With Orion, Kalugal, and Eleanor gone, we have no compellers left to take care of that. We need to wait until at least one of them returns."

"What about Parker?" Shai said. "He's a decent enough compeller."

Onegus gave him an incredulous look. "You are kidding, right? Parker is a kid."

"So what? He's a tested and proven compeller. We can bring him along to lunch or dinner with Darlene, test his ability to compel her, and if it works, we can tell her about her chance at immortality. She needs a strong motive to leave Leo."

Cassandra sighed. "That's another thing I don't want to pressure her to do. We might think that Leo is a bastard, but that's our opinion of him. Darlene might love the guy despite him being an asshole. Maybe he has redeeming qualities we don't know about."

"Like what?" Geraldine asked.

"He might be great in bed, or he might be good at telling jokes, or whatever. There is no accounting for taste."

Onegus's lips twisted in a grimace. "I'm sure she will change her mind about her hubby after she finds out that he sold out their son for reward money."

That was news to Orion. "What did Leo do?"

"When we arranged for Roni to meet his parents, we took extensive precautions that should have kept him safe. We couldn't understand how the meeting place was compromised until Andrew discovered that Leo told the agents in charge of Roni's investigation where the meeting would be."

"Bastard." Orion's fangs punched out. "Why would he do that to his own son?"

"There was a big reward offered to whomever provided information that led to Roni's capture," Shai said. "Apparently, Leo loves money more than he loves his son."

"Roni might not be his," Geraldine said. "When we talked about the genetic testing, Leo made some snide remarks about wanting to see Roni's results. We think that he suspects Roni might not be his son."

Orion rubbed a hand over the back of his neck. "Darlene was married to Leo for many years before they had Roni. Perhaps they couldn't conceive, and she used a sperm donor without telling Leo?"

Cassandra crossed her arms over her chest. "I hope the sperm donor was the total package and that Darlene got the donation the natural way. That would serve Leo right. Even if Roni is not his biological son, he still raised him as his, and he should act as a father, protecting his son, not selling him out. The guy must be a total douchebag to do that."

Alena

⁑

As Alena and Orion arrived at the village's parking garage, a small crowd was already gathered, ready to board the bus. The two teams leaving for two separate destinations in China were heading to the clan's airstrip, where one team would board Kalugal's executive jet and the other the clan's.

Alena watched Mey and Jin hug and shed tears as if they were parting for months, which was kind of silly since they were sharing a ride to the airstrip and were not parting yet. After that, they would be separated for only a week or two, so that wasn't a big deal either, and it was certainly nothing to shed tears over. But then she and Annani hadn't done any better.

They had said their goodbyes in the house, and both of them had fought tears, not because of the upcoming trip and the short separation, but because they were keenly aware that it might be the first of many goodbyes if Alena and Orion bonded and she had to leave the sanctuary.

After spending twenty centuries together, she and her mother didn't know how to live without each other and adjusting would be difficult. Annani had done a much better job of putting on a brave face than Alena had managed, but then she was doing the right thing by encouraging her daughter to live her life to the fullest, and she wasn't the one leaving.

Alena, on the other hand, was overcome with guilt.

"I don't like traveling by bus," Kalugal grumbled as Okidu opened the vehicle's door. "The ride to the airstrip would have been a perfect opportunity to show off my new limousine."

Chuckling, Kian clapped him on the back. "Stop being such a snob. The seats on the bus are just as comfortable as the ones in the limousine."

"Perhaps in yours, but mine is newer and more luxurious."

"You'll have plenty of opportunities to show it off when we return," Jacki said.

Next to Kian, Syssi sighed. "I wish I was going with you."

Amanda nodded. "Me too, sister, me too." She wrapped her arm around Syssi's waist. "Perhaps in a year or two, when our daughters are a little older, we will travel somewhere exotic together. I've never been to Tibet, and I would love to see it."

As if to remind them that she was there, Allegra kicked her little pink blanket off and made a sound that was a clear demand to be picked up. It wasn't a whine or a cry, but a mixture of a huff and a gurgling growl.

Alena laughed. "She's becoming more like her daddy by the day." She reached into the stroller and picked her niece up. "Aren't you, sweetie?" She kissed both warm cheeks, inhaling the baby's scent and getting drunk on it.

Science called it an oxytocin rush, a hormone that was responsible for the bond between mothers and their babies, and Alena was definitely addicted to it. Some people got high on drugs or drunk on alcohol; she got high on babies.

Catching Orion looking on with a smile on his face and softness in his eyes, Alena walked over to him. "Would you like to hold her?"

He shook his head. "I've never held a baby. I don't know how."

"Did you ever hold a puppy?"

He nodded.

"Then you'll do fine." She handed him Allegra.

Immediately, Syssi and Kian both stepped up to Orion, hovering within catching distance in case he dropped their precious bundle.

But they shouldn't have worried. Orion's instincts worked perfectly, and as he held Allegra against his chest and smiled down at her, she smiled back and reached with her tiny hand to grab his hair.

"Ouch." He laughed. "Her grip is surprisingly strong for such a small hand."

"That's my daughter," Kian said proudly but didn't offer to help poor Orion, who didn't know what to do.

Syssi took the little fist between two fingers. "Let go of Uncle Orion's hair, Allegra."

The baby gave her a defiant look and held on.

"Let go." Syssi pried the tiny fingers apart and then took the unhappy Allegra from Orion. "She's also stubborn like her father and doesn't like to be told what to do."

"She's a leader," Kian said.

"Master." Okidu bowed. "All the luggage is safely stowed. Should I ask everyone to board the bus?"

"Yes." Kian tore his eyes from his daughter. "I wish you all a safe, successful, and enjoyable trip."

Alena embraced Syssi and then Amanda. "Don't you dare go into labor while I'm gone."

"Don't you dare not be here when I do," Amanda countered.

Next, Alena hugged Kian. "Do me a favor and try to visit Mother more often. She's going to be lonely without me."

"We will," Syssi said. "I'm going to make sure that she never dines alone. Unless she's meeting other clan members over dinner or lunch, she will dine with Kian and me, or just me when Kian is at work."

"Hey," Amanda pouted. "What about me? I'm her daughter too."

"We'll share," Syssi offered. "Or we can all dine together every day."

"That would make Mother very happy." Alena gave her sister one last kiss on the cheek before taking Orion's hand. Together, they boarded the bus and sat down behind Mey and Yamanu.

"Have a safe voyage, everyone," Kian called out as Okidu closed the door.

Orion

As the bus cleared the tunnel, Orion expected the windows to clear, but they stayed opaque. Was it because they weren't as sophisticated as the ones in the private cars? Or did they function just as well, but he and the others weren't supposed to know where the clan's airstrip was?

His bet was on the second one.

Despite Kian's claims of tight budgets due to the expenditure on humanitarian efforts, the clan seemed very well off, and what Orion found admirable was that the wealth seemed to be more than fairly distributed among the members. Everyone got a share, whether they contributed to the community or not, but those who worked for the clan got compensated according to their contribution. The beauty of the system was that everyone was free to pursue their dreams and interests whether they were profitable or not, but work was still incentivized, and so was education.

According to Shai, young clan members had to be twenty-five to be eligible to share in the clan profits, but if they were full-time students in good academic standing, they got their share as soon as their first semester was successfully completed.

He wondered what happened when someone dropped out. Did they lose their share and have to wait until they reached the age of twenty-five?

Orion had a feeling that Kian wouldn't have left such a loophole for youngsters to take advantage of. The guy was pragmatic, and he wouldn't allow anyone a free ride, but he was also generous.

According to Cassandra, Guardians were very well paid, and Shai, who was just an assistant, had quite a nest egg saved up. Kalugal and his men probably didn't get a share in the clan's profits, but did they become eligible when they mated a clan female?

Orion still had so many questions, and hopefully some would be answered during the trip. He also needed to learn the names and positions of most of his fellow travelers.

Leaning closer to Alena, he whispered in her ear, "I don't know half of the people on this bus."

She chuckled. "I'm such a bad host. It's just that it feels so natural to have you with me that I keep forgetting you are new to all this. Let me introduce you." She motioned for him to get up.

First, she stopped next to the couple sitting in front of them. "I'll start with Mey and Yamanu. Yamanu is a very special Guardian. He has the power to thrall thousands at one time, and the same goes for shrouding. His ability equals or maybe even surpasses that of the most powerful gods."

The guy grinned. "You're making me blush, Alena. Orion and I have met before." He winked at him. "But you might not remember me. That tranquilizer shot knocked you out before we had a chance to get introduced." The guy offered him his hand. "No hard feelings, eh?"

"None." Orion shook the guy's hand.

He remembered the Guardian, but he hadn't known what Yamanu was capable of.

"I'm impressed by your ability. I'm a first-generation immortal, and I can't do even a fraction of that. How did you become so powerful?"

"It's a long story," Yamanu said. "The gist of it is that I channel all of my energy and focus it into the thrall or the shroud, and I need others to shield me when I'm in that state. One day, I'll tell you how I discovered my ability."

"I'm looking forward to it."

"I'm Mey," his mate said as she offered her hand. "It's a pleasure to meet you, Orion."

"You are the one who can hear echoes in the walls." He gently shook her elegant, long-fingered hand.

She smiled. "That's me."

As an idea popped into Orion's head, his hold on her hand tightened. "How do you feel about a trip to Paris?"

Looking confused, she cast a questioning glance at Alena. Her mate's reaction was more extreme. The friendly smile was gone, and Yamanu looked as if he was about to tear Orion's throat out.

"I'd better explain," he said as he quickly let go of her hand.

"Yes, you'd better," Yamanu hissed from between elongated fangs.

Were all immortals that fang-trigger happy? Or was it territorial posturing when another male was perceived as showing interest in their mate?

Orion's control over his fangs was much better than that, and he doubted that they would elongate even if someone flirted with Alena.

Right. He was such a hypocrite. Only yesterday, he'd been battling feelings of anger and resentment when thoughts of her former lovers flitted through his head.

Casting an apologetic smile at Yamanu, Orion took a step back. "The reason I suggested Paris was that I would like Mey to listen to echoes at a townhouse my father stayed in many years ago. I'm sure you're aware who he is."

Mey nodded. "The god Toven. By now, I doubt there is anyone left in the village who hasn't heard about him."

"I met him nearly four decades ago in Paris. It was a chance encounter that he wasn't happy about, and he got rid of me as soon as he could. The Clan Mother wants to find him, and it has just occurred to me that you might find out more about him from listening to the echoes in that house."

"That depends," she said. "I only hear echoes of highly charged emotional moments. Do you know how long he lived there?"

The surge of hope in Orion's chest took a nosedive and got crushed on the rocks suddenly filling his gut. "Not long, and I doubt he could get emotional over anything anymore. There are probably no echoes of him left."

"I'm sorry." She offered him a consolatory smile. "In any case, I'm willing to give it a try." She looked at her mate. "I would love to visit Paris again. Especially since this time, it will be with you."

His friendly expression back on, Yamanu took his mate's hand and kissed the back of it. "As soon as this assignment is over, I'll request time off so we can go to Paris."

Leaning over, she kissed his cheek. "Let's wait for spring, my love. Paris in the winter is not as pleasant."

Alena

"This is Jin, Mey's sister," Alena introduced Arwel's mate next. "The clan sprung her from the government's paranormal program, but that's also a story for another time."

"Hi." Jin offered Orion her hand. "Welcome to the clan."

"Thank you. What is your special talent, if I may ask?"

"I can tether people. I tie a string of my consciousness to theirs, and I can see and hear everything they see and hear. That's how I captured Kalugal."

"That's how you tried to capture me," Kalugal corrected. "Instead, I ended up capturing your mate and your best friend." He wrapped his arm around Jacki's shoulders. "The best catch I've ever made."

By the time Kalugal had finished telling Orion the story of how Jin had tethered him in a club, how the clan's plan had gotten spoiled by a crazed human with a gun, and everything that had followed until he'd moved his base into the village, Okidu had parked the bus at the clan's airstrip.

After they'd disembarked and waited for the Odus to unload the luggage and then load it into the jets, Yamanu put his enormous hand on Orion's shoulder. "Before we go our separate ways, let me introduce Vrog."

The Guardian seemed to have forgotten all about the misunderstanding regarding the Paris offer and was back to his usual friendly self.

"Vrog, this is Orion. Orion, this is Vrog." Yamanu grinned. "Vrog should be thankful to you. When we caught you, Kian authorized Vrog's move to the village because he needed the dungeon apartment for you."

"Thank you." Vrog shook Orion's hand. "You and I have a lot in common. We are both newcomers to the clan, and we are both leaving before we've had a chance to acclimate." He smiled at Alena. "The notable difference is that you are leaving with your true-love mate, while I'm leaving alone."

Orion didn't correct Vrog's misconception. Instead, he clapped him on the back. "Your one and only is somewhere out there, waiting for you. The good news is that as an immortal, you will never run out of time to find her."

"I wish that were true, but I'm not immortal, only long-lived compared to humans. Hopefully, though, it won't take me that long to find the one I belong to."

"I hope that you don't mean Jade," Arwel said.

"No, of course not. I meant the female who will own my heart, not just my vow of loyalty."

"You are Kra-ell," Orion said. "It took me a while to connect the dots."

"I'm half Kra-ell and half-human."

"Yeah, that's what I meant." Orion regarded the guy with curiosity in his sapphire blue eyes. "Are you hoping to find a Kra-ell female? Or are you hoping to catch the eye of someone in the village?"

Vrog lowered his eyes. "I don't think I'll ever find a Kra-ell female, and even if I did, she wouldn't want me. The pureblooded females don't take half-breeds into their beds, and neither do the hybrid females. The only way a half-breed can have long-lived children is if she invites a pureblooded male to breed with her."

"I see." Orion seemed lost for words.

"Don't look so glum." Yamanu squeezed Vrog's shoulder. "You're much better off with a clan female. They don't bite." He laughed. "Much."

As Yamanu's group separated from theirs and headed to the clan's jet, Kalugal led the rest to his. "Ladies first," he said as he motioned for Alena to follow Jacki up the stairs and then Jin.

"Wow." Alena looked at the plush armchairs. "This is even fancier than my mother's jet, and it's bigger than the clan's largest plane." She turned around to look at Kalugal. "What do you need such a large jet for?"

He chuckled. "If your brother were here, he would have said that I'm a competitive bastard and that I need to have everything bigger than his."

She arched a brow. "Is that really why you got it?"

"Among other things." He motioned for her to take a seat. "I enjoy luxury, and I love showing off, but I also love a good bargain. This beauty was for sale at a bargain price because the guy who'd commissioned it needed the money for something else. It's a little too big for what I need, and it barely fits in the clan's hangar, but I couldn't refuse such a sweet deal. I quickly grabbed it before someone else had a chance to."

As the others got on board, Kalugal finished the introductions. "This is my second-in-command, Phinas."

"I'm his third." Phinas shook Orion's hand.

"Not true," Kalugal said. "You and Rufsur are both my seconds." He turned to Orion. "Rufsur is mated to the lovely Edna, whom you had the pleasure of meeting."

Again, Orion didn't contradict him. "Indeed. But I didn't meet Rufsur. He must be an impressive fellow to snag such an important member of the clan."

Kalugal chuckled. "Rufsur is not nearly as smart as Edna, but he has other qualities she appreciates." He motioned for his other two men to step forward. "This is Shamash, who holds a position similar to Shai's, and this is

Welgost, who's my equivalent of Anandur, sans the red hair and about six inches in height and breadth, but no less deadly."

"Well met." Orion shook both men's hands. "I'm looking forward to spending the next couple of weeks with you all."

Annani

Annani could have walked to Ingrid's new design center, but without Alena by her side, it felt awkward to amble through the village. It was a silly sentiment. She had visited the village without Alena, and before that the keep, and she had never felt strange about taking a walk by herself.

Well, usually Kian had a guardian or two trailing her, but she had paid them no attention. Curiously, he had not assigned any to her during this visit. Or maybe he had, but they were keeping their distance?

She hoped none had to chase the golf cart on foot.

As Oshidu parked the cart in front of the house that Ingrid had converted into her workplace, the woman trotted out on her high heels with a big smile on her face.

"Clan Mother." She bowed. "It's such an unexpected honor to have you come visit my new design center."

Annani accepted Oshidu's hand to step out of the vehicle. "Congratulations." She pulled Ingrid into her arms. "With how hard you have been working for years now, you should have gotten some staff to help you out a long time ago."

"Most of the time I didn't need help," Ingrid admitted as she led Annani up the steps to the front porch. "And whenever I did, I asked for the Guardians' assistance, and they never refused me. But with the newest section of the village nearing completion and Kian wanting everything done yesterday, I need a dedicated crew. I just hope I will have work for them after the project is completed."

"I'm sure you will." Annani looked around the living room that had been converted into a design showroom.

Framed photographs of Ingrid's various projects hung on the walls; a few were of houses in the village, but most were of the clan's hotels. Furniture catalogs and fabric samples were strewn over two presentation tables, but from the artful way they were arranged, they had not been just randomly tossed there.

"Knock, knock," a male's cheerful voice sounded from the other side of the door. "May I come in?"

Ingrid arched a brow. "I have no idea who that might be." She sniffed the air and frowned. "I smell chocolate cake, do you?"

Annani nodded. "Open the door, dear. I think someone came with some sweet offerings for you."

Ingrid hesitated. "I didn't invite anyone. I have the next two hours blocked off for your visit."

Another knock sounded on the door. "Is anybody in there?"

Annani smiled. "Your secret admirer is persistent. I do not mind meeting him, especially since he came bearing sweet gifts."

Reluctantly, Ingrid walked over to the door and yanked it open. "Atzil, what are you doing here?"

"I brought you a cake." He thrust a baking dish into her hands. "To celebrate the new design center."

Annani had a feeling that the man was not aware of her being inside, which was a testament to how enamored he was with Ingrid.

Usually, Annani's power radiated so strongly that everyone in her vicinity was aware of her presence unless she deliberately tamped it down.

"Thank you," Ingrid said. "That's very kind of you, but I have a visitor right now. Can you come later?"

"Nonsense," Annani called out. "I want a taste of that chocolate cake."

As Ingrid opened the door all the way, the stunned expression on the man's face made Annani smile.

"Do not look so shocked, Atzil. Please, come in."

"Clan Mother," he whispered and then bowed nearly all the way down to the floor, but did not move an inch. "I should leave."

"Come in." Annani imbued her voice with command, not to compel the poor man, but to release him from his paralysis.

"Yes, Clan Mother." He bowed again and then took a few steps in before halting in the middle of the room.

Ingrid seemed as lost as he was, standing next to him with the cake in her hands. "Would you like some tea with the cake, Clan Mother?" she asked.

"That would be lovely." Annani walked over to the couch and sat down. "Atzil, come sit with me." She motioned to one of the armchairs facing the couch.

"Yes, Clan Mother." He sat on the edge of the chair with his hands clasped in his lap and his eyes downcast.

"You can look upon my face, Atzil. I promise that you will not go up in flames."

That got a little smile out of him. "I am so sorry for coming here unannounced. I thought that since it was a place of business, that was okay. I wanted to thank Ingrid for the beautiful job she has done on my house."

Annani tilted her head. "I thought that you lived with Kalugal and Jacki?"

"I do, but I also have my own place if I wish to sleep there." He cast a quick glance toward the kitchen, where Ingrid was preparing tea. "Kalugal doesn't need me all day long. If I want, I can prepare the meals and leave. Others can take care of the cleanup, but I like to supervise. A kitchen needs to be kept clean at all times. I never compromise on that."

"That is admirable." Annani smiled. "But then it goes well with your name."

When he looked confused, she realized that he might not know the meaning of it. "Your name means noble, which implies high moral and ethical standards."

"In which language?"

She waved a hand. "Several of the ancient ones." She looked up at Ingrid, who came into the converted living room carrying a tray with three teacups, a teapot, and artfully arranged chocolate cake squares. "These cake pieces look almost as good as they smell." Annani cast Atzil a sidelong glance. "Between your baking skills and Ingrid's design flair, you could produce masterpieces together." She clapped her hands. "Like wedding cakes."

Ronja

"You're doing great, Ronja." Kri loaded weights to one side of the barbell and then to the other.

Ronja doubted she could even lift one of those plates or whatever they were called. She chuckled. "I'm using just the bar with no weights on it, and I can do no more than twelve repetitions. How much weight did you just put on yours?"

"I'm not going too heavy because I don't want to bulk up too much. It's a total of one hundred pounds. Fifty on each side."

Did Kri realize how ridiculous that statement sounded? Ronja hadn't visited the gym while still living in the human world, but she was quite sure that male body-builders didn't put much more weight on their barbells. Or maybe they did?

She wouldn't know.

"I find it funny that to you, a hundred pounds is a light weight. I can't imagine being able to lift that much even after years of training."

"Human females can lift that and more, but you are a beginner, and for a fifty-something human who has been training for only six weeks, your progress is impressive. Watching how well you're doing makes me less anxious about you attempting transition."

Ronja felt her cheeks reddening. Did everyone know her plans?

"I'm just trying to get healthier. I haven't decided yet if I'm going to attempt it."

"Yes, you did." Kri lifted the barbell effortlessly.

"I did what?"

"You've already decided that you're going for it. Otherwise, you wouldn't be here every day at seven in the morning, doing something you really don't like doing." She gave her a sly smile. "Don't try to deny it. I see you walk into the gym every morning, looking like you'd rather be anywhere but here."

Ronja wondered whether she'd been so obvious or Kri was very good at reading people. She'd only spoken with the Guardian a few times, and their conversations had been brief and not personal.

At first and second glance, the female was intimidating, but if she cared enough to fear for Ronja's safety then perhaps there was a soft heart beating under all that muscle.

"You're partially correct," Ronja admitted. "I'm about fifty percent sure that I want to attempt it." She shook her head. "No, that's a lie. I'm a hundred percent sure that I want to transition, but I'm also a hundred percent terrified of attempting it."

"That's perfectly understandable, but you should not wait too long. Do it while the Clan Mother is here."

It was a little ridiculous for an advanced society of people to believe in the power of blessings. Ronja had trained as a nurse and had been married to a doctor. She knew first-hand that spirituality only helped to relieve anxiety but didn't deliver miraculous healings.

"With all due respect, I don't put much faith in blessings, even those given by a goddess."

"Don't belittle it." Kri put the barbell down. "It's not superstition, and it's not anything mystical. Think about it this way. If Annani's mere presence induces transition in young Dormant girls, then it makes sense that the power she radiates has something to do with it. It might not be enough to induce transition in an adult, but it must be the boost that helps them through when difficulties arise. It worked for Syssi, Andrew, and Turner. All I'm saying is that you shouldn't dismiss anything that might help you, and don't attempt transition without Annani being nearby to offer you her blessing. Unlike compulsion, her blessings don't work over phone lines."

"Your theory is the first one that actually sounds logical." Ronja set the bar back on the rack. "Thank you."

"You're welcome." Kri turned to look at the gym's double doors a split second before they were pushed open, and Merlin walked in. "Thanks to you, our doctor looks terrific too." The Guardian winked at Ronja before sauntering over to the next station in her morning circuit.

"Hello, gorgeous." A grin splitting his handsome face, Merlin walked over to Ronja and kissed her cheek.

"Hello to you too. What took you so long?"

After their morning run, Merlin had gone back to his house to check on a potion he'd left brewing over a very low flame. It shouldn't have taken him more than a few minutes, but more than half an hour had passed, which meant that he'd either gotten distracted by something or someone needed his help or advice.

"During the run, I had an idea that I wanted to check on. It took me a while to find the right book."

She arched a brow. "What's the idea?"

He picked a dumbbell from the rack and started working his left bicep. "I remembered reading about an Indian recipe that combined several herbs and spices and was supposed to help longevity. Originally, I dismissed it as just another folk remedy, but yesterday I stumbled upon a scientific study that was done on that combination of herbs." He smiled sheepishly. "I wanted to take another look at the ingredients, but then I got distracted and forgot all about it, until this morning when you mentioned the curry dish you were planning to cook later today. Curry is one of the ingredients in that remedy."

That was Merlin to a tee, and she was willing to bet that he'd forgotten about the potion. "Did you remember to check on the potion brewing in your kitchen?"

His eyes widened. "Damn. I forgot all about it." He put the dumbbell back on the rack. "I need to go."

He was such a classic smart guy, with so many thoughts and ideas crowding his head that he couldn't keep them all straight.

"I'll come with you."

"I don't want you to miss out on your workout because of me."

"We can jog to your house. That counts as a workout, right?"

His lips quirked up in a smile. "It sure does."

Merlin

Merlin was a good actor who had honed his skills over many decades of working with human patients, but he didn't know how much longer he could pull this off.

It was getting harder and harder to treat Ronja as a friend and not make any sexual advances.

For a male, it was impossible to hide his desire even from a human with a weak sense of smell, so there was no way she'd missed the evidence of his arousal every morning when she showed up on his doorstep wearing those tight exercise pants and figure-hugging small shirts.

Even Lisa had noticed.

Several times, he'd caught the minx smiling knowingly and averting her eyes.

Ronja, however, was either clueless or pretended not to notice. In either case she chose not to react, and he had to respect her wishes, but he was running out of patience.

Even now, as they jogged to his house, he found it impossible to keep his eyes from being drawn to her bouncing breasts and his mouth from watering as he imagined his lips on her nipples after he'd gotten rid of what was covering them.

Fates. He shouldn't think such thoughts. It was only making him more miserable.

"You're awfully quiet," Ronja said as they neared the house. "Still thinking about that Indian recipe?"

"Not quite."

"What's on your mind?"

"You," he admitted.

"What about me?"

Did she really have to ask?

"You look very beautiful this morning. Is this a new exercise outfit?"

She smiled shyly. "I'm surprised that you noticed. You're usually oblivious to things like that."

He was, but not when the décolletage dipped so low. Her other exercise outfits were more modest.

Was that a hint?

Should he ask?

Ronja jogged up the stairs ahead of him and opened the door. "Nothing's burning, so that's a good sign."

Except for him, nothing was on fire.

In the kitchen the potion was bubbling on top of the low flame, but that was what it was supposed to do. Once most of the liquid evaporated and all that remained was the paste, it would be ready for the next step in his experiment.

"I was wondering." Ronja leaned against the kitchen counter. "Who are you going to test the poultice on? Immortals don't need it."

He shrugged. "I'll find a volunteer or two in the city."

Her eyes widened. "Are you going to just walk into a hospital, find injured people, and use the poultice on them?"

He shrugged. "I've done that many times before. This is an improvement on a tried and tested formula, so there is no chance of me doing them any harm. I'm only going to help them heal faster."

"Test it on me."

"You're not injured."

"I'll make a cut on my arm, and you can treat it with your poultice."

"Never." As he walked over to her, the urge to kiss her was so strong that he doubted he would be able to refrain from taking her lips. Cupping her cheek, he looked down into her pale blue eyes. "I will never allow harm to come to you."

Staring into his eyes, she swallowed. "Yes, you will. If you induce my transition, you might be the one to harm me."

Merlin recoiled, his erection deflating in an instant. "Are you trying to push me away?"

She shook her head. "I'm only stating the obvious. We have been tiptoeing around the subject for weeks, and I appreciate it that you gave me space and didn't push me to decide one way or the other, but I can't keep going on like this, pretending as if there is nothing between us and we are just friends." She reached for his hand and pulled him to her. "I want you too much."

Thank the merciful Fates.

His arousal kicking back up, he pressed himself against her and took her lips in the gentlest of kisses.

Moaning into his mouth, she cupped the back of his neck and kissed him back. He'd expected Ronja to be shy or hesitant, but she proved him wrong, thrusting her tongue past his lips and exploring the way he wanted to explore her.

With a groan, he wrapped his arm around her waist and brought her flush against his chest. Rubbing himself against her softness, he deepened the kiss, devouring her with his lips and his tongue until she pushed on his chest, and he realized that she needed to come up for air.

Letting go, he leaned his forehead against hers. "We can use protection. Sex does not have to equal induction."

Still panting, Ronja lifted her eyes to him. "I don't know what to do. Kri said that I shouldn't wait. She said that I need to do it while the Clan Mother was in the village so she could give me her blessing and help me pull through if needed. Before, I thought that it was just a spiritual thing, and that Annani couldn't really help me, but Kri made a valid point. If the little girls transition just from being around the goddess, then she must radiate some kind of power that induces transition. It's not strong enough to induce an adult Dormant, but it can help me pull through."

Merlin had his own suspicions about the Clan Mother's so-called blessings, but right now, he was focused on only one thing—getting Ronja naked and exploring her lush body like he'd dreamt of doing for months.

Except, he was a doctor first and a male second, and Ronja's immortal life was his first priority. His raging erection would have to take a back seat to that.

Leaning away from her so he could collect his thoughts, he ran a hand over the back of his neck. "Kri made a very astute observation. Naturally, it has occurred to me before, but the Clan Mother has avoided discussing it with Bridget or with me, saying that not everything in the universe has a scientific explanation, and that we should have faith as well. She seems to care very much about you, so perhaps if I request an audience with her and ask her more questions about the way she induces the girls' transition, she might actually give me some answers this time."

Vrog

"Welcome home, Mr. Wu." Doctor Wang inclined his head. "Mr. and Mrs. Williams, it's a pleasure to see you again, and I'm delighted that you loved our school so much that you decided to invest in it."

Mey smiled and shook the guy's offered hand. "We were indeed impressed, and when we met with Mr. Wu in the States and heard more about his future plans, we decided to come back and give the place another look."

The principal cast Vrog a worried glance, but he didn't inquire about those plans or his place in them. That would probably come later when they were alone.

Vrog and Yamanu discussed thralling Wang to forget that he'd ever seen them before, but they'd decided to wait until the end of their visit to erase his memories. Frequent thralling was harmful to humans, so it was better to do it only once. In fact, the entire faculty would need to be thralled after interacting with the Americans for several days, but Yamanu said that he could handle that in one go.

The guy was incredibly powerful in that regard, probably as much as Jade. Vrog was curious which one of them would have emerged triumphant if they were to compete. From what he'd surmised, the Kra-ell ability worked a little differently than what the clan used. It had an element of compulsion in it that thralling didn't have.

Thralling could change people's memories and make them think that they made the decisions the thraller wanted them to make, but they still retained their free will, and if they realized that the thoughts in their head weren't their own, they could theoretically resist.

"Let me show you to your rooms." Dr. Wang motioned for them to follow him.

Since classes were still in session, they didn't encounter any of the teachers on their way to the staff quarters, saving Vrog the need to introduce them twice. He planned to do that tonight over dinner in the staff dining hall.

Wang opened the door to the first room. "This one is for the three gentlemen." He motioned for Alfie, Jay, and Morris to enter. "It is right next door to the Williams' room."

Three narrow beds had been squeezed into the small space, with two chairs serving as nightstands. There was no other furniture or decorations.

Looking at the room through their eyes, Vrog felt embarrassed about how spartan it was compared to the lavish accommodations in the village, or even in the clan's dungeon. "I apologize for the modest size and decor. It has its own bathroom, though."

"It's perfectly fine." Jay walked in and sat on the narrow bed.

Alfie opened the door to the bathroom, took a look at the shower curtain, and closed the door.

Wang looked at Vrog with worry in his eyes. "These are the best rooms we have."

"That's okay. The Williamses knew not to expect luxury."

"I'm sure we will be comfortable." Mey smiled at him. "I wasn't always wealthy. I grew up in a very modest home."

Reassured, Wang opened the door to the other room. "I hope that meets with your approval."

At least the room had a double bed, but even though it was a standard length, it was not long enough for Yamanu. Vrog was not as tall, and he had a special bed commissioned for himself. Yamanu wasn't going to be comfortable, but he didn't seem concerned.

"Perfect." He rolled his and Mey's luggage inside the room.

Wang looked relieved. "I took the liberty of arranging a welcome dinner for our guests. All the teachers are eager to meet the American investors."

"Thank you." Vrog was impatient to end the tour. "Our guests are tired from their trip and would like to rest."

"Yes, of course." The principal bowed. "Dinner is at six."

That was in less than an hour, which didn't leave them much time for what Mey wanted to do.

"We will see you at dinner, Doctor Wang," Vrog said. "Thank you for taking care of all the arrangements."

When the principal finally left, Vrog let out a breath. "Would you like to freshen up before I take you up to my suite? I suggest we make that our headquarters."

"Lead the way." Yamanu motioned.

His place was not much fancier than the rooms they'd been given, but it was more spacious and had its own sitting room. It was also more private. Vrog had made sure that no one could eavesdrop without him knowing.

When they entered his apartment, he walked over to his bar cabinet and opened the doors. "Can I offer anyone a drink before dinner?"

"What do you have?" Yamanu sidled up to him.

"Rum, whiskey, wine, but no beer. I don't have a refrigerator up here. I should get one."

"No worries." Yamanu pulled out a bottle of wine and turned to his mate. "Would you like some?"

"I'd rather have some water if you have any."

"It's not chilled." Vrog opened a drawer and pulled out a bottle.

"That's fine." She took it and sat on the couch. "Where do you suggest I start listening to echoes tomorrow?"

"Where did you listen to them before?"

"Two of the school dorm buildings. I got the best results from the kitchen and from a storage room."

"There are two storage buildings that survived the fire. You can try your luck there."

Alena

❦

It was a little after six in the evening when the limousine pulled up in front of the lakeshore hotel. Kalugal had hired two of the most luxurious vehicles available, along with drivers that would stay with them for the entire duration of their trip. As expected, the hotel he'd booked for them was the fanciest the lake had to offer. It was comprised of several buildings that monopolized the entire peninsula. The hotel was surrounded by water on three sides, offering a panoramic view of the lake.

As Alena stepped out of the limousine, the hotel's front door flew open, and a small figure with a mop of blond curls rushed out, squealing all the way it took her to reach them.

Alena braced for impact, but at the last moment Carol beelined for Kalugal, nearly tackling the guy to the ground as she leaped into his arms.

"I missed you all so much." She let go of Kalugal to embrace Jacki with a little more care and then leaned away. "Let me see that belly." She put her hands on Jacki's slightly rounded abdomen. "How is my nephew doing? Do you feel him moving around already?"

"All I've felt so far are little bubbles, but Amanda and Syssi tell me that this is how it feels in the beginning, and that soon I will start feeling him move."

"How far along are you?"

"Twenty-one weeks, give or take a couple of days."

"Time flies."

"When you're having fun, right?" Jacki waved at Lokan, who was leisurely strolling over, a big grin spread over his handsome face.

"Working with Lokan on a new fashion line is fun, but I miss you all terribly."

As Lokan and Kalugal embraced, clapping each other on the back, Carol walked over to Alena and Orion. Hugging Alena with much less enthusiasm than she'd hugged Jacki and Kalugal, she gave Orion a thorough once-over.

On the one hand, Alena was glad that her cousins had become such an integral part of the clan, which was nothing short of a miracle. The sons of their archenemy had become close family, and that was wonderful. But on the other hand, she felt slightly offended by Carol's preference for her mate's brother and his wife. After all,

Alena had been Carol's several times great-grandmother for much longer than Kalugal had been her brother-in-law.

In a way, it was Alena's own fault. She'd never emphasized her role as the clan's foremother, had never wanted any titles or special treatment just because the Fates had gifted her with incredible fertility. But perhaps she should remind her family of their lineage from time to time.

She turned to Orion. "Let me introduce my five-times great-granddaughter, Carol." She smiled sweetly. "Carol, this is Orion, Toven's son."

The slight jab seemed to fly over Carol's head.

"Hello." She offered Orion her hand. "I've heard a lot about you and your sister." She sighed dramatically. "I miss home and being part of everything that's happening in the village. Hearing about it secondhand is not the same."

Sidling up to Carol, Lokan wrapped his arm around her shoulders. "You hurt my feelings, love. Am I not keeping you happy?"

Carol kissed his cheek. "You are." She pulled out from under his arm to greet Jin, Arwel, and Kalugal's men.

Alena waited for Lokan and Orion to shake hands and introduce themselves before asking what was probably on everyone's mind. "Aren't you taking a huge risk coming to the lake?" She glanced around. "We are out in the open where anyone can see us."

"Don't worry about it, cousin." Lokan tilted his head back and breathed in. "The road you took to get here is the only one leading to the lake. If anyone was following us, we would have seen them coming from miles away."

Carol came over and leaned against her mate's side. "As far as everyone is concerned, Lokan and I are meeting potential investors." She glanced around and then leaned closer. "Chinese intelligence is no doubt aware of where we are, but Navuh has no access to it, so we are good."

"Let's move the party inside." Lokan started toward the front door. "I have a couple of tables reserved for us in the restaurant."

As the Odus and Kalugal's men hefted the luggage, their group headed to the hotel's lobby.

"You can leave everything here," Carol said. "Or have the Odus carry it to the rooms. Do they know what goes where?"

"Of course, mistress." Ovidu bowed.

"I'd rather finish checking in first," Kalugal said. "Dinner can wait a few more minutes." He leaned closer to his brother. "This place looks even better than the pictures on its website. I love the vaulted glass ceiling. It reminds me of my new house in the village. The difference is that the vaulted skylight is the only source of natural light to the great room that's belowground."

"I can't wait to see it," Carol said. "I need to come home for a visit." She threaded her arm through Lokan's. "But not without my mate. We need to find a way to smuggle him out safely."

As the discussion about a possible visit continued, Alena tuned it out and looked at the lobby's architectural details and design touches.

Syssi would have approved of the architecture, and Ingrid would have approved of the decor.

The soaring vaulted ceiling was supported by massive stone columns and had murals painted on it. The marble floor was polished to perfection, and the Chinese-style furniture seemed of the finest quality.

The hotel's main building looked like a Chinese palace.

"This is the most luxurious hotel in the entire area," Carol said. "And since we are talking Chinese scale, that means hundreds of miles in each direction. The rooms are spacious, the beds are luxurious, and the water pressure in the shower is great."

"How is the food?" Orion asked. "Did you have a chance to sample it?"

"I've had better," Carol admitted, "but the service is incomparable. They are really doing their best to impress their guests."

As an army of bellboys descended on the Odus and Kalugal's men, taking the luggage off their hands, the Odus looked to Alena for instructions.

"You can go up and start unpacking," Alena said. "After you are done, you can retire to your room."

"Yes, mistress," they said in unison before pivoting on their heels and following the bellboys.

When their group headed to the hotel's restaurant, Orion leaned closer to her. "This was the first time that I've observed them acting like robots. I wonder if I would have suspected something was off about them if I didn't know that they were cyborgs."

"You would have excused that as their familiarity, being twins, or training. The mind likes to organize things in familiar patterns, and when something doesn't make sense, it just reshapes it until it fits the preconceived mold."

Orion

Once dinner was served, Kalugal cast a shroud around their table so they could talk freely, but Orion couldn't understand how Kalugal had solved the problem of the staff seeing them talking soundlessly. Since none of his dinner companions seemed to be concerned, it was either a different kind of shroud than the one he'd experienced Alena casting, or Kalugal planned to thrall the waiters later.

"How does your shrouding work?" Orion asked. "The waiters can't hear us, but they can see our lips moving. I assume that you have a solution for that."

"Naturally," Kalugal said. "What we say sounds like gibberish to them, and they assume that we are talking in a foreign language they've never heard before."

"What happens if they ask us something? Do you have to drop the shroud?"

Smiling, Kalugal shook his head. "My shrouds are very sophisticated. If you look directly at them when you speak, they will understand you."

"Once again, I'm impressed with your ability. I'm not even going to ask how that's possible because I still don't know how shrouding works. Is it similar to compulsion?"

Kalugal smoothed a hand over his neatly trimmed goatee. "The best description I can come up with is that it's thralling with an element of compulsion. I imagine what I want the humans to hear, and then I will that into their minds." He smirked. "But that's not the impressive part. As you know, my shrouding works on immortals as well as it does on humans. What's truly marvelous is that I can pick and choose who I'm shrouding. While everyone around this table can hear and see each other, the humans cannot. It's a very delicate and complicated operation. In addition, once I cast the shroud, I can maintain it effortlessly while enjoying my dinner and conversing with you."

Kalugal loved to show off, but he was entitled to his bragging rights. "Is there a chance you can teach me how to do that?"

"I don't know that I can, but I'm willing to give it a try."

Lokan put his chopsticks down and dabbed at his mouth with a napkin. "Kalugal told me that you inherited the compulsion ability from your father, and that you can also compel immortals."

"I can."

"How many people can you compel at once?"

"I don't really know. I think twelve was the most I've ever attempted, but those were humans. I have no idea how many immortals I can compel at the same time. Are you asking because of your father's island?"

Lokan nodded. "The only way to wrestle control from him without causing a much bigger problem is for someone to step in and take his place. Over time, after a long re-education effort, the need to keep all the warriors on a tight leash might diminish, and hopefully, one day it won't be necessary at all."

"My brother is an optimist," Kalugal said. "A dreamer."

Lokan didn't dispute Kalugal's claim. "I want a better life for everyone on that accursed island." He looked his brother in the eyes. "You know how bad it is. What they do to the Dormants and the other women they bring over to serve in the brothel. And the thing is that they are not even aware of how bad they have it because they are all either thralled or compelled into thinking that they have it good." Lokan smoothed his hand over his straight dark hair before shifting his eyes to Orion. "Can you blame me for wanting to make it better?"

"No, I can't. And if I could do something about it, I would. But I don't think that I can control a hundred immortals, let alone several thousand. I'm not your solution."

Orion wondered whether Toven could take over for his nephew.

How powerful was the god?

He probably wasn't as powerful as Navuh, or he wouldn't have failed so miserably at all his attempts to bring civilization to the savages.

If he was, Toven could have just compelled them to abandon their bloodthirsty ways until the behaviors he wanted to instill in them became so ingrained that no further compulsion was needed.

That was what Lokan envisioned for the island's hoodlums, and he was right about the method, just not about the means to achieve it.

Orion was not his solution.

"How about your father?" Lokan asked.

Orion smiled. "I was just contemplating the same thing. Toven is a compeller, but I don't know how strong. He told me that he'd failed in all of his attempts to improve the lives of humans, and that they always managed to twist his teachings into horrific acts of cruelty. If he was as powerful as your father, he could have forced the savages to be peaceful."

"Perhaps it didn't occur to him to try," Carol suggested. "Lokan has had a long time to think about the best way to rehabilitate these warriors and turn them into decent males."

"Toven has had even longer," Alena said. "But it's not fair to compare his situation to Navuh's. Controlling the island's population with compulsion is possible only because Navuh also controls who can get in and who can leave. There is practically no outside influence. Toven didn't have that luxury."

"The Brotherhood's home wasn't always on the island," Lokan said. "Its first home was Mortdh's stronghold in Baalbek, and there were at least five others before Navuh bought the island and moved the Brotherhood there. That being said, even before the island, the warriors had not been exposed to much outside information, firstly because it wasn't freely available, and secondly because they were kept too busy training and fighting to ponder or question anything."

Alena

❧

After everyone was done with their meal, and the waitress came over to offer them a dessert menu, Alena was curious to test Kalugal's claim about his shroud.

"What do you suggest for dessert?" she asked while looking directly at the woman.

"Here is the dessert menu." The waitress pulled a stack of red cardboard cards from her apron pocket and distributed them around the table.

The card was printed in Chinese on one side and English on the other, and as Alena went over the selection, she felt Kalugal drop the shroud. She had to admit that his was subtler than hers. The difference between having the bubble he'd created around them and its absence was barely discernible, while her silence shroud felt like being in a fish tank.

Leaning back, Kalugal regarded the young woman with the usual one-sided tilt of his lips that made him look as if he was smirking. "Min," he read her name tag. "My friends and I would like to take a tour of the lake. Can you recommend a guide?"

The hotel had a concierge service, so Kalugal didn't need the waitress's recommendation, and Alena suspected it was just a conversation starter intended to make her feel at ease so he could ask her more questions.

"The boat rental place is a good place to start. They offer a great rowing tour. There are also walking tours around the lake, which is a good way to see the scenic beauty of the surrounding area. There are several old temples along the lake's shores, and beautiful vista points to take pictures of the lake from."

"Is it a difficult trek? My wife is expecting, and I don't want her to exert herself."

"There are two guided treks. One takes a day, and the other is more leisurely and takes three days, but if you prefer something less tiring for your wife, perhaps a horseback tour would be better."

"What is there to see other than the spectacular nature?" Carol asked.

"Oh, many things." Min smiled. "The trek passes through the Lusoshui village of the Mosuo, several temples, pyramidal stupas, and altars. The hotel concierge can make the reservation for you, and a guide will come to pick you up from the lobby. They can also book the rowing tour for you." She turned back to Kalugal. "What would you like to order for dessert?"

As Kalugal looked at the menu and made his selection, Jacki put down the brochure she'd picked up in the lobby and looked at Min. "It says here that Lugu means falling into water. Do you know who fell into the water? Is there a legend about it?"

"There are many legends about the lake, but not about anyone falling into the water. The most well-known one is about the spirit Goddess Gemu who had many lovers among the male spirits of the area. When one of them came to visit and found her with another, he felt humiliated and turned his horse around. She ran after him, but all she found was a hoofprint at the foot of the mountain. Gemu was sad that he'd left and started crying. She cried so hard and for so long that the hoofprint filled with her tears and turned into a lake. When the male spirit saw that, his heart softened, and he threw a few pearls and flowers into the water." Min smiled. "The tear-filled hoofprint is Lugu Lake, and the pearls and flowers are the small islands scattered throughout it."

Jin chuckled. "The legend reflects the sexual practices of the Mosuo."

The waitress kept her expression neutral. "There are several variations of the same legend, but in all of them, Gemu had many lovers."

When Min had left with their orders, Kalugal cast the shroud again. "Aside from their female-dominated society, the Mosuo have several other beliefs and customs that echo those of the Kra-ell. They have taboos on needless killing of animals and felling of trees. From what Emmett told us about the Kra-ell, they drink the blood of animals but don't kill them. Killing an animal and eating its flesh is not forbidden, but it's considered wasteful, and when it's done, a portion of the meat needs to be offered as tribute to their goddess, the Mother of All Life."

"What about the falling into the lake?" Arwel asked. "That got me more intrigued than the other silly legends about the goddess's tears filling up a hoofprint. What if a group of Kra-ell landed in the lake?"

"How deep is it?" Jin asked.

Lokan pulled out his clan-issued phone. "Its maximum depth is 307 ft. It's about six miles long and three miles wide. I don't know how large their pods were, and whether it's deep enough for a massive craft to splash into it from space. But let's check." He typed the inquiry into the search engine. "Ha, that's interesting. Apparently, most of the space capsules that have splashed into the ocean only went six to eight feet down before floating to the surface. The Freedom 7 Mercury capsule went all the way to the bottom, but it doesn't say how deep that was."

Leaning back, Kalugal supported his elbow with one hand and smoothed the fingers of the other over his beard. "Alien landing pods would be much more sophisticated than the primitive capsules human early space exploration employed. I bet they were amphibian and possessed navigation abilities. Probably flying capabilities as well. They were most likely modestly sized and not very long-ranged, but they had to have some mobility."

"Where are you going with this?" his brother asked.

"Oh, I'm just letting my imagination soar. What if the Kra-ell created an underwater base in the lake? What if they did that in many places around the world? There are numerous accounts given by credible witnesses of unidentified submerged objects. I always dismissed them as hallucinations, the same way I did sightings of unidentified flying objects, but perhaps it's worth looking into. My dismissal was mainly due to the familiar terms the witnesses used to describe what they'd seen, which often matched the technology of the time or the science fiction they'd been exposed to. But what if they'd been thralled or compelled to see things not as they appeared? We know that the Kra-ell possess those abilities, and according to Emmett, some of them could compel entire herds of animals." He smiled. "Since humans exhibit many traits of a herd-like mentality, that applies to them as well."

Orion

"Not too shabby." Orion walked over to the chaise and sat down. "I've been in plenty of hotel rooms during my travels, and this is nicer than most." He beckoned her to join him.

Her hands on her hips and her head tilted to the side, Alena remained standing in the middle of the room. "It's fancy alright, but the soundproofing is bad. I can hear Jin and Arwel talking in the next room over. Kalugal got the presidential suite on the third floor for him and Jacki, so at least they have some privacy."

Apparently, his mate had been preoccupied with the same thoughts that had kept him busy throughout dinner. After the long journey during which they hadn't done more than hold hands, he couldn't wait to get to their hotel room and make love to Alena.

His lady wasn't a meek lover, and she could get quite loud when in the throes of passion. He wouldn't have it any other way, but given the circumstances, they would have to get creative.

"Do they have another suite? I'll gladly pay for an upgrade."

"I don't think they do." She walked over to the balcony and opened the French doors. "It's freezing." She closed them and looked out through the glass. "The lake is so dark at night."

Pushing to his feet, Orion walked up to Alena and wrapped his arms around her. "We will just have to be very quiet." He put his lips on her neck and inhaled. "I love your scent," he whispered in her ear before taking the soft earlobe between his lips.

As his hands roamed over her sides and his lips trailed the column of her neck, a soft moan escaped Alena's lips, and her head dropped back on his shoulder. "Let's get into the shower. The water will mask the sounds of our lovemaking."

"I can be silent as a mouse." He cupped her breasts and trailed kisses up her neck. "Can you?"

She shook her head. "Not for long."

"Then I'll have to do this." He turned her around and fused their mouths.

Kissing her, he reached for the curtain and pulled it closed, and then made quick work of getting her naked. When he was done, all that was left were her shoes.

Taking a step back, he admired the beauty before him. "The best of sculptors could not have created such perfection."

Alena wasn't shy, and the pose she struck was more about looking sexy than trying to shield her ample breasts. Smiling confidently, the fingers of her right hand lightly touching her left arm and her head slightly tilted downwards, she gazed at him from under lowered lashes.

His eyes caressed every inch of her, starting with her beautiful face, down her long neck to her substantial breasts, her narrow waist, the flare of her generous hips, her long legs.

"Did you have your fill?" she murmured.

"I will never get enough of this." He put his hands on her waist and lifted her, intending to take her to bed.

"Shower," she insisted. "We've had a long day of travel."

"It's small."

Most of the bathroom area was taken up by a big tub, but Orion wasn't keen on submerging himself in one that had served many guests before him, and the shower was not built for two.

"We will make it work." Alena kicked her shoes off and nipped his ear.

Orion knew better than to argue.

"Yes, mistress," he mimicked Ovidu's subservient tone.

Alena gave the impression of being a soft, accommodating female, and most of the time she was precisely that. But in the short time he'd been with her, he'd discovered the steel core underneath. Alena didn't compromise on what was important to her, and right now, it was showering before making love.

Changing directions, he crashed his lips over hers and carried her into the bathroom.

As he set her down, Alena stepped into the enclosure, cranked the faucets all the way, and reached for the soap. Slowly lathering her skin, she taunted him with a seductive smile as her hands ran all over her lush body.

In seconds, he shucked his clothes and joined her inside. They were both statuesque, substantial people, so even with their chests flush against each other, their bottoms hit the shower's glass enclosure on both sides.

He had a feeling that the whole thing would fall apart as soon as things got heated.

"There are only two ways this can work." He cupped her bottom. "Either like this." He lifted her and let his shaft tease her entrance. "Or like this." He turned her around, her back to his front. "What's your preference, princess?"

She chuckled. "Why do I have to choose when I can have both?"

"True." He slid down her body until his face was flush with her round bottom.

With his hand on her inner thigh, he lifted her leg to the side and dove in. His fingers digging into her glorious ass, he kept her in place as he lapped, kissed, and nibbled. She tried to move, her hips undulating in response to the onslaught, but he held her firmly in place. Releasing one side, he wrapped his arm around her and touched his finger to that most sensitive bundle of nerves at the apex of her thighs.

As he speared his tongue into her wet sheath and applied gentle pressure to her clit, the tiny inner muscles rippled around his invading tongue, and then she bucked against him, the orgasm exploding out of her with a muffled groan.

After helping her ride out the aftershocks, he kissed her soft petals and pushed to his feet, sliding up her silky skin. "Wait in bed for me," he commanded in her ear. "I'll wash up and join you in under a minute."

Panting, her hands pressed against the glass enclosure, she turned her head around and kissed the underside of his jaw. "Yes, sir."

Alena

❦

The climax Orion had wrangled out of her notwithstanding, Alena felt disappointed as she padded to the bed with a towel wrapped around her. In her fantasy Orion would take her from behind in the shower, but practicality prevented her fantasy from materializing.

The shower was too cramped, and the enclosure too flimsy for a couple of immortals in the throes of passion. They would have demolished the thing, which she wouldn't have minded paying the hotel for, but broken glass would have not been conducive to lovemaking.

Looking at the four-poster bed though, she had an idea for how she could still have some of her fantasy, just without the water and the glass.

In addition to the four posts, the bed had a tall headboard and a matching footboard. If she waited for Orion leaning against either one, he would guess what she was after. He might be in a bossy mood, but she knew he would follow her cues nonetheless.

Her male was eager to please, which was a very good quality for a mate to have. Alena was a generous lover, and she expected the same in return.

Dropping the towel, she climbed on the bed and knee-walked to the headboard. The top provided a good grip for her hands, but given how powerful immortal love-making got, that position would make the bed bang against the wall while she was trying to minimize noise.

Leaning against the footboard might produce similar results, though.

The chaise would have to do.

In fact, the way it was built was perfect for a very naughty pose. One side was higher than the other and curved, providing a perfect perch for her belly, and the other side didn't have an armrest at all.

Smiling, she quickly got off the bed and assumed the pose she'd envisioned on the chaise lounge.

As the door opened and Orion stepped out, naked and magnificently erect, her core clenched in anticipation.

The hiss he emitted had her shiver in the most delicious way.

"I wish I had my father's talent." He walked over and smoothed a hand over her arched back all the way to her behind. "But I would never show the drawing of my Venus to anyone."

The god had no place in their hotel room, but she felt like commenting nonetheless. "He never intended anyone to see the drawings he made of his lovers."

"True. And yet, he drew them partially covered." Orion's hand traveled down the swell of her buttocks, his fingers lightly brushing against her lower lips. "I would draw you completely nude." He dipped his head and kissed one cheek and then the other before delving into her with his tongue.

That wasn't what she wanted. As talented as he was with his tongue, she needed that magnificent shaft of his inside of her.

As if reading her mind, or maybe tasting her need, Orion climbed up behind her. "Gods, I need this." He teased her entrance with his erection, coating it with her juices before surging into her in one powerful thrust.

Despite herself Alena cried out, not because the penetration was painful, but the opposite of that. It felt perfect, and as he started pumping into her, she gripped the curved armrest and readied for the ride.

Holding her hips with both hands, he pistoned in and out of her with the power of a freight train. The lewd sounds their bodies were making as they slapped against each other only added to the experience, and as she clamped her teeth on the armrest to muffle her moans, his lips closed on her shoulder to stifle his groans.

At some point, he pulled her upright, her back flush against his chest, and kept riding her hard. When his tongue swiped over the spot his lips had claimed moments ago, the anticipation of what was coming next ripped an orgasm out of her, and as his fangs pierced her skin, she cried out, not caring about who heard her.

Cassandra

⁓

Geraldine tapped Onegus's shoulder. "Where is that restaurant you are taking us to?"

Why was she asking him, the one behind the wheel, and not Shai who was sitting next to her in the backseat?

Besides, Cassandra had told her twice where they were meeting Darlene, once before she'd called her sister to invite her to lunch, and a second time after they'd set the time.

Geraldine was getting better, there was no doubt about it, but whenever she was stressed, her memory issues resurfaced.

"It's a private lounge in one of the clan's hotels," Onegus said.

"Isn't that dangerous?" Her mother's tone was bordering on panicked. "What if Darlene is followed? We don't want to bring the government to a property that belongs to the clan."

Cassandra had explained that too, but Geraldine either didn't remember it or was too stressed to recall their conversation from yesterday.

"I have a Guardian trailing Darlene. If he notices that she's being followed, we will cancel the lunch."

"What if she has her phone on, and they follow the signal?"

"Cassandra made the arrangements with Darlene over the phone, so they already know where Darlene is going, who she's meeting, and why." Onegus had the patience of a saint. "The only reason they might have to follow her is if they suspect that Roni will be there. But they have no reason to think that."

By now, the agents keeping an eye on Darlene in the hopes of finding Roni knew about her two recently discovered cousins. Thanks to Leo, though, they also were aware that Cassandra knew how to reach Roni. But when she'd called, Cassandra hadn't mentioned him, or even told Darlene that Onegus and Shai were joining them, and the reason she'd given her sister for the meeting was that she and Geraldine missed her and wanted to see her.

The lunch meeting necessitated her taking half a day off work, but there was no avoiding that if they wanted to see Darlene without her hubby present. During the day, Leo was busy at the gallery and couldn't join them, so lunch was the best time to talk to her privately.

Clutching her purse, Geraldine looked tense. "Forgive me for asking so many questions, but I still think it looks suspicious. Why would three cousins who live in the same city meet in a hotel for lunch?"

"The hotel is a public place," Onegus said. "No one knows that it belongs to the clan because it's held by a subsidiary of another larger company, which belongs to yet another one abroad, and the connection to the clan is very well-hidden. The hotel restaurant is open to the public, and in addition to the hotel's guests, business-people from nearby office buildings dine there. The private lounge is just a room inside the restaurant that is frequently used for business meetings. Even if Darlene's phone is being tracked, and her location is known, all they will see is her going into the hotel restaurant."

Cassandra turned around to look at her mother. "You're overthinking it, Mom. By now, they are keeping a minimal lookout for Roni. He's eluded them for so long that they should have given up already."

"And yet they offer a reward for information that would lead to his capture." Geraldine sighed. "I don't know how we are going to tell Darlene that Leo sold out his own son for that reward money."

Shai took her hand. "That he didn't get because we were careful and changed plans as soon as we noticed agents snooping around Nathalie's café. We are just as careful now, so you have nothing to worry about."

"That's not true," Geraldine said. "Of course, I have reason to worry. Darlene is going to be devastated when she hears that. I don't want her to be in pain."

Cassandra huffed. "I think this plays beautifully into our plans. Hearing what scum Leo is will make it easier for her to leave him. We can bring her to the village, and she can find a nice immortal male to console her. If Roni is right, the only reason she hasn't left Leo yet is that she's afraid of having no options and being alone. If we convince her that she'll be a most desirable catch for the immortal males in the village, it will give her the courage to leave the jerk."

"We're making too many assumptions," Shai said. "What if Darlene is happy with Leo? What if Roni is wrong and his own opinion of his father is coloring his opinion of their relationship? What if Darlene knew about Leo selling Roni out? Today's meeting is about getting answers to these questions. We will decide how to proceed only after we know what Darlene wants and where she stands in regard to Leo's betrayal of Roni."

"My daughter would never betray her son," Geraldine said. "I might not remember her and the kind of person she is, but she is my and Rudolf's daughter. I would have never done such a thing, and after meeting Rudolf, I know he wouldn't either."

"It's the classic nature versus nurture argument." Cassandra sighed. "You and Rudolf were not the only influences in her life, and genetics don't determine everything. I want you to mentally prepare for the possibility that Darlene knew about Leo's betrayal of Roni."

Geraldine

For the rest of the drive, Geraldine didn't ask any more questions. Cassandra seemed annoyed with her, probably because she'd forgotten what she'd already told her, but that was what usually happened when she got anxious. Her mind just stopped working right, and Geraldine wasn't even sure that it was a memory problem. She just couldn't handle stress well, or at least not as well as others.

If only she was more emotionally resilient, life would have been easier. She worried about telling Darlene about Leo's treachery and how it would affect her. And she worried about Darlene attempting transition at forty-nine. She worried about Shai's son, and whether he carried the immortal gene after all, and whether the clan would find a way to activate his Dormant genes with the help of that new gene-editing technology that was named crisper, or was it crispr? It was probably an acronym, but she didn't know of what.

Perhaps with Shai at her side, she shouldn't be as worried, but despite his eidetic memory, he didn't have the answers to everything. He just knew a collection of facts that was sometimes useful.

Too much had happened too fast for her to adjust, even if it was all good. She'd found a true-love mate, she'd found a new home where she belonged, and she'd found her brother. But what if her good fortune ran out?

What if pushing Darlene to leave Leo and attempt transition was the wrong thing to do?

"What's wrong?" Shai squeezed her hand. "You're very quiet."

"I'm not sure that we should tell Darlene about Leo. What if it makes her so upset that she keels over? I don't know anything about her medical history. She might have a heart condition, or diabetes, or whatever else humans her age suffer from. She's forty-nine."

Shai chuckled. "She'll be fine. If you're worried about shocking her, we can tell her about it in a roundabout way. Besides, she's not going to remember it after we are done with her, so if she gets overly upset, at least it's not going to last long."

Geraldine nodded. "I try to tell myself all those things, but I can't stop worrying anyway. She's my daughter, and I want what's best for her. The problem is that I don't know what that best is."

"That's simple," Cassandra said. "You can't beat immortality. If she has even a slim chance of achieving that, it's worth the risk."

As Onegus pulled up into the valet station, Geraldine's heart started racing, and her palms got sweaty. "I'm scared."

"I know, love." Shai kissed the top of her head. "Let's just take it slowly, okay? We are not going to drop it on Darlene right off the bat. Let's enjoy lunch first."

"Okay." She took his offered hand and stepped out of the car.

"The restaurant is on the seventy-second floor." Onegus led them to the elevators. "This building is a new concept that combines hotel rooms with offices. The guest rooms are on the top ten floors, and the rest are office suites."

The elevator to the top floor was so fast that Geraldine felt her ears pop, and as the doors opened and they walked out, the view that greeted them was spectacular. The entire metropolis was spread out before them, or at least most of it.

Onegus stopped by the hostess's station. "MacBain. I reserved the private lounge."

The woman made a show of checking her ledger and then lifted her head with a smile. "Welcome to the Seventy-Second, Mr. MacBain." She pulled out five menus and then looked over their party of four. "Are we waiting for another guest?"

"She should be here at any moment," Cassandra said. "We can either wait for her here, or you can show her to the private lounge when she gets here."

The hostess was about to answer as the elevator door opened, and Darlene stepped out. "That was quite a ride." She patted her ears. "I can't hear anything."

"Hi." Cassandra gave her a one-armed hug. "Blow your nose. That will clear your ears."

"Yeah, that's what I do on flights." Darlene turned to look at Shai and Onegus. "I didn't know that you two were coming as well. I'm glad that you are joining us, but I'm surprised."

"It was a last-minute decision." Shai leaned toward her and kissed her cheek. "Onegus and I had a meeting nearby, so we thought why not combine business with pleasure. I hope that you don't mind."

"No, of course not."

"Let me show you to the private lounge," the hostess said.

That got Darlene's attention. "Are we dining in a private lounge?"

"Working for a very rich guy has its perks." Onegus winked.

Cassandra

❧

Normally Cassandra was a straight shooter who didn't mince words, but the situation with Darlene needed a more nuanced approach. She could let Onegus handle it, which he would no doubt do better than she could ever hope to, but Darlene wasn't his sister, and it wasn't his responsibility to tell her about her scum of a husband or offer her immortality.

She should hear it from her family.

Another complication that had somehow escaped Geraldine's list of worries was that when they told Darlene about her chance at attempting immortality, they would also have to reveal that Geraldine and Cassandra were not her cousins.

Cassandra had no doubt that the shock of learning that Geraldine was Darlene's long-presumed-dead mother would be much worse than her sister learning about her husband's treachery. She hadn't pointed it out to Geraldine because her mother was already stressed enough.

"Let's make a toast." Cassandra lifted her wine glass. "To family."

Looking a little confused, Darlene lifted her glass and clinked it with Cassandra's. "To family, old and new."

"I bet you're wondering why the four of us cornered you into this private dining room." That wasn't the soft delivery Cassandra had hoped for, but they didn't have all day to dance around the issue.

Darlene put her glass down. "I had a feeling that the story about the business meeting wasn't true. What's going on?"

"We've learned something very upsetting about Leo."

Darlene swallowed. "Does he have a mistress? Is that why he goes on all those business trips?"

"He might, but that's not it. Did you know that there was a substantial reward offered to whoever provided information that led to Roni's capture?"

She shook her head. "How substantial?"

"Half a million dollars."

Darlene smiled proudly. "My Roni is worth a lot more than that, but I'm sure he's tickled silly by that amount. What does it have to do with Leo, though?"

Unless Darlene was an excellent actress, she really didn't know about the reward money or about Leo selling his son out.

Cassandra leaned forward and reached for her sister's hand. "Do you remember that we changed the meeting place with Roni because agents were snooping around the original place?"

She nodded.

"We couldn't figure out how they'd found out about it. Later, we learned that Leo had sold Roni out. He was the one who told the agents where the meeting was about to take place."

For a long moment, Darlene just gaped at her, and then the waterworks started. "Oh, my God. I can't believe that he did that. What a colossal jerk." She fisted her hand. "If he were here, I would punch him right in the teeth. How could he?"

Next to Cassandra, Geraldine sniffled. "I didn't want to tell you. I knew how upset you would be."

"How did you find out?" Darlene asked Cassandra and then turned to Onegus. "Was it through your security connections?"

He nodded. "After Leo's comment about wanting to see Roni's DNA test results, I suspected that he had something to do with compromising our meeting location. I have agent friends who work for a different department than the one Roni worked for but have access to the same files. I asked one of them to check, and he provided the information."

"When did you find out?"

"A while ago," Onegus admitted. "We debated whether to tell you or not. Geraldine was afraid it would upset you."

"Of course, it upsets me." Darlene sighed and picked up a napkin to dab at her eyes. "But it shouldn't have surprised me. Leo has always suspected that Roni wasn't his, but he never had the guts to demand a DNA test."

"Was he right?" Cassandra asked.

Darlene nodded. "We've always had relationship problems. Well, not in the beginning, but after years passed and I couldn't get pregnant, he blamed me, assuming that I was the infertile one because nothing could be wrong with him. I went to the doctor, and when she couldn't find anything wrong with me, she suggested that Leo might be the infertile one. He refused to get checked, saying that the doctor was incompetent and that I should go see a specialist. I was angry that he wasn't willing to even consider that it might be his fault. We fought over this and many other things, and finally, I got fed up and left. He didn't even try to stop me." Darlene dabbed her eyes again. "I think that he was happy to be rid of me."

"You met someone," Cassandra guessed.

Darlene nodded. "I wasn't ready to file for a divorce yet, but I was hurt and angry, and my confidence was shot. I needed to prove to myself that I was still desirable. I wasn't picky, and I said yes to the first guy who offered." She chuckled. "He was a geeky software engineer who couldn't believe that I said yes. I didn't know that he was a genius, but I guess I got lucky. Roni wouldn't be nearly as smart if Leo was his father."

Geraldine

Geraldine had so many questions she wanted to ask her daughter, and more than that, she wanted to take her into her arms and console her, but she could do neither since the waitress had returned with their order.

When the woman left and closed the door behind her, Onegus asked, "How long were you and Leo separated?"

"Not long." Darlene unfurled the napkin and spread it over her knees. "A couple of months, maybe even less than that. I still worked back then, and Roni's father was the IT person for the firm. I didn't know that he'd been mooning after me for the entire year and a half he'd known me. We went out a few times, but it wasn't serious. Not on my part anyway. I still loved Leo and hoped that he would come to his senses and apologize for being such a dick. But it didn't happen."

"What did you do when you found out that you were pregnant?" Geraldine asked.

"I freaked out. I didn't want to divorce Leo, so I called him and suggested that we go to couples therapy. Surprisingly, he agreed. I took it as a sign that he missed me and wanted me back but had been too proud to initiate the reconciliation. Naturally, I did everything to be the perfect wife he wanted, and we got back together. When I told him that I was pregnant a month later, he was overjoyed. Frankly, I don't think he started suspecting anything until Roni's superior intelligence started manifesting. They have similar coloring and the same slim build, but neither Leo nor I are that smart. When Roni got a little older, and his contrary character started to become more apparent, he and Leo fought nonstop. I think that was when Leo started suspecting that Roni wasn't his."

"Did he confront you about it?" Shai asked.

Darlene sighed. "Many times. I denied it, of course. When I called him paranoid and pretended to encourage him to take a paternity test, he backed off, only to bring it up again when we had yet another fight. But I never thought he would go as far as selling Roni out. He raised him as his son. How could he have done that?"

Cassandra crossed her arms over her chest. "A better question is why did you put up with him for so long? Leo is obviously a prick."

"Guilt. Fear." Darlene wiped tears from her eyes. "What am I going to do now? How can I stay with him after he did a thing like that?"

"Do you love him?" Geraldine asked gently.

"I don't know. I'm used to him, and I don't want to be alone."

"What if I could promise you a better future?" Cassandra said. "What if you could live next to Roni and his mate, have handsome men vying for your attention, and all of your needs met? Would you leave Leo then?"

"Sure, but you can't promise me all that."

Cassandra smiled. "Yes, I can, and much more than that. I can offer you immortality."

Darlene's tears dried in an instant. "You're either crazy, or you think that I am, in which case, I really resent you for making fun of me."

"I wouldn't dream of it." Cassandra uncrossed her arms. "But I see that you are not ready for the red pill yet. Let's eat first, and when you feel up to it, I'll tell you precisely how you can have all the wonderful things I've offered you."

"What red pill?"

"Didn't you see *The Matrix*? The red pill represented the willingness to learn a potentially life-altering truth, and the blue pill represented staying ignorant. Which one would you choose?"

"I remember now." Darlene reached for a glass of water with a shaking hand. "The truth was much worse than the fantasy, and one character betrayed the rebels in exchange for erasing that knowledge from his mind. So maybe choosing the blue pill is the smarter option."

"Not in this case." Cassandra grinned. "The red pill we offer you will reveal a truth that is better than your wildest fantasies."

Geraldine wasn't sure Cassandra had it right. The truth in the so-called red pill could tempt Darlene with a promise of eternal life but also deliver premature death.

Kian

⌒✦⌒

"Come in," Kian said as a knock sounded on his office door.

He was expecting Edna sometime that afternoon, but not this early. Perhaps she'd cut her workday short. After all, it was Friday, and people were getting ready for the weekend.

"Hello, Kian." The judge walked in and sat down on one of the chairs in front of his desk. "I didn't see Shai on my way in. Did he take a day off?"

"He's in a lunch meeting with Geraldine's daughter." He looked at his watch again. "I wonder how it's going. They are supposed to tell her about her possible shot at immortality, get her reaction, and then thrall the memory away."

Edna lifted one sculpted brow. "That's an odd way to go about it. Now that we have several compellers in our midst, it would have been better to compel her silence instead of thralling her."

"I agree. The problem is that except for Parker, all of our compellers are away at the moment, and Cassandra didn't want to wait. I think she hopes that Darlene will just decide on the spot and come back with them to the village, but that's unrealistic."

"I don't know the woman, but without a very compelling reason to jump ship, most reasonable people would need some time to mull over a decision like that."

Kian nodded. "How is translating Toven's journal going?"

Edna sighed. "I haven't read anything in Aramaic in a very long time, and my initial progress was painfully slow. It's going faster now, and I have about half of it translated. He recorded detailed descriptions of his lovers, including their full names, the month, year, and location of the encounter. I bet that Orion looked into that and checked whether these women produced children nine months later, but what I found more interesting was the pattern I discerned."

"That the women were all artistically inclined? Orion said that Toven had a thing for artistic females."

"That too. Toven wasn't moved by physical beauty alone. He preferred ladies who piqued his interest, who were creative and were independent, or as independent as the times allowed women to be back then. He also preferred big cities, and during the time period that particular journal covered, he visited the US many times. So far, the cities mentioned in the journal were New York, Boston, Chicago, Philadelphia, San Francisco, Houston, Miami, and Honolulu. In Europe, the only cities mentioned were Paris and London, and there were none in East Asia or Africa or South America. That doesn't mean that he didn't visit there, though. He might have just not taken lovers while there. It makes perfect sense. Women were more progressive in the West, and large cities provided him with the anonymity he needed."

Leaning back in his chair, Kian crossed his arms over his chest. "How does that help us find him, though?"

"I think he's in the US, probably on the East Coast. We know what he looks like, but not precisely enough to use facial recognition software to find him by his driver's license or passport. I wonder if William can tweak the program to broaden the match. It might produce thousands of results, but it shouldn't take too long to sift through them. If he can include British and French databases in his search that would be even better."

"That's a very smart idea. I'll ask him if that's possible. Anything else that you found and took note of?"

"For now, that's it. I'll work on the rest over the weekend and make a list of all the cities his affairs took place in and the corresponding dates. Perhaps I can narrow it further."

Kian nodded. "The problem is that the last entry was made nearly four decades ago. Toven might have moved to a new territory."

"It's possible," Edna said. "But for now, that's all we have to work with. What about the other idea of locating his novels by his writing style?"

"Turner's guy is searching through Russian libraries and used books stores for the title Orion remembered seeing at Toven's place. Their cataloging system is not nearly as thorough as the one we have here. We will also use your translation of the journal. I hope that Aramaic translates well into English."

Edna grimaced. "It does not, but Toven has a very distinctive writing style that I doubt he was able to change enough for the novels he published. Once I'm done with the translation, it's worth a try to run it through a style-detecting software."

"Of course." Kian uncrossed his arms and leaned forward. "I wonder if Eva and Geraldine have more in common than they realize. What if Eva wasn't induced by Kalugal but was born immortal?"

Edna shook her head. "Eva said that she'd thought it was the flu. She wouldn't have gotten sick if she were immortal. She also remembers her parents, and she wasn't adopted."

"Perhaps she just felt down emotionally and thought that it was the flu?"

Kian knew that he was grasping at straws, but that nagging suspicion that there was more to Eva's story refused to abate. "Also, record keeping back then wasn't as efficient, and her parents might have opted for a private adoption without any intermediaries. That was also done back then."

"What about her senses? Did she always have super strength and super hearing, or did she start noticing that after her so-called flu?"

"That's actually a very interesting question. Eva thought that her powers were the result of tampering with her DNA that was done during her training with the DEA."

"As far as I remember her story, she was oblivious until she cut her finger one day, and it healed almost instantly. She was probably blocking her super senses like Geraldine did, or thought that it was normal to hear and see as well as she did. Personally, I don't think the Fates would have sent Kalugal Eva's way if she didn't need activation. But if you still have doubts, you can call her and ask."

Despite his nagging suspicion, Kian had to accept that all the evidence confirmed Eva's induction by Kalugal.

Perhaps Eva's grandmother was Toven's daughter?

"No, you're right. The simplest explanation is usually the right one. We know for certain that she and Kalugal hooked up, and there was no way he wouldn't have noticed her strength and stamina when he had sex with her. She must have been still human back then."

Annani

The house felt empty with Alena and Oridu gone. Annani still had Ogidu and Oshidu, so she wasn't alone, and she had been trying to distract herself by making back-to-back appointments with various clan members, but she could not fill every moment of every day.

Besides, she needed time to rest and gather her thoughts, or so she had been telling herself, but the truth was that she was very happy about Merlin's request for an audience. Not only did it fit in nicely between two appointments, but she also enjoyed the quirky doctor's company.

Merlin was a positive male with a good sense of humor and a seemingly bottomless trove of knowledge. He was always a pleasure to be around, and he was entertaining.

Except, she had a good idea why he had requested an audience with her, and there was nothing amusing or entertaining about that. She could not tell him the truth about her blessing, but she wanted to reassure him that it was helpful and had proven to be highly effective in aiding Dormants' transition.

Merlin was smart, and he might figure it out, but as long as she did not admit the truth, he had no proof and did not know it for a fact. If he was ever captured by their enemies or by humans who sought the secret of immortality, he had a better chance of withholding information he was unsure of.

When the knock sounded at the door, Oshidu walked over to open up for Merlin, and Ogidu rushed out of the kitchen with the tea and canapés she had requested him to prepare for the meeting with the doctor.

"Good afternoon, Clan Mother." Merlin bowed his head. "Thank you for agreeing to see me on such short notice."

"It is always a pleasure to talk to you, Merlin. I was very glad to grant your request." She motioned to the armchair. "Please sit down and help yourself to some canapés."

Ogidu lifted the teapot and poured tea into Annani's cup.

"Would you like some tea, master?"

"I would love some." Merlin lifted the cup for the Odu to fill.

After taking a few polite sips, he put the cup down and smiled. "I promised to update you on Ronja's progress."

"Indeed." She put her cup down as well. "I saw her on Wednesday, and I was amazed at the transformation. If I did not know better, I would have thought that she had already transitioned. You look amazing as well, Merlin."

He inclined his head. "Thank you, Clan Mother. Ronja and I have been working very hard, exercising, eating healthily, drinking plenty of water, and of course, my health-boosting potions had something to do with it as well."

"Do they work on immortals?"

"We don't need them because our bodies are programmed to operate optimally, but I believe that there is always room for improvement." He flexed his muscles. "I'm proof of that. I was perfectly healthy, but my posture wasn't great, and I was a bit on the scrawny side. After training alongside Ronja, I look much better, and I feel better as well. But as far as health-boosting potions go, I don't think they have much effect on immortals. Unless we abuse our bodies on a daily basis, they repair whatever needs fixing on autopilot. Humans, on the other hand, need all the help they can get." Leaning forward, he looked into her eyes. "Speaking of help, I would like to find out more about your blessings and how they help Dormants transition."

She arched a brow. "Is Ronja ready to attempt it?"

A sly smile lifting his lips, Merlin nodded. "My new and improved physique has proven to be a very effective aphrodisiac. Ronja admitted that she could no longer resist me. But joking aside, the reason she finally capitulated was a conversation she had with Kri."

"Good for Kri." Annani lifted her teacup. "That girl does not mince words. What did she tell Ronja to convince her?"

"Kri advised Ronja to attempt transition while you are in the village."

"I told her the same thing." Annani crossed her feet under her long skirt. "I would think that my word would carry more weight than Kri's, but apparently, it is not so."

"Ronja thought that the blessing was a spiritual thing and that the effect it had on transitioning Dormants was a psychological rather than physical one. Kri had an interesting observation that convinced Ronja the blessing was much more than a mood booster for the transitioning Dormant and his or her mate. She said that if your presence alone is enough to activate the dormant little girls, then you must be emitting something that activates their dormant genes. It might not be enough to induce transition in an adult, but it can provide the extra boost to get them over the most difficult part of it."

"Kri is a smart girl." Annani took a sip from her tea and waited for Merlin's question. When it did not come, she leveled her eyes at him. "Was there a question in that story which I missed?"

He nodded. "Are you aware of emitting something that activates the Dormants?"

"Of course." She put her cup down. "Well, I do not feel it, if that is what you are asking, but I have been told by many that being in my presence is like being next to a small nuclear power source." She laughed. "Thankfully, I am not radioactive despite having glowing skin. But I am radiating something. Blessedly, it has only positive effects and no negatives."

She had not lied. Everything she had told Merlin was the truth, just not the whole truth.

"Is that all?" Merlin asked. "What do you do when you bless a Dormant? Do you concentrate that power somehow? Do you put your hands on them to imbue them with your power? Forgive me, Clan Mother, but as a scientist, I like to know how things work."

"I forgive you." She gave him an indulgent smile. "But I keep what I do to channel my power a secret for a reason, and I have no intention of letting anyone witness the ritual. What I can tell you, though, is that spirituality is only one component of the blessing, and it is more for my benefit than the transitioning Dormant. It helps me concentrate and channel my power. What I can also tell you is that without my blessing, those Dormants I helped might not have made it. If I were a totalitarian ruler, I would have forbidden you from inducing Ronja without me being nearby to help if needed. But since I do not like to assert my will on others, and I prefer people to listen to my advice because that is the prudent thing to do, I leave it up to you and Ronja to make the final decision."

Merlin dipped his head. "Thank you, Clan Mother. You are as wise as you are gracious."

Darlene

Leo had warned Darlene that there was something wrong with her newfound cousins. He'd said that their stories didn't add up, but she'd been so happy to have found them, or rather at having been found by them, that she'd ignored the seeds of doubts he'd planted in her head.

She'd done a little online research and found plenty of information about Cassandra, but none about Geraldine. She didn't know Shai's last name, so she couldn't check up on him, but she found Onegus's while reading an article about the gala where he and Cassandra had met.

What was written about him didn't match what he had told her and Leo at all. According to the article, he was a reclusive billionaire, the founder of the charity that helped rehabilitate rescued victims of trafficking.

He was not the head of security.

Still, their story had been plausible enough until Cassandra had started pushing her to leave Leo and talking about that immortality nonsense. If it was only Cassandra, Darlene would have dismissed it as the blabbering of a crazy person, but the others hadn't denied her claims.

They were all in on it, and they had ganged up on her while Leo was away, spinning lies about him.

Telling them about Roni's real father had been so stupid. Now they could use it against her, forcing her to do things that she wouldn't otherwise agree to.

She was such a stupid cow.

She'd just proven Leo right and justified all the times he'd called her that.

How was she going to get out of the mess she'd created?

"Stop stressing," Cassandra said. "Your nervous energy is killing my appetite."

"I can't help it." Darlene shoved another piece of chicken into her mouth.

When she was nervous or unhappy, she ate more, not less. No wonder Cassandra looked like a supermodel while she looked like a pumpkin. And just to prove that she wasn't only a stupid cow but also a fat one, when there was nothing left on her plate, she reached for the last piece of bread in the basket and shoved it into her mouth as well.

Cassandra pushed her half-eaten entree away from her and picked up her wine glass. "So here is how it's going to happen. I will tell you a lot of things that you are probably not going to believe, and then I'll ask you to make a decision. After that, Shai is going to erase your memory of this entire conversation, and we will take it from there." She glanced at her watch. "I'm just waiting for Roni to get here."

Darlene frowned. "What do you want from him?"

"I thought that you would be more inclined to believe your own son than a cousin you've just met." As Cassandra turned to Geraldine, her eyes softened. "You know what's coming, right?"

Tears glistening in her eyes, Geraldine nodded.

"Are you ready?" Shai asked. "We don't need to do this today. If you need more time, that's fine."

Why were they all coddling Geraldine?

If anyone needed reassurance it was Darlene, the woman who they were trying to deceive, the one who was outnumbered and alone.

Roni was coming, but would he stand by his mother's side? Or was he going to stick with these strangers that claimed to be related to him?

"I need to visit the ladies' room." Darlene pushed to her feet.

Perhaps she could duck into the elevator before they could notice.

Could they really erase her memories?

"I'll go with you." Cassandra got up.

Darlene sized her cousin up and realized that she didn't stand a chance against that Amazon woman. With heels on, she was well over six feet tall, and she looked toned. Darlene hadn't visited the gym in years, and her idea of exercise was pacing around the kitchen island, which was sizable, but given that she usually snacked while doing it, it really didn't count.

God, if she got out of this bizarre situation without losing her husband or worse, she was hitting the gym, and to make sure that she actually followed through, she was going to hire a personal trainer.

As dreams of a better, stronger body and a brighter future eased some of her anxiety, Darlene gave Cassandra a forced smile. "I can find the way to the bathroom on my own."

"I know you can." Cassandra put her hand on Darlene's arm in a gesture that might have been intended as reassuring but came across as threatening. "I need to visit the ladies' room as well."

Darlene doubted that, but it wasn't as if she could get rid of her imposing cousin. "Let's go. I want to be back before Roni gets here."

"Same here." Cassandra took hold of her arm and led her out of the private lounge. "It was difficult enough to drag him out here. I promised him that it wouldn't take long and that we wouldn't waste his valuable time."

"Does he know what this is about?"

"I only told him that you would need someone you trust to tell you the story. I wish I had thought of that ahead of time, but I didn't expect you to panic. It will also make it easier on Geraldine." Cassandra pushed the door to the ladies' room open.

"Why is everyone so concerned with her?" Darlene asked. "She is not the one that is getting slammed with nonsense from *The Matrix*."

"Let's wait for Roni." Cassandra opened one of the stalls and motioned for Darlene to go in. "I'll be right here if you need me." She winked.

Cassandra

As the door to Darlene's stall closed, Cassandra leaned against it to make sure the little mouse didn't get any ideas of escape into her head.

Pulling out her phone, she texted Roni. *When are you getting here?*

His reply text came in a minute later. *At the valet. Will be there in two.*

Cassandra let out a breath. She should have thought of bringing Roni along, but it hadn't occurred to her until Darlene revealed her big secret. That was the reason she'd stalled and told Darlene that they would continue talking after the meal. She'd needed to give Roni enough time to get there. He would be so glad that Leo wasn't his biological father. He didn't like the guy, and the feeling was mutual.

Even if Roni wasn't Leo's biological son, the guy had still raised him from infancy into adulthood. He should have loved Roni even though he suspected that he wasn't his. But Leo was a jerk who hadn't been a good husband or father, and yet Darlene clung to her marriage despite everything.

Did she love him, though?

When the toilet was flushed in the stall behind her, Cassandra pushed away from the door and waited for Darlene to step out.

"Roni should be here in a minute."

Darlene nodded and walked over to the row of sinks to wash her hands. "I thought that you needed to use the bathroom yourself." She looked at Cassandra through the mirror.

"I thought I did, but when I got here, the sensation passed."

Raising a brow, Darlene turned the faucet off and dried her hands with a towel. "Just admit that you accompanied me to make sure that I didn't escape."

Cassandra shrugged. "What can I say. You caught me."

"Why is this so important to you? Why do you care if I stay with Leo or not? It's none of your business."

"I just want what's best for you." Cassandra took Darlene's arm and led her back into the lounge.

Roni came in a moment after they'd sat down. "Hi, everyone." He walked over to Darlene and leaned to kiss her cheek. "How are you holding up, Mom?"

"I'm confused and worried. Cassandra told me that you have all the answers."

Roni gave Cassandra an accusing look. "Thanks, auntie."

"She will be more accepting of what we need to tell her if it comes from you."

"Right." Roni motioned for Cassandra to get up and let him sit in her chair. "So here is the thing, Mom." He took her hand between his two. "You and I carry godly genes. Mine were activated, and I am now immortal. Yours can be activated as well, but not without risk. The transition into immortality is dangerous for older Dormants, and you are pushing the limit of what's safe, but I still think that it's worth the risk."

Darlene gaped at him. "Are you on drugs?"

He grinned. "I knew that you would think that. Just look at my teeth." He closed his eyes, and soon his fangs started elongating. He'd probably imagined making love to his mate, or maybe attacking another immortal male.

"What the hell?" Darlene's eyes widened. "Are those prosthetics?"

Roni sighed, and his fangs retracted. "I hoped that I wouldn't have to do this, but you leave me no choice." He pulled out a small switchblade from his pocket, flipped it open, and plunged it into the palm of his hand.

"What are you doing?" Darlene shrieked.

"Just watch my hand," he commanded.

As the skin started knitting together, Darlene sucked in a breath, and when the cut disappeared, she gripped Roni's hand and wiped the few drops of blood away with her finger. "It was a trick. You used one of those prop knives and dripped a few droplets of blood on your hand."

"You've seen the skin knitting together, but here," he handed her the switchblade. "Check it out for yourself."

Darlene turned the miniature weapon this way and that, opened it, closed it, opened it again, and then handed it back to Roni. "I can't believe it."

"I know you can't." Roni took her hand again. "But it's real, and it could be yours, but you can't stay with Leo. He doesn't have the godly genes, and when you transition into immortality, it will be really difficult for you to hide it. You'll be stronger, faster, your hearing and eyesight will improve, and your wrinkles will disappear. You will look much younger."

"You should have started with that," she murmured. "How, though? Where did we get it from? My mother wasn't immortal, and my father's aging process is just as predictable as any other human's."

"Actually," Geraldine said. "Your mother is an immortal. I am not your mother's twin sister's daughter, Darlene. I am your mother."

Darlene

Darlene felt as if someone had kicked her in the gut. The young woman who she'd believed was her cousin, the one who looked years younger than her, was her mother?

"Prove it. What was my favorite dessert?"

Tears slid down the imposter's face. "I don't remember. The day you thought I died, I almost did. I must have collided with a boat and suffered a severe brain injury. If I hadn't been immortal already, I would have died. In fact, a normal immortal would have died from an injury like that, but I wasn't just any immortal. I'm the daughter of a god, and the amazing healing abilities I inherited from my father saved my life. But since I regrew a large chunk of my brain, all my memories from before the accident were gone. I had to learn everything from scratch, even how to speak. Fortunately, my brother found me and took care of me. He chose not to tell me about the family I had before to save me from having to go through the anguish of leaving you later on. I wasn't aging, and eventually, I would have been forced to really fake my own death and disappear. Orion thought that he was doing the right thing, but I wish he hadn't kept me in the dark. I wish I had spent a few more years with you, at least until you were old enough to go to college. But what was done is done, and I only discovered recently that I had another daughter. You can't imagine how upset and heartbroken I was about it. So much so that I was convinced it couldn't be true and that I really had a twin sister who was your mother." Geraldine reached across the table for Darlene's hand.

Darlene leaned back, pretending not to notice the gesture. Even if everything Geraldine had said was true, she still wasn't ready to forgive her for the charade she'd pulled, pretending to be her cousin. She'd had plenty of opportunities to come out and admit who she really was.

"Who is your other daughter?" Darlene suspected who she was, but she wanted her suspicion confirmed.

"Cassandra is my younger daughter," Geraldine, or rather Sabina said. "You and I lost so many years, but we can have eternity to make up for it. All you have to do is decide whether you are willing to take the risk, and whether you are willing to leave your old life behind. From what I've heard so far, leaving Leo shouldn't be a great heartache for you."

"Why do I need to leave him?" Darlene narrowed her eyes at the woman claiming to be her mother. "Why is it so important to all of you?" She turned to Roni. "Do you hate your father so much?"

As the words left her mouth, she wondered whether anyone present had already shared her confession with Roni.

"He sold me out for money," Roni hissed, the fangs he'd shown her before elongating once again. "Leo doesn't think that he's my father, and even though I look like him, I don't think he is either. I can't remember him ever hugging me, or giving me a ride on his shoulders, or coming to any of my school events, or congratulating me when my science project won first prize in the entire county. I thought that he was just a cold bastard, but to sell me out was a new low that I'm not willing to ever forgive him for. He doesn't deserve the title of father."

Every word was true, and each one was like a punch to her stomach. Leo had always been cold, but she'd blamed his upbringing for it. His parents were two dry sticks who looked down their noses at everyone because they were rich, and their grandparents had been the founders of whatever.

"You are the smart one in our dysfunctional family, Roni. What do you want me to do?"

"I don't want you to do anything that you don't want to, but I want you to know that you have options, and I want you to choose what's best for you."

"I don't know what's best for me. What do I need to do to start the transformation to immortality? And what are the risks?"

Roni grimaced. "That's not something I'm comfortable explaining to my mother. Cassandra should do that."

Darlene turned to her sister. "Well? Do I need to get bitten by a werewolf or something?"

"That was actually a very good guess. You need to get bitten by an immortal male while having sex with him, and if you really like him and bond with him, that makes your chances of transitioning even better."

"You can't be serious." Darlene looked at Roni. "Don't tell me that you had to have sex with a male to transition into immortality."

Roni chuckled. "Thankfully, male Dormants only need to fight an immortal male to activate their genes. The venom needed for the induction gets produced in response to aggression as well as to arousal."

If it were anyone but Roni, Darlene would have suspected that they were pulling a joke on her and that at any moment, someone would shout, you've been pranked! But she'd known Roni all of his life, and he wasn't a good actor, nor was he a jokester.

"What are the risks?" She looked her son in the eyes.

He was the only one she trusted.

"The clan's doctor says that the older Dormants have a difficult time, and that the transition could be potentially deadly for them, but so far, everyone who has attempted it made it through. For some, it was easy, while for others it was more difficult, but no one has died."

"How old was the oldest person who transitioned?"

"I think Turner was forty-seven." Roni looked at Onegus. "Or was it forty-eight?"

"He was forty-six at the time," Onegus said. "But Turner was also sick. He had cancer."

Cassandra waved a dismissive hand. "Everyone knows that women are more resilient. You're forty-nine and in good health. You'll be fine. Besides, you are the grand-daughter of a god, which means that your genetics are superior. Your transition should be easy."

"A god? What do you mean by that?"

"Do you remember what you learned in school about Greek and Roman mythology? Both are based on a more ancient pantheon of gods that originated in Sumer. Those so-called gods were genetically enhanced humanoids who came from somewhere else in the universe, and like it says in the Bible, they took human lovers and produced us—immortals who possess a diluted version of their powers. Long story short, our grandfather is the god Toven. He and two other goddesses were the only ones who survived the cataclysm that destroyed all the other gods."

Darlene's head was spinning enough as it was, and adding an alien grandfather to the mess was too much for her to absorb all at once.

It was easy to focus on the details than on the big picture.

She shifted her gaze to Cassandra. "Did you transition?"

Her sister nodded. "It was an easy process for me, which is why I'm confident that it will be easy for you as well."

Roni

Roni struggled to keep his expression neutral and not let his mother see the storm brewing inside of him. She needed to choose between him and his father, between living a second-rate life or grabbing the opportunity given to her with both hands and joining him on the other side.

What would it be?

So far, she'd chosen Leo at every juncture. She'd never come to Roni's defense when his father had been mean to him, and when he'd confronted her about it in the past, her defense had been that parents needed to show a united front. That might be true if both parents were doing what they were supposed to, but not when one was being an asshole and the other a doormat who'd never stood up for herself or for her child.

Would his mother finally grow a pair and show some backbone?

"So, what's next?" Darlene asked.

"It depends on what you decide," Onegus said. "If you don't want to leave your husband and would rather spend the rest of your human life with him, we will respect your wishes and thrall you to forget this entire exchange. Cassandra and Geraldine will go back to being your cousins, and you'll continue believing that Roni works for some secret organization. However, if you decide that you want to jump on the opportunity right away, you can leave your old life behind today and come with us to live in our secret community. You'll have plenty of immortal males to choose from, and once you find one you like, you can start the process. But if you need more time to think it through, that's totally understandable. We will thrall you to forget what you've learned today, but the next time we meet we will bring a compeller along. When we release your submerged memories of today and answer more of your questions, the knowledge will be secured by a compulsion to never utter a word about it to anyone outside of this group. That will give you time to think it through."

Darlene cast Roni a sidelong glance. "Why didn't you bring that person along today?"

He'd wondered the same thing. "You should ask Cassandra. She's the mastermind behind this."

Cassandra pinned him with an incredulous stare. "Did you forget that we have a shortage of compellers at the moment? The only one available is Parker, and he's just a kid. I didn't want to drag him into this unless it was absolutely necessary."

"Right. I did forget." Roni turned to his mother. "If you want my opinion, just come with us now. Leo can rot in hell for all I care. Don't even pack a suitcase, so the agents watching the house won't know that you're going anywhere. I can replace everything that you leave behind. The clan pays me very well for my services."

Looking into his eyes, Darlene shook her head. "I guess Cassandra told you about Leo not being your father. Otherwise, you wouldn't be talking like that."

"She told me no such thing." He turned to Cassandra. "What is my mother talking about? And why didn't you say something before?"

Cassandra lifted her hands in the air. "Don't blame me. I had my suspicions, but until your mother confirmed them today, I didn't know that Leo wasn't your real father."

Roni shifted his eyes to his mother. "Does he know?"

She shook her head. "He suspects, but he's never had the nerve to test it."

"Who is my real father?"

She smiled. "He's just a guy I dated for a couple of weeks while I was separated from Leo. He doesn't know, and I'd like to keep it that way. By now, he's probably married with two and a half kids. He was the IT person in the firm I worked for at the time, and he was very smart and very sweet." His mother chuckled. "You inherited your smarts from him, but not his personality. In that, you were more like Leo—sarcastic, judgmental, and you have a superiority complex."

A growl started low in Roni's throat. "I'm nothing like that jerk. I was thrown into the adult world much too early, and I had to survive. My crusty attitude was my shield, my armor."

Onegus cleared his throat. "If that were true, you would have turned into a sweetheart after joining the clan. But we both know that didn't happen."

Roni shrugged. "It was too late for me to change." He turned to his mother. "How do you want to do this?"

"I don't want my memories erased." She turned to Geraldine. "So, the memory issues you and Cassandra said plagued your mother were actually yours?"

Geraldine nodded. "My brain healed, but not completely. When I get stressed, I still forget the most basic things. It's not a good feeling."

"I believe you." Darlene sighed. "But how can I just leave everything behind? And what about Leo? It's true that he hasn't been the best of husbands or fathers, but he wasn't a monster. He deserves an explanation."

"Call him or write him a letter," Cassandra said. "Admit that Roni is not his and file for a divorce."

For a long moment, Darlene chewed on her lower lip, and then she shook her head. "I can't do it like that. I'm sorry. Can you let me walk away with my memories intact if I promise not to breathe a word of it to anyone?"

"We can't," Onegus said. "After Leo sold Roni out, we are even more wary than usual."

"I understand." She lowered her eyes. "Then do what you must and let's all meet at a later time. You will have to explain everything to me again when you bring along that compeller of yours to ensure my silence."

The boulder in Roni's gut dropped to the bottom. His mother was once again choosing damn Leo over him.

"As you wish," Onegus said.

Darlene lifted her eyes to Roni. "I just need a little more time to think things through. Can you understand that?"

"Yeah. I guess." He pushed to his feet. "I need to get back to work." He forced a small smile. "Do you need me for anything else? Or can you handle the rest without me?"

Roni still couldn't thrall, so he would be no help to them in taking care of his mother's memories. In a way, it was a relief that she wouldn't remember any of that.

He wished he could forget it all as well.

Alena

As the canoe gently glided through the lake's placid water, Alena leaned her head on Orion's arm. "This is one of the most beautiful places I've ever visited, and I've been all over the world."

"I agree," Kalugal said. "Lugu Lake is a hidden gem."

After breakfast, they'd taken the waitress's suggestion to book a boat trip on the lake. The simple dugout was larger than the traditional pig troughs, as the canoes were called by the Mosuo. Each of the four benches was just wide enough for a couple to sit snuggled together, and it glided over the water nearly soundlessly, not disturbing the serenity of the lake.

Kalugal's men followed in another boat that Phinas had insisted on renting without a guide. Originally the proprietress had refused, but when he'd offered her double the price, she'd relented. In the unlikely event of an attack, Phinas didn't want to have to worry about the human tour guide.

The two Odus had been left behind in the hotel, which Arwel hadn't been happy about, not because he thought he needed them for Alena's protection, but because Kian would have a fit when he found out.

There were two problems with taking the Odus along. The first was practical. The Odus might be too heavy for the flimsy canoes. The other one had to do with what might happen if they accidentally fell into the water. They wouldn't float and hauling them out would require a motorboat and a cable, which would betray that they weren't human. A lot of mind scrubbing would ensue, and that was not something Alena wanted to deal with on her vacation.

But those were minor considerations compared to a possible reboot. Okidu and Onidu had both rebooted after prolonged submergence in water, and until it was proven that their following emergent sentience didn't pose a risk to the clan, Alena didn't dare risk Ovidu rebooting. If she was ever forced to decommission him because he was dangerous, it would break her heart.

"Why is the boat called a pig trough?" Carol asked Lamai, the pretty Mosuo girl who captained their boat. She was young, no more than eighteen or nineteen, and dressed in her people's colorful traditional outfit, including flowers in her hair and strings of beads around her neck.

"It's because of the legend," the girl said in heavily accented English. "A long time ago, there was no lake here. One day the water came from the Gamu mountain and flooded the valley. When that happened, a mother was feeding the family's pigs with her children playing next to her. When she saw the water coming, she put her children in the pig trough and saved them. She died in the flood, but the children who survived became the ancestors of the Mosuo people. That's why we call Lugu Lake the Mother Lake." She smiled proudly. "The mother's courage and sacrifice was the foundation of our matriarchal society."

Orion leaned and whispered in Alena's ear. "I wonder if some ancient Kra-ell visitors caused the flooding or it was a natural phenomenon."

Smiling, Alena lifted her head off his shoulder and turned to look up at his handsome face. "It's just another legend that explains how the lake was formed. It's a little more believable than the mountain spirit's tears filling a giant hoofprint, but it's probably just as untrue."

"You never know." Amusement danced in his eyes. "People think that the Sumerian legends are made-up stories as well."

With his lips hovering so close and that dimple in his cheek making him look so roguishly attractive, Alena wanted to kiss him long and hard for all to see, not just because she craved him nearly nonstop, but because the tour guide was eyeing Orion with hunger in her eyes.

Why had the girl set her sights on him when the other males in the boat were nearly as handsome?

Kalugal had the vibe of a rich man about him, and he had the bad boy charm most women found irresistible, Lokan looked elegant and sophisticated, and Arwel had the most unique colored eyes and misleadingly vulnerable expression that made women want to take care of him. And yet, out of all these magnificent males, Lamai coveted Orion.

Well, he was the most handsome of the four and the kindest, but he was just as taken as the others, and Lamai was out of luck.

"I don't think that the Kra-ell are that technologically advanced," Kalugal said quietly enough for the girl not to hear but loud enough for the immortals.

"It's not complicated to do," Arwel said. "If they had explosives, which given that they were space travelers, I'm sure they had, they could have caused an avalanche that formed a natural dam. The water wouldn't come in a torrent, but it would gradually rise until it filled the valley."

"Lugu Lake is one of the deepest natural lakes in China," Lamai continued her tour guide speech. "The average depth is forty-three meters, and the deepest is ninety-three meters. If you look over the side of the boat, you'll see that the water is very clean. You can see for many meters down."

"But not all the way down," Lokan murmured. "If I was part of an ancient expedition to earth and feared the local savages, I would have built a subterranean base and then flooded the basin to hide it."

"The Kra-ell are different from us," Arwel said. "They don't like living underground. Emmett was miserable in the keep."

"One male's preferences are not indicative of the entire species," Kalugal countered. "Don't forget that he's half-human, and the human side of him might not have liked living underground while the Kra-ell might have loved it. Besides, safety comes before comfort, and we know that a subterranean base is not a bad idea. I would love to explore the possibility."

Alena let out a breath. "We decided to wait with the investigation until Monday and enjoy the weekend sight-seeing. Can we give the conspiracy theories a rest for a while?"

"Why?" Kalugal sounded amused. "They are so much fun."

"I want to hear more about the lake and the Mosuo culture," Jacki said, loud enough for the girl to hear.

"I'll be delighted to tell you more about my people. Our main industries are tourism and fishing. The lake is rich with fish, and its beauty attracts many visitors. It is said to be like a quiet, beautiful girl. The lake changes colors like a girl changes dresses. In the morning, the sun paints it gold, during the day it is a beautiful blue and green, and when the sun goes down, it is dark green. The lake has five islands and three semi-islands, which are compared to a girl's jewels."

As their boat reached the middle of the lake, one of the guides on a nearby boat started singing in their native language. Even though it sounded like Chinese, it wasn't. Soon after the first girl began singing, all the other guides, including Lamai, joined her, their song rippling over the surface of the lake.

"One thing is for sure," Jin said. "The Mosuo women are not like the Kra-ell females. They seem so nice and gentle."

"Seem is the operative word," Kalugal murmured. "You need to ask their men how they are in bed."

Jin chuckled. "Are you curious?"

"Of course, I am."

Was Orion curious as well? He must have noticed the looks the girl had been sending his way.

"The Mosuo are human," Alena said. "We don't even know if their customs were influenced by the Kra-ell, but even if they were, the Kra-ell sexual practices just don't fit human nature and would have served no purpose. The Mosuo didn't suffer from a shortage of females that needed to be compensated for, and their survival didn't depend on producing the strongest, most aggressive offspring. Besides, if the men weren't happy, they would have rebelled. I think that they had a sweet deal in the Mosuo culture, and that's why it survived for so long. The women take care of pretty much everything."

Jacki snorted. "That's no different from most human cultures. Women work, take care of the children, pay the bills, clean the house, and the men think that they are saints for helping out when they feel like it."

"Excuse me?" Kalugal protested. "Is that your experience with this male?" He pointed at himself.

"I'm pampered silly. But I wonder what would have happened if we weren't rich and we didn't have Shamash and Atzil to take care of all the housework. Do you even know how to operate a washing machine?"

"I don't have to know. With my brains, there is no way we could have ever been poor enough not to afford domestic help."

Alena stifled a laugh. Kalugal was such a snob. She'd had a butler from the day she was born, and yet she knew how to cook and how to operate modern household appliances. The difference between them was that she didn't consider housework beneath her, while Kalugal obviously did.

Orion

■—↔—■

As their boats neared the second of the seven islands on their tour, an older guy wearing a Hawaiian shirt and a rumpled tweed jacket waved at them.

"I wonder what he's doing there all alone." Carol waved back. "There are no boats moored at the dock." She turned to Lokan. "Can you sense if there are any more people on the island?"

Lokan shook his head. "I only sense him. Besides, I wouldn't call this rock an island."

Orion didn't sense the presence of anyone else either. "Perhaps there is a dock on the other side as well."

"There isn't," their guide said.

As their boats docked, the guy grinned. "Hello, fellow travelers."

"Hello," Alena answered. "Are you stranded here? Where is the rest of your group?"

"Oh, I'm not stranded. I asked the young lady who brought me here this morning to leave me so I could explore at my leisure. She'll pick me up when she returns with another group of tourists. I thought that it was her, but your guide is a different young lady."

"We can offer you a ride back." Alena glanced at Phinas, who was shaking his head.

If the man wanted to hitch a ride with them, they would have to twist Phinas's arm to allow him on his boat.

"That's very kind of you." The guy smiled. "But I still have some exploring to do, and Milu will be worried if she comes back for me and I'm not here." He leaned closer to Alena. "I promised her a generous tip for picking me up. I don't want to disappoint her." He straightened and offered Alena his hand. "Doctor Herbert Neisman at your service." He smiled. "But call me Herb, and don't expect me to know anything about medicine. The only service I can offer is to put you to sleep with talk about ancient languages. I'm a doctor of philology, not a medical doctor."

"I happen to find old languages fascinating." Kalugal offered Herb his hand. "Which ones do you specialize in?"

"The Kra-Dai languages. The Kra family of languages in particular."

The small hairs on Orion's neck prickled. "Kra-Dai? What languages are those?"

"It's a family of tonal languages found in mainland South Asia, South China, and Northeast India. It's spoken by roughly ninety-three million people and includes ninety-five languages, the majority of which belong to the Tai branch. The modern Kra language family, however, is only spoken in southern China and northern Vietnam. There are about twelve Kra languages, with about eight thousand speakers, and they include at least four mutually unintelligible varieties."

That didn't sound like a lot of people and given how much they drifted apart as to be unintelligible, the original language was probably very old.

"Fascinating." Kalugal smoothed a hand over his goatee. "What does Kra mean? Is that a name of the people speaking it?"

"The word Kra in Porto-Austronesian means human, and as you know, Austronesian is one of the world's major language families."

Orion had never even heard the term, and he thought of himself as a well-informed man with well-rounded general knowledge.

Had Kalugal heard about it? As an amateur archeologist, he might have.

The guy was nodding sagely as if he knew precisely what Doctor Herbert Neisman was talking about, but that didn't mean much. Kalugal could be completely clueless and still pretend as if he was knowledgeable in the subject.

"What's particularly interesting about the Kra languages," Herb continued, "is that they contain words for metalworking, handicrafts, and agriculture that do not correspond to any of the other languages in the broader category of the Kra-Dai languages family. That suggests that the Kra people developed technological innovations independently from their contemporaries, or perhaps preceded them."

Orion hadn't been emotionally invested in the Kra-ell investigation, but as more pieces were added to the Kra-ell puzzle, he was starting to get excited.

"I have to admit that I've never heard of the Kra languages." Kalugal didn't show even the slightest reaction to the doctor's explanation. "I'm more familiar with other ancient languages—Sumerian, Hattie, Minoan."

When Herb's eyes widened with delight, Kalugal lifted his hand. "I'm just an amateur archeologist, and my knowledge of these languages is rudimentary."

"He's being modest." Jacki wrapped her arm around Kalugal's middle. "He can translate ancient texts written on crumbling tablets with half of the symbols missing. That requires much more than just a rudimentary familiarity with those languages."

"What tablets?" Herb asked.

"Fragments of tablets is more like it," Kalugal said dismissively.

Orion remembered Kian saying that the artifacts on display in the village's entry pavilion had been illegally smuggled out of the countries they'd been excavated in. No wonder Kalugal was being evasive.

"Which hotel are you staying in, Herb?" Carol asked, probably to change the subject for Kalugal's sake.

"The Lake Lodge."

"It's only a few minutes' walk from our hotel," Kalugal said. "You should join us for dinner tonight. I would love to hear more about the Kra people and their languages."

"I would be delighted. What time?"

"We are late diners," Jacki said. "Is seven too late for you?"

"No, it's perfect. I'm a night owl myself."

"Tell me, Herb." Kalugal started walking down the path toward the island's interior. "What are you researching on this little jewel?"

"The temple, of course. Unlike the others in the area that are Buddhist, this one is dedicated to the goddess, and it's much older." He smiled at Kalugal. "As an archeologist, I'm sure you will find it fascinating, and since I'm one of the few who can translate the inscriptions, you're very lucky to have bumped into me. I can translate them for you."

"Indeed. Are you up to showing my friends and me the temple today?"

Herb beamed. "It would be my pleasure. Follow me."

Orion leaned closer to Alena and whispered in her ear, "Can this be a coincidence? An ancient language named Kra?"

"I don't think so," she whispered back. "I got goosebumps when Herb said that Kra means human in that language. Ell means god in a lot of the languages spoken around the Mediterranean. Maybe Kra-ell means people who are half-human and half-gods."

"But that describes us better than the Kra-ell."

"I know. The pieces of the puzzle don't fit yet, but as we collect more of them, we might be able to discern a pattern."

Alena

❦

As the philologist led them to the ruins of the goddess's temple, Alena held on tight to Orion's hand. Not all of the lake's islands and peninsulas were covered in such dense greenery, but this one was uninhabited and overgrown with bushes. Fates only knew what crawled under the thicket, and Alena wasn't fond of snakes and spiders and other creepy-crawlies.

The climb to the top of the hill took a good twenty minutes, not because it was so steep or the distance long but because there was no path.

"It seems that the goddess doesn't have many followers," Kalugal said. "Given how everything is overgrown, no one comes to see her temple, not even the tourists."

"It's not in any of the tour guides," Herb said. "The locals are all Buddhists with a twist. Some of their old traditions and legends are intertwined with their particular brand of Buddhism."

As they climbed the last several feet, the ruined remains of the temple looked more like a heap of rocks than a structure, but it was obvious that it had never been more than a small shrine.

"I know that it doesn't look like much," Herb said. "But I discovered something that you might find interesting." He pushed aside several branches to reveal an engraving in the stone. "If you look closely, you can see that it's a woman's face, and she looks fierce. The symbols are in better condition, and I wonder if they were added at a later time. 'Oh, Mother of Life, death and destruction, be pleased with me, oh dreaded one, be pleased with me, you who shapes the world, be pleased with me, you who are beyond comprehension and time.'"

Pulling out his phone, Kalugal snapped a picture of the engraved rock face and then moved aside to let the others get closer.

Not much of the original face engraving remained, but the mouth with a pair of fangs protruding over it was unmistakable.

As goosebumps rose over Alena's arms, Orion rubbed his hands over them. "Is it common for goddesses to be depicted with fangs?" he asked Herb.

"I'm a philologist, not a historian, but I'm a fan of mythology, so I know a thing or two about the various gods and goddesses. Several Indian goddesses are described as skinny, small-breasted, and bearing fangs and fierce expressions. Their depiction represents their ever-present primordial hunger and their power of destruction and death. There is also Wadjet, the fanged cobra goddess of ancient Egypt, or Nehkbet, the vulture-goddess of Upper Egypt. But unlike the Hindu goddesses, they were not bent on destruction and death. Wadjet and Nehkbet were the protective goddesses of the king, and Wadjet was nurse to the god Horus, helping his mother, the goddess Isis, to protect him from his uncle Seth."

Herb scratched his balding head. "I'm sure I'm forgetting someone. I think that some of the Native American goddesses had fangs as well."

"I wonder if I could get a permit for a dig here," Kalugal said.

Herb shook his head. "The locals don't even allow motorboats on the lake. They don't want to disturb its tranquility or pollute the water. The Chinese government pushed hard for it, and motorboats were delivered to the lake, but there was so much opposition that their use was quickly discontinued. The lake isn't big, and the canoe rides provide income for the Mosuo people who live around it. They can't live on fishing alone."

"My partner secured permits for a dig a little farther up the Lugu river," Kalugal said. "There used to be an ancient outpost built on a river island, but that one is much bigger than this one."

Herb looked impressed. "Your friend must be well connected. I wanted to visit the site but was refused entry. Is there a way you could arrange for me to see the excavation?"

"I haven't been there yet." Kalugal wrapped his arm around Jacki's shoulders. "My wife wanted to explore the lake first. I'm probably going to head out there tomorrow, but I need to check with my partner whether it is safe before I allow visitors on site." He smiled. "I don't know how litigation works in China, but even if that's not an issue, I don't want any accidents on my conscience."

"I understand." Herb nodded. "Will you let me know?"

"Of course."

"We should head back," Jacki said. "Our guide is probably getting impatient."

The girl hadn't accompanied them to the top of the hill, preferring to remain with her boat.

"I'll stay here for a little longer." Herb pulled out a handkerchief from his back pocket and wiped his forehead. "Does the invitation to join you for dinner still stand?"

"Of course." Kalugal gave him one of his charming smiles. "It was a pleasure to make your acquaintance, Doctor Herbert Neisman, and I'm looking forward to continuing our conversation over dinner."

After everyone had said their goodbyes, and their group started their descent down the hill, Alena asked, "Is it just me, or did that engraving look a lot like what I imagine a Kra-ell female would?"

"I had the same thought," Kalugal said. "That's why I took the picture. I want to send it to Vrog and to Emmett and ask them if she looks anything like the Mother of All Life that the Kra-ell worship. I'm also curious whether the symbols resemble the Kra-ell language."

"Are we coming back here tonight?" Arwel asked. "We can bring some tools and dig around for clues. If the Kra-ell worshiped their goddess on this hill, they might have left some tributes that we can date. It will give us an idea when they'd arrived here."

"If they ever did," Kalugal said. "As Herb said, a depiction of a fanged goddess is not such a rare occurrence. Kali, one of the Hindu main deities, is always drawn with fangs and with a long, protruding tongue."

"Why the tongue?" Carol asked. "What does it symbolize?"

"Hunger, most likely," Jacki said. "The warrior goddess who devours her enemies and licks their blood."

Carol shivered. "All this talk about blood freaks me out." She leaned closer to Jacki. "That's why I'm not fond of the newest additions to our clan. Did you meet Vlad's father?"

Jacki shook her head. "I didn't."

"I did," Arwel said. "He's a decent fellow. Don't hold his heritage against him. After all, he contributed half of Vlad's genes, and Vlad is one of the best people I know."

"True." Carol nodded. "Will I get to meet him during this trip?"

"It remains to be seen," Arwel said. "If we find something that we think he should take a look at or vice versa, and pictures are not enough, then I might suggest that he and the team investigating the school join us."

When they were back on the boat, Kalugal pulled out his clan phone again. "Let's see what we can find about the goddess Kali."

Jacki leaned closer to him to look at the screen. "Aren't you going to send the photo from the shrine to Vrog first?"

"It can wait." Kalugal peered over his phone for a long while, uttering all kinds of surprised sounds and nodding as if what he was reading confirmed his suspicions. "The goddess Kali is considered to be the master of death, time, and change. She is said to be the supreme of all powers, and the ultimate reality. She is also the mother of all living beings." Kalugal lifted his head and looked behind him. "Sounds familiar?"

Arwel shook his head. "You are all getting carried away. I can accept that the Kra-ell influenced the lifestyle choices of the Mosuo, but I'm not buying that they also influenced the entire Indian culture. That's taking it too far."

"Why?" Alena said. "A small group of gods influenced the entire Western civilization from a small settlement in Sumer. A small group of Kra-ell who settled in a different corner of the globe might have influenced the cultures of the people of that part of the world."

They no longer bothered to speak quietly, and their guide was following the conversation with curious eyes. "Who are these gods you talk about?" the girl asked.

Kalugal cast her an indulgent smile. "We are talking about legends and mythology. Those are all just fantasies that people came up with to explain the world to themselves. It's like your legend of how the lake was formed. No one truly believes that it's made from a goddess's tears, right?"

The girl smiled. "It's a nice story."

"Indeed." Kalugal went back to reading on his phone. "There are even more similarities between Kali and Jade. Kali is often depicted as standing on top of her husband, Shiva, who lies prone on the ground. It says here that it's never Kali who calms Shiva when he's misbehaving, but Shiva who must calm Kali. Her eyes are often described as deep red with rage and maybe intoxication, her small fangs sometimes protrude out of her mouth, and that lolling tongue." He chuckled. "The Indian patriarchal society had trouble reconciling Kali's dominant pose with her husband lying literally under her foot, so they came up with an explanation. Kali was called to destroy a demon army, which she did, but with her blood lust out of control, she couldn't stop rampaging. Shiva was called to stop her, and as he lay under her feet, Kali realized that she had stepped over her husband's chest and was so embarrassed that she extended her tongue in modesty and shame."

Jin snorted. "Right. To me, the foot over Shiva's chest and the lolling tongue look like signs of triumph and dominance."

"I think so too." Kalugal returned the phone to his pocket. "It would be fascinating to discover the origins of that story—the Sumer of the East."

Vrog

The files Vrog had recovered from the safes were locked in a fire-proof cabinet in his office. If he'd learned anything from the fire that had destroyed the compound, it was that Jade had been smart to lock all important possessions and documents in the two safes. She probably hadn't expected fire or flood, only theft, but Vrog had taken the lesson to heart.

Anticipating the worst and preparing for it was smart. Hoping for the best was not.

Vrog's hand trembled as he opened the cabinet and pulled out one of the ledgers. Taking it with him to the desk, he sat down and opened it at the first page. It was handwritten in the Kra-ell language, and he wondered whether Jade had preferred to record their tribe's accounting the old-fashioned way, handwritten with pen on paper, as a security measure or because there was no way to program the Kra-ell language into accounting software.

The fact that she'd kept the ledgers locked in a safe suggested that she'd been worried about privacy, and no one could hack into handwritten books. The question was who she'd been protecting the information from, humans or another Kra-ell.

As he flipped through page upon page of neatly written columns, he also wondered whether it was Jade's hand-writing or did it belong to one of the other females. He doubted she would have entrusted any of the males with so much information. The Jade he remembered kept things close to the chest, so to speak.

It felt strange to allow Kian to have a look at the ledgers, and probably Shai and the clan's hacker as well. Kian wouldn't do the investigative work himself. He would assign it to his assistant and others who knew how to follow a money trail.

Vrog should have done it himself a long time ago.

He'd excused his reticence as lack of resources, but the truth was that he'd been afraid to attract attention to himself by following the money and looking into the tribe's various holdings.

As long as no one tried to recover the tribe's riches, whoever had sacked the compound wouldn't suspect that anyone had survived the attack and wouldn't come back to finish the job. But twenty years was a long time, and perhaps it was safe to do so now.

Or not.

Was he signing his own death sentence by giving the journals to Kian?

As soon as the clan started investigating what happened to all that money, the killers might come back. Vrog could potentially hide in the clan's village, but what if they harmed the students or the staff?

Could he risk that?

It was too late to change his mind. He'd promised Kian to deliver the files, and Vrog wasn't the kind of male who went back on his word. Not intentionally anyway.

When his clan phone buzzed with an incoming message, he picked it up expecting it to be Mey. Earlier, he'd left her in one of the storage buildings, with Yamanu and the two Guardians watching over her as she listened to the echoes. Perhaps she'd found out something new.

But the message wasn't from Mey. It was from Kalugal.

At first, all he saw in the picture the guy had sent him was a brown-grey rock covered in moss, but when he read Kalugal's explanation, he enlarged the picture with his fingers and took a closer look.

Kalugal asked whether the carving looked anything like the Mother of All Life that the Kra-ell worshiped, but it was hard to tell. The full lips and the small protruding fangs could have belonged to a Kra-ell female, and they could have been a rudimentary drawing of the Indian goddess of time, doomsday, and death. Since there was no body, and just a few lines of the face had survived the elements, it was impossible to tell. If it was the goddess Kali, she would have four or ten arms and some sort of a headdress.

Lugu Lake, where Kalugal and his team were visiting, was close to Tibet, so discovering a shrine dedicated to Kali wouldn't be overly surprising.

He texted back, explaining why he couldn't say for sure that it was or wasn't the Kra-ell deity, and that it was most likely the Hindu goddess Kali.

His phone rang a moment later.

"Can you talk?" Kalugal asked.

"I'm alone if that's your concern."

"Could Kali be based on a Kra-ell female or on legends of the Mother of All Life?"

"I will have to look into the stories about Kali, but what I can tell you for sure is that the Mother of All Life had only two arms. She had fangs, she was thin and tall, and she was dark-haired, but that's where the similarities end."

"What about her dominant pose with her foot over the prone body of her husband Shiva?"

Vrog chuckled. "Unlike the Mother of All Life, Kali didn't have a harem of husbands to serve her needs."

"Those variations are to be expected," Kalugal said. "Just as Western cultures adapted the stories about the gods to fit their religion and their world view, Eastern cultures might have done the same to a Kra-ell influence. The Indian culture was and still is patriarchal. They made Kali as fearsome and as dominant as their world view allowed. I'm not saying that Kali is for sure based on a Kra-ell deity or living female, but it's worth pondering."

Ronja

R onja had spent the afternoon planning, or rather attempting to plan, how she was going to seduce Merlin. Not that she would have to work hard for it, but she wanted to make it special, elegant, refined —a night to remember for eternity, and not because she was embarrassed by it.

Without a plan, she was bound to attack him.

Not that Merlin would mind.

He wanted her, he'd made it quite obvious, and since he hadn't left the village without her, she also knew that he hadn't been with anyone else. For an immortal male that showed extraordinary restraint, and she loved him all the more for it.

Except, she hadn't told him that she loved him yet, not in so many words, but he shouldn't have trouble guessing her feelings. Over the past two months they'd spent many hours together, and they had all been enjoyable despite the undercurrent of sexual tension, or perhaps because of it.

It might have not been love at first sight, but then that was reserved for the young and naive, not a middle-aged woman who'd been married twice, cheated on by her first husband, and widowed by her second.

Merlin had grown on her gradually, but Ronja had known she was in love with him for weeks.

What was there not to love?

He was brilliant, handsome, funny, and he needed her, not just as a friend and a sex partner, but for organizing his messy life. She wasn't nearly as smart as he was, but she had a methodical mind while Merlin's was all over the place, which made them perfect for each other. With her monitoring everything he worked on and keeping his house from falling into disarray again, she freed him up to think. His mind could wander in whichever direction he pleased without worrying about all the things he might have forgotten.

Merlin had told her many times about how invaluable she'd become to him, and that since she'd taken over organizing his work and everything else in his life he'd become so much more productive.

It was a good feeling to know that, in her own way, she was contributing to the creation of great things. With her, Merlin might come up with new cures that would help countless people. After all, most of his research wasn't on how to heal immortals but on how to cure humans.

Fates, she felt so absurdly happy and fulfilled that she was afraid to rock the boat and introduce a new variable that might ruin the good thing they had going. Then again, the clock was ticking both on her window of opportunity to transition and on Merlin's patience, and frankly, hers as well.

Ronja had always been a passionate woman who'd enjoyed sex, and going without for so long was frustrating, especially when it was offered to her on a silver platter with a cherry on top.

As much as she wanted to honor Frank's memory and mourn his death for a full year, she was reaching a breaking point and could no longer wait.

"Bye, Mom." Lisa kissed her cheek and then pranced toward the door.

"Where are you going?"

"To Parker's house." Lisa paused with her hand on the door handle. "Magnus bought a movie projector, and we are going to watch all the Harry Potter movies."

"That will take all night."

"I know." Lisa smiled. "Don't wait up for me. I'm going to try to stay awake for as long as I can, but as the only human among five immortals, I stand no chance. I'll probably fall asleep on their couch."

"Five? Who else is joining the Harry Potter marathon?"

"Ella and Julian."

"That sounds like fun. Say hello to Parker's family for me."

"I will." Lisa opened the door. "Hey, why don't you call Merlin and invite him over? That way, I won't feel too guilty about leaving you alone on a Friday night."

Ronja felt her cheeks heating up. "That's a good idea. Perhaps we can watch something as well."

As the door closed behind Lisa, Ronja released a breath.

The stars seemed to be aligning in formation tonight, all pointing in one direction—her bedroom.

As Merlin had said, sex didn't have to mean induction. They could use protection. Perhaps they should start with that. It definitely made the decision to go for it much easier.

Well, easier did not mean easy.

Ronja had only been with two men in her life, and she'd been married to both for a very long time. She'd been just a young girl when Michael had seduced her, beautiful, desirable, and as perfect as a human girl got to be. She'd still been beautiful and desirable when she divorced Michael and started dating Frank, so getting naked with him had not been a problem.

But she was much older now, and despite all the progress she made over the past several weeks, all the excess weight she'd lost and the muscle she'd gained, she was still a middle-aged woman who'd had three kids, and her body was far from perfect.

Heck, she didn't remove her bra until it was time for bed, even if she was alone in the house, and not just because her large drooping breasts didn't look good. They were uncomfortable.

How was she going to bare herself to Merlin, who looked like a male model in his mid-twenties or early thirties?

He'd only ever seen her dressed in flattering outfits, push-up bras, and tummy control panties that streamlined her silhouette and concealed the flabbiness. Without those props, she wasn't as good-looking as he thought she was.

What if he got turned off when he saw her naked?

Closing her eyes, Ronja sighed. One way or another, it was going to happen, and since Annani was in the village, the sooner the better.

Hopefully, Merlin was starved for sex enough to overlook all of her imperfections.

Mey

~~~

Mey walked out of the storage building and shook her head. "There was nothing of interest in there."

That wasn't entirely true, but what she'd heard in the echoes had nothing to do with the Kra-ell, and a lot to do with the current inhabitants of the school. As it turned out, the storage building had been frequently used for amorous encounters between teachers, administrators, groundskeepers, delivery people, and Fates knew who else.

Mey was still trying to shake off what she'd heard, and the sounds of passion hadn't even been the worst. There had been screaming arguments about broken promises, crying fits about real and perceived betrayals, mean-spirited gossip, and evil plotting against this one or that.

It was good that the faculty had no idea what she could do, or some members would have been very worried.

Yamanu pushed away from the wall he'd been leaning against and put his arm around her shoulders. "If you didn't find anything, why are you shaking your head?"

"People are nasty when they think no one can see or hear them, and I was never into pornography. This storage building was used more as a shag-pad than to store stuff."

Both his brows shot up. "Is that so? Who shagged whom?"

"It wasn't the Kra-ell, and thankfully, not the students. I only saw and heard adults, and given their clothing and vernacular, they were all contemporary. I wonder if Vrog knows what's going on under his nose. It seems that everyone is shagging everyone else, people are plotting and scheming to get promoted and to get others demoted, and don't even start me on the drama."

Yamanu sighed. "It's a shame that you can't share what you see and hear with me. I could have used the entertainment. I'm so bored that I'm reduced to watching reruns of old episodes of *South Park*."

"My poor baby." She leaned closer and kissed his strong jaw. "You don't need to trail after me. I'm perfectly safe on my own here."

She felt awkward with Yamanu and the two Guardians following her around. It was a school, not an enemy camp.

"Stella and Richard thought that they were perfectly safe in that sleepy little town, and they got a nasty surprise. I'm not gambling with your safety. Especially not here."

"Why? Do you sense anything?"

Yamanu wasn't empathic, but he was very intuitive, and it would be a mistake to ignore his intuition's warnings.

He shook his head. "It's a general feeling of things not being right about this place, but it might be because of what happened here two decades ago. I think the impact it left on the compound is overshadowing any current or impending threats." He rubbed a hand over his jaw. "I wonder if that's why my intuition didn't warn me when Vrog planned his attack on Stella."

"Maybe you didn't feel anything because he wasn't going to harm her. The Fates had no reason to sound the alarm."

"I didn't consider it from that angle, but you might be right."

Smiling, she looped her arm around his waist. "Of course, I'm right. I always am."

"Naturally." He grinned. "You're as wise as you are beautiful, my mate, and I'm always awed by you."

He stopped next to the second storage building. "Do you want me to come in with you?"

"What for? All you'll see is me sitting on the floor with my eyes closed. I look like I'm meditating."

"Can't you narrate what you're seeing and hearing? That would be very entertaining."

"I wish I could, but I can't. It would break my concentration." Looking over her shoulder at Alfie and Jay, she had an idea. "Why don't the three of you play cards or something while I'm inside. You could entertain each other."

"As I said, my mate is brilliant. We don't have cards, but we could play the stone game, provided that we can find a fourth player." Yamanu turned his head to look over his shoulder. "And here he comes." He smiled at Vrog, who was heading their way. "What's up, buddy?"

"I came to ask the same of you. Did you hear any interesting echoes?"

Mey grimaced. "Yes, but not the ones I was hoping for. Do you know what the faculty has been using that storage building for?"

Vrog frowned. "Other than storing classroom or janitorial supplies?"

Mey had a feeling that the guy had no clue. Dalliances between the staff members were prohibited, and given how straitlaced Vrog himself was, he probably expected everyone to uphold the same standards.

"Let me put it this way. You should really relax the rules and allow the faculty and other staff to have intimate relationships. That way, they wouldn't have to sneak into the storage building to have fun."

His eyes widened. "Are you sure it was the current staff?"

"Positive. And the drama, oh, my. You have no idea."

"No, I don't, and I prefer it that way."

"Why don't you allow it?" Yamanu asked. "These people live and work here, and they didn't sign up for a monastery."

"I can't allow it." Vrog sighed. "It would be like opening Pandora's box. My major concern is sexual coercion, with senior faculty members taking advantage of junior members. Then there are the squabbles, the lovers' spats, the jealousies, you name it. If they are not supposed to be doing any of it, they can't complain to me about it."

"Forcing them to live like monks is not the solution, though." Mey pointed to the door of the other building. "I hope this one will have less of what I saw in the other storage building, and at least a scrap of what I'm looking for."

"Perhaps the Kra-ell didn't leave echoes because nothing emotionally charged happened in there." Vrog started toward the other building. "Which makes sense. I don't think the purebloods bothered with fetching supplies. That's what the human servants were for."

"You mean slaves," Yamanu said. "If they weren't allowed to leave and weren't paid for their labor and for their blood donations, then the right term is slaves."

"True." Vrog sighed. "But things are not much better for many people in this part of the world. I'm not saying that to excuse what the Kra-ell did, and they would have probably done the same if they settled in the West, it's just that most of the humans living on the compound didn't think that their lot in life was so unfair or terrible. Some even appreciated the health benefits of occasionally donating their blood to the Kra-ell."

Mey didn't know much about the local population's attitudes, but people were the same everywhere, and no one enjoyed having their freedom taken away from them or serving as breeders for aliens.

"What kind of things were stored in there back then?" Mey asked. "I assume that there was no need for school supplies, not in these quantities." She waved at the building they'd come from.

"Dry goods, extra clothing for the humans, bedding, bathroom supplies, etc. When I got here, there was almost nothing in these buildings, and whatever was left was saturated with smoke. I disposed of it."

"That's odd. If the compound was taken in a surprise attack, then the storage building should have been full. Your leader sounds like the type who would not allow supplies to dwindle. She would have been on top of that."

Vrog nodded. "Jade was like a general, and she ran the place efficiently. She probably put one of the pure-blooded males in charge of inventory to make sure that no one was taking more than they were supposed to. But don't forget that the compound stood in ruins for months before I got back here. The locals probably took everything that was salvageable."

"Makes sense," Mey agreed. It wouldn't even have counted as looting because there had been no one left to claim the goods.

"Why would Jade be concerned with people taking more than they were supposed to?" Yamanu asked. "What would the humans have done with extra supplies? It's not like they could have smuggled stuff out of the compound."

Vrog smiled. "Never underestimate the ingenuity of people."

Yamanu looked doubtful. "If they couldn't smuggle themselves out, how could they smuggle supplies and what for?"

"They were thralled to fear leaving. The fear instilled in them was so powerful that their hearts would give out if they tried."

"A simple solution to prevent theft would have been to thrall them not to steal." Mey sniffed the air as they got closer to the other building. "It smells nice. Was it converted to serve as the school's laundry?"

Vrog nodded. "I turned the back part of this building into a laundry and kept the front for storage of maintenance supplies."

"Can I go in there?" Mey asked. "Or are people working there?"

"For now, you can listen to echoes in the storage part. You can check out the laundry during the weekend." He typed in the code and opened the door.

Mey stepped over the threshold. "Wish me luck."

Vrog didn't let go of the door. "Before you go, I wanted to give you a quick update about the other group's progress at Lugu Lake."

"Did they find anything?" Yamanu asked.

After giving them a summary of his conversation with Kalugal, Vrog pulled out his phone to show them the photo Kalugal had taken. "What do you think?"

Mey lifted her eyes to him. "You're asking me? I've never seen a picture of the Kra-ell goddess."

"Have you seen pictures of Kali?" Vrog asked. "She's the Hindu goddess of time, doomsday, and death."

"Of course," Mey said. "Who hasn't? She is the blue goddess with a long red tongue and four arms."

"She also has fangs." Vrog took his phone from her and typed Kali in the search field. "Like in this picture."

Mey took the device. "I've never noticed the fangs before. The necklace of severed heads must have distracted me."

"What I don't understand," Yamanu said, "is why would anyone worship such a terrible goddess."

"Kali is both terrible and wonderful," Vrog said. "According to legend, she became terrible only when she was called to defend her people. She used her power to defeat demons and assist the gods, and she's revered for it. She's also the goddess of life, and some refer to her as the Mother and the essence of all existence."

Merlin

A bouquet of flowers in one hand, a bottle of wine in the other, and six packets of condoms in his pockets, Merlin left his house and headed to Ronja's.

After she'd called him, he'd made a mad rush to the city to purchase the necessary items for a night of seduction.

Hopefully, he hadn't forgotten anything—

Damn, he should have gotten her chocolates. He had a stash of Godiva boxes at home, which he kept on hand for his fertility patients. Should he turn back and get them?

Nah, it was bad luck to re-enter the house, and even though Merlin wasn't superstitious, tonight he wasn't taking any chances.

Because tonight was *the* night.

Annani had confirmed that what she did for the transitioning Dormants wasn't a morale boost that had a placebo effect but was a real exchange of energy. She had refused to give him specifics, but what she'd told him was enough to reassure him that she could save Ronja if her transition became life-threatening.

Then Ronja called to invite him for dinner at her house, emphasizing that Lisa would be gone all night and that they would have the house to themselves. He couldn't have hoped for a clearer message than that.

Well, if she told him to bring condoms that would have been clearer, but Ronja was old-fashioned, and unlike the young women of today, she still believed that subtlety was classier.

He wondered whether Lisa's absence was what had prompted Ronja to take the plunge tonight. Privacy hadn't been the reason behind her reluctance to take their relationship to its natural next step because his house was always available to them. Since Ronja had taken command of it, his bedsheets were clean, smelled fresh, and his bed was always made, so that shouldn't have been an obstacle. But perhaps Ronja felt more comfortable seducing him in her own place?

Damn, if his erection became any harder, he would require hospitalization.

He needed to deflate that bad boy, or it would ruin the evening.

Perhaps going over the list of symptoms and various forms of nephrotic syndrome would do the trick, and if that didn't work, he had plenty of other lists he could go through, and the more troubling the disease, the better.

High blood pressure, swelling in the feet, hands, and around the eyes, weight gain with fluid retention and swelling— Merlin went through the list of symptoms twice, and by the time he reached Ronja's house, he had everything under control.

Ringing her doorbell, he was sure that he wasn't going to embarrass himself, but as soon as Ronja opened the door, that conviction evaporated into thin air.

"You look stunning." He gaped at her lush body that was encased in a sexy, form-fitting black dress, and those black stiletto shoes—damn—they made her legs look so good —

All he could think about was Ronja with nothing on except for those shoes, her legs wrapped around his waist, and him buried deep inside of her.

Forcing his eyes to shift to her face, he focused on her pale blond hair, which was gathered in an elaborate updo, with soft curling strands left loose to frame the long diamond earrings that shimmered with every move of her head.

With the outfit and the hair and the makeup, she looked like a pinup, and she had done it all for him.

Ronja definitely had seduction on her mind.

Should he go over the list of epidermal parasitic skin diseases? That was a sure erection deflator. *Scabies, pediculosis, tungiasis...*

"Thank you." She took the flowers and the bottle of wine from him. "You look very handsome yourself." She walked over to the kitchen and pulled a vase out of the cabinet. "When did you have time to get these? I called you less than two hours ago."

"I made a quick run to the city."

She smiled. "Just to get me flowers?"

"And wine. Don't forget the wine." He'd spent a small fortune on that bottle. "I hope it goes with whatever you made that smells so good."

Ronja smiled. "Today's meal is not perfectly aligned with your health guidelines, but it's not terrible either. I made almond-crusted trout with mashed potatoes and grilled vegetables."

"That sounds healthy and delicious."

She chuckled. "Not really. There is a whole stick of butter in the dish, but that's what makes it so tasty."

"Butter is the secret of life," he quoted. "What movie?"

"*Last Holiday.*"

"That's my girl." He leaned and kissed her cheek.

Ronja

❦

"This is delicious." Merlin cut another piece of the fish and arranged the almond slices, so they covered the morsel evenly. "I love everything you cook, but this is your best one yet."

"I'm glad you like it."

Ronja pressed her fork into the mashed potatoes, making a lattice design. She was too nervous to eat, or maybe she just wasn't hungry because she'd been snacking while she cooked, or maybe her control-top panties were too tight.

It had been a mistake to put them on. They made the dress look ten times better on her, smoothing out her muffin top and creating the hourglass figure she'd once taken for granted. But she should have considered her plans for later tonight and worn something looser that didn't leave red compression marks on her skin.

Perhaps she should excuse herself and go change into a robe? It would take at least an hour for the marks to fade.

"Ronja," Merlin said quietly. "Why aren't you eating?"

She forced a smile. "I'm not hungry. I snacked while I cooked."

"You haven't touched your fish." He pulled her plate toward him and cut a nice little piece. "Just one bite. Once you taste it, your appetite will awaken."

Reluctantly, she opened her mouth and let him feed her the small piece of fish. It was good, even better than she'd imagined, but her stomach was still tight like a drum, and not just because of the damn compression panties.

"Good, right?"

She nodded.

"Have another one." He quickly cut another piece and put it in front of her mouth. "Open wide." When she took it, he nodded his approval and cut another piece for her.

Ronja shook her head. "Stop feeding me. I cooked for you, and you're not eating."

"I like feeding you." He made small circles with the fork in front of her face. "Please, for me." His eyes were bright like twin flashlights as they focused on her lips. "I love seeing you eat."

Was he imagining her lips closing around his erection? Was that why his eyes were glowing?

Was this a kind of foreplay?

Neither of her husbands had ever fed her, and she had to admit that she liked Merlin being so focused on her, watching her so intently, taking care of her.

As something loosened deep within Ronja, she smiled and opened her mouth. Merlin growled his approval and kept feeding her until there was nothing left on her plate, and she felt like her belly was going to win the war with her panties and burst them at the seams.

"No more." She lifted her hands. "Now, you finish yours."

His eyes still trained on her lips, he put the fork down and leaned closer. "You are mine." He put his lips on hers, his tongue penetrating her mouth and stroking leisurely.

She was breathless when he leaned back and looked at her. His glowing eyes were full of sexual promise, and then he was kissing her again, his tongue invading, probing, caressing, elaborating on that carnal promise.

Ronja was on fire, her breasts and her core tingling, aching with need. It had been so long, and she was so damn hungry. She gasped when his fangs scraped her lower lip, not expecting them to elongate that quickly. It was a little scary, but the small fear only added fuel to the inferno raging inside of her. He was careful though, and as his lips left hers to trail down her neck, he somehow managed to keep his fangs away from her skin.

Was she crazy for wanting him to scrape her again? To bite her?

Leaning away, he looked at her with hooded eyes. "Can I take you to bed now? Please say yes."

She wanted to, boy, how she wanted him to do precisely that, but her damn inhibitions were raising their head again. There was no way in hell she was letting him undress her and see those granny compression panties. "Can I ask you for a favor?"

"Anything."

"Can you give me fifteen minutes to slip into something more comfortable?"

He seemed understandably confused by her request, but then he nodded and smiled. "Take all the time you need and call me when you're ready."

"Thank you."

When she rose to her feet, he caught her hand and pulled her down onto his lap. "I need one more kiss to tide me over."

As his hand started a slow track from her hip and up her side, she jumped off his lap before he could feel what was under her dress, leaned down, and pecked him on the lips. "This will have to do for now."

Mey

The remaining storage area of the second building was indeed much smaller than the first, no bigger than a four-car garage, maybe even smaller than that. The windows were closed and barred, but because of the laundry on its other side, it lacked the slightly musty smell she'd suffered through in the other building.

The organization style was the same, though. Neat rows of fully stocked industrial metal shelving took up most of the space, holding big boxes of toilet paper, cleaning supplies, bedding, towels, and other bathroom necessities.

The only open area was in the front of the room right by the door, and that was where Mey chose to sit down. Crossing her legs in the lotus position, she closed her eyes and started the meditative process.

She still felt overstimulated from the echoes she'd heard and seen in the other building, as well as from the conversation with Vrog and all the new bits and pieces of information she'd just learned. It took her a long time to quiet her mind enough to reach the state necessary to open herself to the echoes.

When the scenes started playing, she braced for a long and protracted drama-fest similar to what she'd been subjected to in the other building. If she were lucky, the old echoes would have been more emotionally charged than those that had been created after the compound had been turned into a school.

At first, the two ghostly spindly forms that appeared in her mind's eye were not substantial enough to make sense of other than their humanoid form, and unlike most of the echoes that started with a built-in soundtrack playing the moment they popped into her mind, the two forms were utterly silent as they entered the storage building and locked the door behind them.

When the forms became more substantial, Mey realized that they were females, and they weren't human. The two were very clearly Kra-ell and not hybrids but pure-bloods. Even in their semi-ghostly echo form, they looked so alien that Mey wondered how they'd ever managed to pass for humans.

It was difficult to assess their height, but if the entry door was the same size as the current one, the taller female was at least six foot four inches tall, and the other maybe an inch or an inch and a half shorter. They were so slim that they looked almost skeletal, but not gaunt like some of the runway models, just narrowly built. They were both nearly flat-chested, had no hips to speak of, and their waists were so tiny that she could probably close her hands around them and her fingers would touch. Nevertheless, there was power in those seemingly insubstantial bodies, and they moved with the sinuous fluidity and gracefulness of immortals.

Even if Mey hadn't known anything about them, she would have recognized them as predators—dangerous, lethal, even cruel.

Still, despite the lack of feminine curves and the twin hard expressions they wore, they were both beautiful. Long black hair cascaded like a gleaming curtain down their backs, their dark eyes large in their thin faces, too large, and the corners were slightly elongated but not in the same way Asians' eyes were. In fact, the eyes were the females' most alien feature. Well, that was true until they started talking, or rather arguing, and Mey saw their fangs and their tongues, which were definitely more alien than their eyes.

Except for a word here and there, she was unable to follow the rapid exchange in Kra-ell. Giving up, she paid closer attention to those fangs which, unlike hers and Jin's or even those of the male immortals, were quite long in their retracted state. Then again, given the explosive animosity between the two Kra-ell females, their fangs might have been in their elongated state in response to aggression.

Even more interesting than the fangs were their tongues, which had a pattern of dark coloring down the middle that made them look as if they were forked.

Was that a natural feature or were the patterns tattooed?

Mey had seen humans with tongue tattoos, so alien ink wasn't such a far-fetched idea, and since the Kra-ell didn't heal as fast as immortals, perhaps they'd found a way to mark their bodies permanently, which the immortals couldn't do.

None of the hybrid Kra-ell she knew had a pattern of different coloring on their tongues, but maybe because they were mixed the different coloring was less evident. She and Jin had none, but then they were only one-quarter Kra-ell.

In either case, if the tongue marking was natural, it was a recessive trait that didn't get transferred to hybrid offspring.

As the arguing became more heated, the taller female backhanded the other one, the force of the blow sending the shorter female flying across the room and crashing into a shelving unit.

The shelving and everything on it went down, but not the female. It was as if she was made of rubber, bouncing up, and with a roar, launching herself up at the aggressor, flying at her with fully extended fangs and toppling her to the ground.

As the females clawed and bit each other, the savagery was too much for Mey, and she averted her eyes.

At least her suspicion about their fangs being elongated in aggression had gotten confirmed.

Mey managed to keep her concentration and stay in place as long as the ghostly figures kept wrestling and crushing into shelving that wasn't near her, but as the brawling got closer and closer to where she was seated, Mey fought the urge to get out of their way, even though she knew they weren't real and couldn't hurt her.

When they crashed right through her, she lost the battle with her concentration and was thrown out of the echo.

No, no, no. She closed her eyes and tried to calm herself down enough to regain access to the echo, but it was no use.

Mey knew that she had to rest and give it a try another time.

After all, the echoes weren't going anywhere, and they would still be there tomorrow and the day after that, years and decades from now. Even if she hadn't lost her concentration, she would have to watch the replay of the scene many more times before she could decipher the rapid Kra-ell exchange.

She was curious about the impetus for the fight, but even if she never found out what the females had been fighting about, it was a rare glimpse into an alien society of which she was a distant member.

With a sigh, Mey pushed up to her feet and walked to the door.

Outside, Yamanu, Vrog, Alfie, and Jay were seated on the ground, a pile of small rocks between them, looking like a bunch of boys on a school playground.

What would Vrog's students think if they saw him like that?

He would have to thrall their memories away.

Yamanu took one look at her and knew that something had gone wrong. "No luck, eh?"

She crouched next to him. "I wouldn't say that. I struck gold in there. I saw two pureblooded females go at each other's throats, but then they started brawling, their ghostly forms crashed into me, and I lost concentration. I will have to come back another time and watch that echo again."

"What did they look like?" Vrog asked.

"Very tall, very skinny, with long black hair, long white fangs, and black tattoos on their tongues. One was a little taller than the other."

"Those were not tattoos," Vrog said. "The purebloods are born with them. None of the hybrids had the markings, so I assumed it was a trait that manifested only when both parents were pure Kra-ell. Did you notice any other distinguishing features?"

Mey shrugged. "They were both very beautiful but had no feminine curves whatsoever. They both had the same dark hair and the same alien-looking eyes." She chuckled. "Like those little gray aliens with enormous black eyes, except the eyes of the Kra-ell females weren't all black, just too big for their faces and oddly shaped. Other than that, they looked like human eyes, with a pupil and an iris, just very dark." She looked at Vrog. "Was that common for the females to go at each other so viciously? I thought that only the males fought each other for the females, not the other way around."

"I've never seen them fight," Vrog said. "They presented a unified front, but maybe they fought for dominance in private, or maybe they just needed to release some steam. Did you catch any of what they said to each other?"

Mey shook her head. "Is there a chance you could coach me on some more Kra-ell? They were talking so fast, screaming and hissing at each other that I couldn't understand what they were saying."

"It would be my pleasure," Vrog said. "We can work on your Kra-ell through the weekend, and then you can try the echoes again on Monday. I'm very curious about that fight and what it was about."

Ronja

In her bathroom, behind a locked door, Ronja peeled off her dress, unhooked her bra, and then hesitated before shrugging it off.

Should she leave it on?

It was a sexy bra, a black lace and satin pushup balconette that kept her breasts where she wanted them. She had the matching panties somewhere in her lingerie drawer, still with the price tag attached. She could swap them for the control top and that would solve her biggest problem. Merlin would assume that she'd had them on all along.

She hadn't laundered them, though, and she didn't like putting on anything that hadn't gone through the wash yet, but she would make an exception this time. After all, it wasn't as if anyone tried on panties in a lingerie store. They were clean.

With the bra back in place, she peeled off the tight panties and put on a robe before ducking into the bedroom. She found the sexy panties that matched the bra, ducked back into the bathroom, tore the tag off, and put them on. Red marks marred her skin where the other pair had dug into her flesh, but other than that, she looked okay. Not great, but pretty good for a middle-aged mother of three. She'd lost weight, and at her age that meant loose skin, and that wasn't attractive at all, but there wasn't much she could do about it.

Ronja didn't know what was worse, the loose skin muffin top or the padded one she'd had before.

Whatever. Merlin knew that she wasn't a spring chicken, and he wanted her anyway.

After rubbing some lotion over the marks, she spritzed a little perfume on her hair and the panties that still smelled like the store she'd gotten them from and took off the robe.

Ronja planned on waiting for Merlin in bed, so the robe wasn't needed.

Turning the lights off, she quietly opened the door, leaving it slightly ajar before dashing to the bed and slipping under the cover.

"I'm ready," she said barely louder than a whisper, not sure at all that the words were true, but it was time, and she wasn't a coward, so ready or not, she was having sex with Merlin tonight.

Naturally, Merlin heard her. As he pushed the door open, light spilled in from the hallway, and as he sauntered into the bedroom, she saw that he was holding a glass of wine in each hand.

"Are you comfortable, my beautiful Ronja?" He prowled over to the bed, sat next to her on top of the covers, and offered her a glass of wine. "You seem tense and unsure of yourself, and it's not like you. Did I do anything to make you nervous? Do you want to wait a little longer?" He smiled. "It will kill me, but if you are not ready, tell me, and I will go home, or we can go back to the living room and watch a movie."

"I'm ready." She took a sip from the wine and then another one. "I'm just nervous because I'm a vain woman who is no longer in her prime and feels insecure about baring herself to a man who looks half her age."

Merlin frowned. "You are hot, Ronja. Every morning when you show up on my doorstep with those sexy exercise clothes of yours, I get so hard I can barely walk, let alone run. Do you know what I have to do to be able to jog with you?"

"What?"

"I go over lists of conditions and symptoms like I did in medical school. That's the only way I can stop thinking about those bouncing breasts of yours and that magnificent ass that I can't wait to sink my teeth into."

Ronja laughed. "Don't you dare put your fangs anywhere near my ass."

His eyes blazed blue green in the dark. "What about other parts of your body? Can I bite your neck?"

As she imagined that, her new panties dampened. "Yes."

"Where else can I bite you?" He took the wine glass from her hand and put it on the nightstand. "Can I bite your inner thigh?" His hand tugged on the blanket, and as she let go of it, he pulled it down her breasts. "Or here?" He ran a finger over the swell of her breast.

"Just the neck for now," she breathed.

"That's a shame." He dipped his head and kissed each swell before tugging the bra cups down and exposing her nipples. "One day, I'll bite you here." He lightly pinched her right nipple and then licked the small hurt away. "And here." He repeated the same on the other side. "And maybe, when you learn to trust me, I'll bite you down here." He tossed the blanket aside, exposing her fully. "Gorgeous."

Merlin

"So soft." Merlin trailed his finger over the top of Ronja's sexy black panties. Her skin was so pale in contrast. "Will you allow me to kiss you here?" He lowered his head and pressed a kiss to her mound over the satin and lace.

"Yes," she breathed. "Don't you want to undress too?"

"Not yet." He smoothed his finger down the side, eliciting a shiver from her. "I want to take my time with you." He kissed her a little lower, finding her panties soaked through.

"I thought that I would be scared." She reached with her hand and cupped his cheek. "Of your fangs, I mean. Not you."

"And you're not?" He lifted his head and let her see his fully elongated fangs.

The room was dark, but the light coming from his eyes should be enough for her to see what she would later feel.

"I'm not scared. It's you, the same kind male I fell in love with, just with fangs."

His throat dried out in an instant. "You love me?"

She reached for him, winding her arms around his neck. "Wasn't that obvious?"

"I was hoping that you feel about me the same way I feel about you, but I wasn't sure. I didn't want to pressure you, so I held back, but I wanted to tell you for weeks that I love you."

Her smile was radiant as she leaned up and kissed him softly, her tongue darting out and licking around his fangs.

With a groan, he pulled away. "If you keep doing that, I'm going to come in my pants, and I'm way too old for that."

She gazed at him from under her long lashes. "There is no reason to hold back. I'm ready, and I'm aching." She trailed her hand down her belly and pushed past the elastic into her panties. "Right here." Her eyes rolled back as she lightly rubbed her clitoris.

It was the most erotic thing he'd ever seen, and as he snaked his finger under the gusset, her hips bucked up in a blatant invitation.

She was drenched, and as he dipped his finger in her wetness and dragged it up to where her fingers were pressed, she let her hand fall to the side to give him access. "Get undressed, Merlin. I want to see you. All of you."

"Not yet, love. I'm trying to pace myself so I can give you the attention you deserve, and I'm afraid that if I take off my clothes, I will lose control. I can't let it happen. You are still human, and you're fragile."

She chuckled nervously. "You will have to take them off at some point."

"Yes, but I need to prepare you first. It has been a while for you."

"For you as well." She said it as a statement, but there was a slight questioning note in her tone.

"Yes, it has. I've been waiting for you." He kicked off his shoes and stretched out on the bed next to her. "You were worth the wait." Lowering his head, he kissed her deep and long while gently massaging that most sensitive spot on her body.

When he slipped a finger inside of her, she bucked up against his hand, and he swallowed the moan she emitted. As he kept devouring her mouth and pumping his finger in and out of her, the faster he finger-fucked her, the lewder the wet sounds became, and combined with the overpowering scent of her desire, he was on the brink of spilling in his pants or ripping his zipper open and plunging into her with one brutal thrust.

Gathering the last of his self-control, he did neither, but he wasn't going to last much longer, which meant that he had to wrest a climax out of her lightning fast.

Given the churning of her hips and the sounds she was making, that shouldn't be hard to do.

Adding another finger, he let go of her mouth and lowered his head to her nipple, lapping at it once, twice, and sucking it into his mouth. Ronja was almost there, he could feel the small muscles in her sheath rippling against his fingers, and as he added his thumb to the play and gently rubbed her clitoris, she exploded with a scream.

Ronja

The orgasm exploded out of Ronja with the force of a hurricane, and for long moments, she couldn't move, couldn't open her eyes, couldn't even thank the male who'd given it to her.

She hadn't been with anyone since Frank had died, but lately, she'd gone back to pleasuring herself. Heck, she'd done that last night thinking about Merlin and coming hard as she imagined him between her legs and at her neck.

Ronja had hoped that last night's powerful orgasm had taken the edge off, so once she let loose, she wouldn't attack Merlin like a crazed succubus. It had done the job in that regard, but she'd still climaxed like a firecracker after two minutes of foreplay.

A gentle hand on her cheek and a kiss on her lips forced her to open her eyes, and the sight that greeted her was precious. Even though Merlin's eyes were aglow, and his fangs were at the longest she'd ever seen them, he didn't look alien, or scary, he just looked like a man in love.

A very naked and very hard and very thick male in love.

During the scant moments of her post-orgasmic bliss, he'd managed to get his clothes off and mount her, but he made no move to penetrate her.

"Hello, beautiful." He dipped his head and kissed her softly. "I need to ask you a question."

If he wanted to propose, that was wonderful, but it could wait. She needed that thick, pulsating length inside of her.

Ronja lifted her arms and looped them around his back. "Does it have to be now?" She ground herself on his erection. "I might have orgasmed harder than I ever did before, but that only whetted my appetite for more."

His smile was all about male pride and satisfaction as he slipped his hand under her butt and tucked her closer, the head of his erection probing her entrance. "Glad to oblige, my love, but I need to know whether you want us to use protection or not."

That was a tough call.

Ronja had planned for their first few times to be just about making love and not about her transition, and that necessitated the use of condoms. But now that she felt the velvety skin of him, she didn't want to sheath it in rubber.

Damn, she was such an airhead.

The same kind of frivolous behavior had gotten her pregnant with twins at nineteen and forced Michael to marry her. Then again, the twins were a blessing, and she'd been in love with Michael and had wanted him to marry her, so that hadn't been a mistake.

Perhaps this time it wasn't either.

It was the voice of her intuition, and it was telling her that it was time and that her gamble would pay off.

"No condoms." She tightened her arms around him. "I'm a hundred percent in. I want eternal life with you, Merlin, and that life begins tonight."

As the tenderness and love in his eyes became tinged with fear, he lowered his head and rested his forehead against hers. "I love you, Ronja, and I will continue loving you even if you choose not to transition. Are you absolutely sure?"

"I am." She caressed his back. "But I don't want anything to diminish the pleasure of our first time. If wearing a condom would make you less anxious, it's fine with me."

Her only warning was a growl that started deep within Merlin's chest, and then his manhood speared into her with one glorious thrust, filling her so completely, so perfectly, that it brought tears to her eyes.

As Merlin froze above her, his expression of lust replaced by alarm, she shook her head. "You're not hurting me. It just feels so perfect that I was moved to tears."

He smiled, flashing her those dangerous fangs, and thrust deeply. She arched up, meeting him stroke for stroke. As he started a steady rhythm, penetrating and retreating, she gripped him tightly, her fingers digging into his back muscles, her mouth finding a spot on his chest that she just had to lick.

He tasted as good as he smelled.

"You feel so perfect, Ronja."

She didn't answer, not with words, but she did with her body.

As another climax tore through her, she turned her head to the side, exposing her neck, and as she heard him hiss, she shut her eyes tightly, expecting the pain, welcoming it but also fearing it.

When his fangs penetrated her skin, the burn was worse than she'd expected, but it didn't last more than a couple of seconds, and then it was gone, and she orgasmed again, and again, and just when exhaustion began to wash over her, she was hit with a boost of energy and whisked away onto a cloud.

She was soaring high above magnificent landscapes that were totally alien, and yet felt more like home than everything she was familiar with. They were about love and tranquility, about a sense of rightness, of being one with the universe. She was no longer Ronja. She was a goddess, an angel, a free spirit not bound by any laws of men or nature, but she felt safe. She wasn't going to get lost because she was tethered by love, and all she had to

do to find her way back home was to follow that golden
line of light.

Merlin

❦

Merlin held Ronja in his arms for nearly three hours, her head tucked into the crook of his neck, her hair tickling his nose, the scent of their lovemaking permeating his nostrils.

As she soared on the clouds of venom-induced euphoria, or maybe just slept and dreamt, he hadn't dared close his eyes for longer than it took to blink, not because he was worried about her being out for so long, but because of who she was to him and what was at stake.

He'd been with enough human females before to have absolute certainty that the venom bite was not harmful.

On the contrary, once the women woke up, some as soon as an hour later while others took up to six, they felt wonderful. Rejuvenated, satisfied, and relaxed.

He'd always stayed to make sure that they were fine and to thrall the memory of his bite from their minds. They'd remembered spending several hours of passion with the quirky doctor, but they hadn't remembered that the doctor was not human.

If they wondered about the venom-induced trip, they dismissed it as a strange dream, or maybe even suspected him of slipping them a hallucinogenic, but none had ever complained.

Dipping his head, he pressed a soft kiss to the top of Ronja's head. He'd done that many times over the three hours or so since she'd checked out, but so far she hadn't even stirred. This time, though, her lips lifted in a little smile, and yet she didn't wake up. It wouldn't be long now. The smile meant that her consciousness was surfacing, and that her trip was almost over.

He hoped she'd enjoyed the ride, and he had no intention of letting her see how worried he was once she opened her eyes.

Up until now, her transition had been hypothetical, something that needed to be decided on in the future. As such, he could think about it rationally and refer to the excellent statistics the clan had with transitioning Dormants so far—a hundred percent success rate. But statistics didn't mean shit even if they had a one in a million chance of death when that death was of the one you loved.

In his case, it was even worse because if Ronja didn't make it, he would be the one responsible. It couldn't be blamed on some random act of fate or nature, a disease that there was no cure for, or an accident. It would be entirely on him.

If he hadn't pressured her into it, if he hadn't bitten her, her life wouldn't be in peril.

If she died, it would destroy him. He wouldn't be able to go on, and he would have to find a way to end his own life. Jumping off a plane with no parachute should do the trick, but he wouldn't need to resort to such extremes.

After all, he was a doctor, and there were poisons that in the right dosage could kill even an immortal.

With a sigh, he looked down at Ronja's peaceful sleeping face, leaned down and kissed her warm cheek. He shouldn't entertain such morbid thoughts on what should be the happiest day of his life.

Ronja had told him that she was in love with him, and he had known that he loved her for weeks now. There was no doubt in his mind that they were true-love mates, and if so, the Fates were responsible for their mating and wouldn't let anything happen to her.

Right.

Since when did he believe in all that spiritual crap?

He was a scientist, and it was against his religion to invoke the Fates or any other supernatural power. But as the saying went, there were no atheists in the foxhole, or in the hospital, or wherever else people fought for their lives and stared death in the face.

Merlin had cared about many people over the long centuries of his life, immortals and humans, but he'd never been in love before, and it was terrifying.

Orion

~~~

When their group arrived at the hotel restaurant, Orion expected the philologist to already be there, and a frown creased his brow when he didn't see him. "I hope Herb was picked up by his tour guide. I don't think it's safe for a middle-aged human to stay the night on that tiny island. His Hawaiian shirt and tweed jacket do not offer much protection from the elements, and it gets freezing on the lake at night."

Kalugal didn't seem to share his worry as he walked past, following the hostess. "If he doesn't show up in the next half an hour, I'll call the Lake Lodge and ask to speak with him. If he's not there, I'll send one of my men to that island."

"Thank you." Orion pulled out a chair for Alena. "I don't mind rowing over there myself. I could use the exercise."

"I'll join you." Alena sat down. "It sounds romantic."

"It's dangerous," Arwel said. "You can send one of your Odus."

"I don't want them anywhere near water. They are so heavy that I don't know if it's safe for them to be on one of those narrow canoes. Besides, I don't think that they like the idea of being on a boat." Alena pushed a strand of hair behind her ear. "Ovidu seemed very glad to be left behind this morning."

"Did you reboot him?" Carol asked.

"Not yet. Annani and I discussed it, and we decided to wait a little longer and see how Okidu and Onidu are doing and that the reboot doesn't have an adverse effect on them."

Orion followed the conversation with interest. "Do the cyborgs require rebooting?"

"One second." Kalugal lifted his hand. "Okay, you can talk now. I cast a shroud to muffle our conversation."

Jacki kissed his cheek. "You are so talented, my love."

Alena smiled at the couple before turning to Orion. "They don't. In fact, my mother refused to let anyone probe them or test them, fearing that it might cause damage that would be impossible to fix. The first reboot happened by accident when Okidu fell into the ocean, and it took a long time to pull him out. The Odus are very heavy, so he sank all the way to the bottom, and they needed to hook a cable to him and drag him back to the boat, where they used a crane to haul him out of the water. When he woke up, so to speak, Okidu started acting differently. He appeared more sentient, and then one day, he decided to reboot Amanda's butler because he needed help with a surprise he was preparing for Kian's birthday. Now we have two sentient Odus and five who are not."

"What was the present?" Orion asked.

Alena averted her eyes. "It's a very closely guarded secret. I'm sorry, but Kian would have my head if I tell you."

As an uncomfortable silence stretched across the table, Orion tried not to feel hurt. For a newcomer, he'd been entrusted with many of the clan's secrets and even with the goddess's heir. That was much more than he could have expected, and he shouldn't feel offended that they were still withholding information from him. It would have been irresponsible of them to do otherwise.

"That's okay." He lifted Alena's hand to his lips and kissed the back of it. "I don't need to know everything there is to know about the clan. I'm not a member yet."

"Most members don't know about it either," Arwel said. "It's a security issue, and we cannot afford any slackening in that."

"I understand perfectly." He kissed Alena's hand again to reassure her that he wasn't holding it against her.

Even if they had been already mated for many years, he wouldn't have expected her to share everything with him. She was an unofficial leader of her clan, privy to classified information, and there were things she couldn't share even with her mate.

"By the way." Arwel turned to Kalugal. "Did you mean what you told Herb about visiting the dig tomorrow? Weren't we supposed to wait until Monday?"

"I changed my mind," Kalugal said. "I'd rather tour the place and explore it freely without the workers snooping around us and watching what we do. My partner sent me a video of what they've found so far, and I can't wait to see it, but I was serious about going alone. I want to check the safety measures before I bring my pregnant wife there."

"You're not going alone," Jacki said. "Besides, I thought that the Chinese worked seven days a week."

Carol chuckled. "It's a myth. The Chinese are hard-working people, but they are not machines, and they get weekends off just like everyone in the West. If they work in a factory, they have shifts, and in case of an emergency, they stay overtime to solve the problem, but that's no different from how it's handled in the West."

"What about bribes?" Phinas asked. "I read that businesses in China have to pay hefty bribes to operate."

"Speaking of business," Kalugal said. "How are your double endeavors progressing? The fashion line and recruiting high-ranking Chinese officials to work for the Brotherhood?"

Lokan cast a quick sidelong glance at Phinas and Kalugal's two other men who were sitting on the other side of the long table, but then shook his head. "It's going slow, and the bribes are indeed a big problem."

Alena

Alena could understand Lokan's instincts kicking in and making him wary about talking in front of Kalugal's men, but he had nothing to worry about.

Or so Alena hoped.

Annani had compelled all clan members and all of Kalugal's men to not cause harm to one another. But did that include Lokan?

As Carol's mate, he was a clan member, but since he was still serving Navuh and the Brotherhood, it was a loophole someone could use to circumvent the compulsion.

Not that it was likely. Kalugal's men were loyal to him, and they had proven that loyalty countless times. They would never do anything to endanger his brother. Besides, they had as much to fear from Navuh and the Brotherhood as any clan member, probably more. If any of them was ever caught, Navuh would make an example out of them to scare the others into obedience.

"You can get away with not paying the bribes," Jacki said. "Why not compel them to do whatever you want them to do?"

"It's not that simple," Lokan said. "The bribe-takers are well organized, and it's part of doing business in China. I can compel those who come to collect the bribe money, but I have no access to their bosses. If the money doesn't get to them, I can kiss any progress goodbye, or worse." He leaned back in his chair. "Don't forget that I'm a foreigner, and they can kick me out very easily.

"Who do you need to bribe?" Alena said. "Is it like organized crime and you have to pay protection money?"

"That too," Carol said. "The bribe-takers are mostly local officials. We even have to pay to get access to materials, equipment, and other supplies needed to run the business. Perhaps it's not as bad in other provinces, but Beijing is the worst."

"Are Chinese entrepreneurs in the same boat as you are?" Arwel asked.

"Slightly less," Lokan said. "The statistics I read say that Hong-Kong-owned firms pay the most, followed by other foreign-owned firms, and the Chinese firms pay the least. The spread is about twelve percent. The highest bribes are paid by real estate and manufacturing firms. Corruption is a plague, and the government is trying to crack down on it, but it's like fighting trafficking. As long as big money can be made with relatively little effort, the cockroaches will find a way around the strongest of pesticides."

"Ugh." Carol shivered. "Why did you have to talk about cockroaches at the dinner table? It's gross."

"My apologies." He leaned toward her and kissed her cheek.

As the restaurant door opened and the philologist walked in, Kalugal snapped his fingers, letting everyone know that he'd dropped the shroud.

"Doctor Neisman." He rose to his feet. "My companions and I were worried that you were left stranded on that island." He pulled out the chair he'd reserved for Herb. "If you didn't show up just now, I would have called your hotel to check whether you had returned to your room."

"I'm so sorry." Herb sat down. "I started reading up on Kali and lost track of time." He chuckled nervously. "I'm the definition of an absentminded professor."

He hadn't mentioned being a professor before. As far as Alena knew, a person could have a doctorate, but unless they were employed by a university as teachers or heads of research, they weren't called professors.

"Where do you teach?" Alena asked.

"Brown University."

"Lovely place," Kalugal said. "I once dated a girl from Brown."

Jacki elbowed him in the ribs. "You said that you didn't date anyone before me."

He smiled indulgently. "Dated is a figure of speech. I just don't appreciate the modern lingo referencing amorous encounters. The romance is gone from it."

At the mention of romance, Orion's hand found Alena's under the table, and as he teased her palm, the way she knew he would later tease other places on her body, Alena felt her cheeks get warm.

Luckily, everyone's eyes were on Kalugal, and Herb gazed at him with renewed admiration. "It's so refreshing to see a young man like you who appreciates the finer nuances of language."

"Thank you." Kalugal dipped his head. "Language has power, and the words chosen to express feelings feed back into those feelings. We need to be careful in the way we communicate and even in the way we think."

"I couldn't agree more." Herb turned to look at the waitress who'd been waiting patiently to take their order. "If you don't mind, I would like to order and keep discussing the use of language over dinner. I'm famished."

Orion

The sexual tension Kalugal's innocent comment had ignited refused to abate despite the food Orion shoved in his mouth. As his mind got stuck running in circles and replaying all the marvelous moments of him and Alena making love, his appetite for her nullified his interest in the meal he was consuming on autopilot.

The same couldn't be said about Herb, who kept refilling his plate from the communal platters as long as there was anything left on them. He was very polite about it, though, always asking if anyone else wanted the last few bites. Naturally, they had all indulged him by telling him to go ahead.

When the professor finally pushed his plate away and leaned back, the buttons of his Hawaiian shirt strained to hold his bloated belly inside, and a few gray hairs poked through the gaps.

"Thank you for dinner." He rubbed a hand over his belly. "The Mrs. always tells me that it's not healthy to wait until dinner to eat and that I should consume smaller portions throughout the day, but I get so absorbed in my work that I forget to eat until hunger is gnawing at my belly, and then I overindulge."

"Where is Mrs. Neisman?" Carol asked.

"Back in the States. Our youngest daughter is about to have her first baby, and Matilda flew to Seattle to be with her." He smiled sadly. "We have three daughters, and each one of them lives in a different state. It's so difficult for Matilda. I have my work to keep me busy, but she retired a couple of years ago, and she gets lonely."

The guy didn't know how lucky he was. Orion couldn't imagine having one daughter, let alone three. He and Alena hadn't talked about the future yet, but she'd told him that she loved children and would have loved to have a hundred if she could, but it seemed that her fertility had run out, and his hadn't manifested yet and maybe never would.

What were the chances of them having a child together?

Geraldine had told him about a clan doctor who was working on improving immortals' fertility. If things went well and they bonded, perhaps the doctor might be able to help them conceive.

Casting a sidelong glance at Alena, Orion imagined her pregnant with their child, her delicate hands resting on her rounded belly, and happiness illuminating her beautiful face.

"So, Herb." Carol turned to the professor. "What did you find out about the monster?"

He frowned. "What monster are you referring to?"

"Kali, of course."

He seemed offended on the goddess's behalf. "Kali is not a monster. She's vicious but also nurturing. She is complicated, feared, and adored at the same time. She represents all of existence and encompasses the two forces governing it—death and destruction on one side, creation and salvation on the other. She symbolizes death's inevitability, but at the same time, she makes the passage easier by encouraging acceptance and dispelling fear."

The professor's speech was interrupted by the waitress. "Can I take away some of these?" She motioned at the mostly empty platters.

"You can take all of it," Kalugal said. "I would like to see the dessert menu for tonight, and another serving of tea would be great."

"Right away, sir." The young woman inclined her head, and a moment later, several busboys rushed over to clear the table.

"How old is Kali's worship?" Lokan asked.

Orion had wondered the same thing and even planned to search for answers on the internet, but it had been a busy day, and he hadn't had the opportunity. If the myths about Kali originated with the Kra-ell's Mother of All Life, the start of Kali's worship could provide them a rough time estimate for when the first Kra-ell had arrived.

"Kali's name first appears in a holy Hindu text. The oldest estimated age of that text is seventeenth-century BCE, and the most recent eleventh-century BCE. Kali is also described in the Devi-Mahatmya portion of the Markandeya Purana historical texts. What's somewhat confusing about the Hindu pantheon is that one god or goddess can have many manifestations. Kali is also the great goddess Devi, who is also known as Durga. Her other names include, Sati, Rudrnai, Parvati, Kamakshi, and others that I can't recall at the moment."

"Interesting," Carol said. "I don't know much about the Hindu pantheon, but I remember hearing a story about the god Shiva, and a wife named Parvati, and another wife named Kali. I thought he had several wives, but from what you're saying, it's a different manifestation of the same one."

Herb grinned. "Isn't that just brilliant? Women are such complicated and multifaceted creatures, and the Hindu tradition captured the female essence so beautifully. Kali is the goddess of fertility and time. She is the protector and defender who is called upon in times of great calamity. She is the symbol of productivity, the cycles of nature, the creator who takes life to give new life. She's the destroyer of evil, ignorance, and selfishness, and the nurturer of all that is good in humanity."

"I like her," Jin said. "She's a kick-ass goddess."

"Like the Kra-ell's Mother of All Life?" Arwel said so quietly that only the immortals heard him.

"She's a warrior," Herb said. "When demons needed slaying, and Parvati was too gentle to deal with them, she called upon Kali—her fiercer manifestation to come forward. Kali decapitated the demons and swallowed some in her enormous mouth. That's why she is often depicted with blood-smeared lips, holding weapons in her four, eight, or ten arms, and wearing a skirt of severed hands and a garland of skulls."

"She sounds terrifying and horrifying," Alena said. "More of a destroyer than anything else."

"Don't forget that those she slew were demons, real or figurative." Herb pulled out his phone and scrolled through until finding what he was looking for. "This is Kali at a dinner party. As you can see, her plate is painted in reds and purples, reminding us that she drinks the blood of demons."

"Lovely." Alena grimaced and passed the phone to Orion. "I hope that I'm not going to dream about her tonight."

Alena

❧

Alena opened the balcony doors of their hotel room and stepped outside. The two rocking chairs with a small table between them reminded her of Kian. As she imagined her brother sitting outside and puffing on one of his cigars, she wondered what he would have made of their discoveries from earlier today.

Leaning her elbows on the railing, she looked at the lake. Most of it was dark, with the exception of an area that was bathed in moonlight, shimmering with a silver light.

Were they seeing real mythological patterns that aligned with what they knew of the Kra-ell? Or were they mistakenly assigning meaning where there was none?

Orion walked up behind Alena and wrapped his arms around her. "What are you thinking about?" He kissed the side of her neck.

Closing her eyes, she let her head drop back against his chest. "When you are kissing me, I think of nothing at all. I just feel."

He nuzzled her ear. "Is it just me, or does the goddess Kali perfectly fit the Kra-ell deity?"

"Kian always warned us against seeing patterns and giving them unwarranted interpretations. Just like humans, our brains are programmed to see patterns, but that doesn't mean that what we deduce from those patterns is true. Many of the ancient gods and goddesses were depicted as terrifying and destructive, and not all mythologies were based on our ancestors."

As he trailed kisses down her neck, his hands traveled up her sides and then closed over her breasts. "How about we give the scary gods and goddesses of other mythologies a rest for tonight and move to more enjoyable topics?"

Alena smiled. "What topics do you have in mind?"

His fingers teased her nipples. "The worship of one very beautiful goddess who is gentle and sweet and not terrifying in the least."

"I could be terrifying if I wanted to."

"Not a chance." He turned her around to face him. "I'm running the water in the tub. It's probably full by now." He dipped his head and kissed her lightly. "I plan on giving you a very thorough wash, starting with your dainty toes."

Said toes curled inside her ballet flats. "Sounds delightful."

"I'm glad you approve." He lifted her into his arms and carried her to the bathroom.

Alena laughed. "I've never understood what was so special about a male carrying a female, but I get it now. It's sexy as hell."

"Is it, now?" He lowered her onto a chair he'd positioned in front of the bathtub and went to turn the faucets off. "I don't know what's sexy about hell. Isn't hell supposed to be hot?"

"That's the idea." Alena kicked her shoes off. "Maybe it started with hot as hell, which would make sense, and then it morphed into sexy as hell. Or perhaps it started with sexy as sin and turned into sexy as hell."

"We could ask Herb." He knelt at her feet and reached for the waistband of her trousers. "Your new wardrobe is sexy and sophisticated, but I liked your long dresses better."

She arched a brow. "Really? Amanda said that I looked quaint in them."

"So?" He gently pulled her pants down. "You looked like the fairytale princess you are, and the dresses were easy to take off. What more can a male ask for?"

She leaned and kissed the top of his head. "You say the nicest things."

He still hadn't told her that he loved her, but then she hadn't said the words either. Were they in love, though? Or were they still in like and lust?

Orion lifted on his knees and started on her blouse buttons. "Wait until I get you naked. I will have even nicer things to say."

"Oh, yeah? Like what?" She helped him with the last two buttons and shrugged the blouse off.

He sucked in a breath. "Keep the new lingerie when you go back to wearing the soft dresses you like. Talk about hot as sin and sexy as hell. Or is it the other way around?"

It was just a white lace bra, but it was low cut, leaving most of the swells of her breasts exposed. But if it got Orion to look at her like that, she was going to buy it in every color.

"Should I leave it on?" she breathed as he leaned to kiss the top of her breasts.

"As beautiful as it is," he reached behind her and popped the clasp, "it can't compare to the beauty of you in nothing at all." He slid the straps down her arms and tossed the bra aside.

Lifting her off the chair, Orion kissed her long and hard before lowering her into the tub.

Alena scooted to the side. "Aren't you going to join me?"

"Not yet." Orion took a washcloth, squirted liquid soap on it, and knelt by the tub. "Lift your foot." When she did, he took hold of her heel and ran the washcloth over her foot. "You have the prettiest toes I've ever seen." He lifted her foot to his lips and started kissing one toe at a time.

With a moan, Alena let her head drop back on the lip of the tub and closed her eyes. "This feels so good."

His strong fingers pressed into the arch of her foot. "I've only just begun."

Orion

As their limousine bumped and swayed over the unpaved road, their driver swore in Chinese and then quickly apologized for it. Orion couldn't converse freely in the language, but he picked up enough of it to get the gist. Besides, some things were universal, and cussing sounded the same no matter which language it was uttered in.

Kalugal said something about compensating him for damage to the vehicle, which seemed to mollify the guy, and he cussed no more even though the ride got even bumpier over the last section of the path.

When the vehicle finally stopped next to a dusty truck that was parked a hundred feet or so from the riverbank, they all sighed in relief.

"Whose truck is that?" Lokan asked.

"My partner's, Jianye," Kalugal said. "I asked him to meet me here and walk me through the security measures he's taken."

"I'm glad I had a light breakfast," Alena said as she took Orion's hand. "I didn't expect the road to be a goat trail." She cast Kalugal an accusing glance. "Did you know that it was unpaved?"

"Of course."

"So why did you bring us here in the limousines?"

He arched a brow. "Would you have preferred a yak ride?"

"You have a point," Alena conceded.

"I hope my baby is okay." Jacki caressed her small belly. "He got quite a rollercoaster experience today."

"He's fine," Kalugal reassured her. "Right now, he's the size of a banana and is surrounded by protective liquid."

Jacki's lips twisted in a grimace. "Please don't compare our baby to a banana."

"I didn't. All I said was that he was the size of one." For the first time since Orion had met Kalugal, the guy seemed impatient with his wife.

Perhaps it was worry that shortened his temper.

Kalugal had wanted to go to the dig alone, check the safety of the site, and come back to get them only after making sure that it was okay. But Jacki had insisted that it was a waste of time and that he could check the site while the rest of them waited on the riverbank. If it wasn't safe, they would at least get to see the scenic route leading to the islet in the middle of the wide river.

In Orion's opinion, it was worth the nearly one-hour-long bumpy ride to just get a look at the ruins from the riverbank. The ancient trade post had been carved into the rock, starting on top of the high platform and going down.

He wondered how the platform had been naturally formed in the middle of the river, and if the locals had a legend for that as well. The walls of the outpost were at least fifty feet tall, and a massive gate once guarded the only entrance. All that remained of it was the opening, which was about thirty feet tall and had carved pillars on both sides that were more decorative than functional.

As their group walked the last few feet to the bank, Kalugal's local partner waved and smiled from the rope bridge that had been erected between the riverbank and the excavation site. After a short round of partial introductions, the two made their way across the bridge, while the rest of them waited to hear Kalugal's verdict about the site's safety.

"I'm glad that we are immortal," Alena whispered in Orion's ear. "That bridge doesn't look too solid."

Wrapping his arm around her waist, he nuzzled her neck. "How good of a swimmer are you?"

"Not great, and I'm not looking forward to getting wet. The middle rungs of the bridge are submerged. I also don't like the idea of the outpost being carved going down. Kalugal said that this site has been excavated before, and that the previous archeologists dug through several strata of habitation. It made me wonder how deep down they went. If they dug below the river's surface level, the whole place could be flooded."

"Don't worry," Jacki said. "They've been digging here for over two weeks, and nothing's happened. Why would anything collapse just from us walking around and looking?"

"I don't know." Alena rubbed her hands over her arms. "I have a bad feeling."

Orion's shoulders stiffened. "Do you often get premonitions?"

She chuckled. "Very rarely, and I'm usually wrong, so don't mind me. I guess it has become a habit of mine to issue warnings about all possible mishaps. With my mother's complete disregard for safety, I had to be the voice of reason." She sighed. "I hope she's doing okay without me."

"Have you called her since we got here?" Carol asked.

Alena shook her head. "She told me not to call unless it was an emergency. She wants me to enjoy my vacation and not worry about her, but it feels so strange. I want to call her and tell her about how beautiful it is out here, and about all the interesting things we've learned from the philologist."

"So call her," Carol said. "I think your mother wants to prove that she can survive just fine without you, but there is no reason to go cold turkey about it. I think that both of you will feel much better if you talk at least once a day."

"What do you think?" Alena turned to Orion. "Should I call my mother?"

He glanced at the ruins, but Kalugal and his partner had disappeared beyond the gate and were nowhere to be seen.

"Kalugal's inspection of the site might take a while, so you have time to call your mother. The only thing I'm not sure about is whether it is smart to defy the goddess's command. Will she be okay with you disobeying her wishes?"

Alena shrugged. "The worst she will do is pretend to be upset with me, but I think she'll be glad I called." She pulled out her phone and frowned. "That's strange. I have no reception here." She looked up. "And it's not even cloudy. Clan phones are supposed to work everywhere."

"Let's see." Arwel pulled his out. "You're right. Something must be interfering with the satellite connection." He turned to Lokan. "Do you have the Brotherhood's phone on you?"

Lokan shook his head. "I left it in the hotel."

"Damn." Arwel put the phone in his pocket. "I'm going to jog back to the limo and check with the driver if his phone works."

"I'll come with you," Jin said. "I don't think he speaks any English, and you might need me to translate."

"I'll go with you as well," Lokan said. "I speak fluent Chinese."

Alena

❧

"I feel naked." Alena looked at her useless phone. "Does anyone have a theory about why our phones don't work here?"

The driver's phone didn't work either, but that was because the nearest tower was at the lake, and the area of the ruins didn't get coverage. He'd told Lokan that he'd lost reception twenty minutes into the drive. That had probably been another reason for the man's cussing bout.

The satellite phones should have been fine, though.

"Maybe the satellite is malfunctioning," Arwel said. "Although it has never happened before."

"Should we even go into the outpost without our phones?" Carol asked.

Arwel looked conflicted. "I don't think we should. We should buy walkie-talkies and leave someone on the outside with one."

"Where are you going to find them?" Lokan asked. "All you can get around the lake are touristy things."

"The boat operators might have them," Carol said. "I didn't see ours carry a walkie-talkie, but she probably had one. How else is she communicating with her dispatcher?"

"We had no problems using our phones on the lake." Alena lifted her phone again, hoping that by some miracle a signal would show. "The guides can use phones. They don't need walkie-talkies."

It would be a shame to come all the way out here and not visit the ruins just because they didn't have reception. If people worked on that site Monday through Friday without it, their group could manage an hour sightseeing with no connection. People had done just fine without instant global connectivity up until about a decade ago, and now they couldn't function without it?

It was ridiculous.

Alena dumped the device in her purse and crossed her arms over her chest. "We are already here, and we are going to see the damn site with or without reception. It's not like we always had cellular phones. We've spent the vast majority of our lives without them."

"Kalugal is coming back," Jacki said.

As Alena turned to look at the swaying rope bridge, her bravado of only moments ago evaporated. She had no idea how Kalugal was crossing it so calmly. One wrong step and he would plunge into the river's freezing water.

It was good that the Odus had stayed behind. The flimsy bridge would have come apart under their weight.

"It's safe," Kalugal announced. "As long as we don't go inside any of the dwellings, there shouldn't be a problem."

"Our phones don't work," Arwel said.

"I know. There is no reception here."

"That shouldn't affect our satellite phones," Lokan said.

"Jianye says that there's some sort of natural interference in the soil. Supposedly there are large deposits of copper in the river's sediment and in the rock platform." Kalugal smiled. "Although Jianye thinks that the culprit is a naughty spirit. The workers are complaining about their tools and lunches disappearing."

"I don't think it's safe to go in without the ability to communicate," Arwel said. "I don't even like being here, on the riverbank, without a line to the outside world."

"That's fine." Kalugal waved a dismissive hand. "There is no one for miles around, and we are only going to walk through the outpost's main boulevard and look at the artifacts that have been found so far. I don't expect it to take long, and I'll inform the drivers that they should come to look for us if we don't come out in an hour."

"I'll do that for you," Jianye said.

"Thank you." Kalugal offered him his hand. "Thanks for coming out here during the weekend. I appreciate that."

"No problem." The man smiled. "My compensation is more than adequate."

As the two said their goodbyes, Arwel walked over to the bridge and examined it. "The bridge looks well built, but I suggest that we cross it one at a time."

"The water is pretty shallow here," Kalugal said. "If we didn't mind getting wet, we could have walked across. In fact, when they installed the bridge, that's how they did it. Anyway, my long preamble was to explain why I feel it's safe for us to cross two at a time."

Alena wanted to kiss Kalugal on both cheeks. Walking across the rope bridge together with Orion would be much less scary than crossing alone.

"The current is strong," Arwel said. "If anyone falls and loses their balance, they might get carried away."

Jin rolled her eyes. "You probably mean us, the fragile females. I assure you that each one of us can swim against the current. We are immortal, in case you've forgotten."

Alena wasn't sure at all that she could battle the current. She wasn't a strong swimmer, and that was why she never ventured into water that was deeper than she could stand in. Nevertheless, she refused to be the only one who acted scared.

She was Annani's daughter, and she should be fearless, or at least pretend that she was.

Arwel nodded. "Two at a time it is."

"Shall we, my love?" Kalugal offered Jacki his arm.

Brave girl.

Then again, if Kalugal felt that it was safe for his pregnant wife, then Alena really shouldn't worry.

Except, phobias were not rational, and Alena seemed to be afflicted with several.

"Let's go." Jacki took Kalugal's offered arm without a moment's hesitation.

As the two of them made their way slowly across the swaying bridge, Alena held her breath, and when they stepped onto solid ground on the other side, she finally let it out.

"Who's next?" Arwel asked.

"Lokan and I." Carol took her mate's hand and led him toward the bridge.

The two made it across much faster than Kalugal and Jacki had, and since Arwel wasn't going to do it until Alena got safely to the other side, it was her and Orion's turn.

"Don't worry," Orion said. "I won't let you fall." He took her hand.

The next five minutes were the longest of her life. How had the others done it so fearlessly?

The gaps between the wooden slats were so wide that one wrong move could end up with her plunging into the water, and the whole thing swung like a pendulum. Holding Orion's hand on one side and the rope railing on the other, Alena concentrated on putting one foot in front of the other and not thinking about the water below.

By the time she made it safely to the other side, she was drenched in sweat and shaking.

"I don't know why I was so scared." She smiled apologetically. "Even if I fell, I would have just gotten wet and cold. The current doesn't look that strong, and even I could swim ashore."

"I blame your mother." Carol patted Alena's arm. "Just don't tell her that I said that."

"What does my mother have to do with my anxiety?"

"Because of her shenanigans and your constant exposure to stress, you have developed low-level anxiety. Two thousand years of trying to tame a mischievous goddess would do that to a person."

Alena was about to deny Carol's observation when she realized that there might be something to it. She was aware that most of her fears were irrational. She had no reason to fear compellers when her mother could free her of compulsion if needed, and she had no reason to fear the rickety bridge because a fall from it would be harmless. But knowing something intellectually was not the same as internalizing it and believing it on a visceral level.

Perhaps she should have a talk with Vanessa and see what the therapist thought of Carol's observation.

Orion

As they crossed what used to be the outpost's gate, Orion was glad to see that Alena's anxiety had been replaced by curiosity.

"Please stay on the main boulevard and don't walk into any of the structures," Kalugal warned.

What he called a boulevard was actually a trench. From what Orion could see, the ancient builders had started digging down in the middle of the plateau to carve out the main throughway, and then continued carving on both sides to form the homes and shops and other structures. It was quite ingenious. First of all, they hadn't needed to bring any building materials to the site, and secondly, the steep sides of the plateau provided a natural barrier, so they hadn't needed to build protective walls either. What he found curious, though, was that the outpost had only one gate. For strategic reasons at least two gates were needed, one on each side of the islet, and preferably an escape tunnel that ran under the riverbed.

"All I see are piles of rocks," Jin grumbled.

"Let me explain what you are seeing," Kalugal said. "Most of the dwellings are underground, and they were excavated from the top down." He motioned for them to get closer. "These steps are hewn out of the rock, and they lead into a hidden entrance." He took the steps down and crouched. "This one is blocked, either on purpose or because of crumbling rock." He pushed up and took the steep steps out of the small tunnel.

"Did they find any homes that were easy to access and not walled off?" Jacki asked.

"Jianye said that they found some dwellings that survived nearly intact. The workers erected a tent at the end of the boulevard to house the artifacts they found, and that's where we are heading."

"How old are these ruins?" Orion asked.

"About twenty-one to twenty-three hundred years old."

Alena chuckled. "They are not much older than me and there isn't much left of them. It always amazes me that our bodies can keep regenerating as they do."

Over the many years of his life, Orion had often thought about how his body's regeneration worked, what was special about it. Except, everything that had to do with science usually went over his head, and when he tried to educate himself about human biology, he'd usually given up after a page or two of explanations that had his eyes glazing over.

Given that his father was the god of knowledge, he should have been better at the sciences, but evidently, he'd inherited his mother's brain and not his father's, just without her talent. He had a good eye for art and appreciated it, but he couldn't create it.

It occurred to him that he hadn't tried many forms of artistic expression yet. He might have a talent for sculpting, or glass-working, or pottery, or songwriting, or any of the other creative endeavors he planned to experiment with one day. As an immortal, Orion had endless time to explore his talents, but that was also why he hadn't yet. There was no rush to do anything.

His body was going to keep repairing itself and serve as housing for his soul for a very long time.

"Kian said something about the gods being genetically engineered. Is that fact or a hypothesis?" he asked Alena.

"It's a strong hypothesis," she said. "Another hypothesis is that the Kra-ell are an older version, perhaps even the original, and that we are a later development."

"Do you have anything to substantiate the belief that they came from the same place as the gods?"

She shook her head. "We don't, but it makes sense."

As they kept their leisurely stroll down the avenue, and Kalugal pointed out another set of stairs leading down to a residence, Jacki stopped.

"Check if the doorway is still intact. I want to see one of those dwellings."

"It's not safe." He carefully descended the stairs and crouched to look through the opening. "This one is not blocked, but it's a twenty-foot drop down. The people who lived here probably had a ladder that they could detach in case of an invasion. Anyone trying to go down this hole would have been immediately killed or injured, either by the defenders or by the fall."

Orion followed Kalugal down and took a look through the hole. "I wonder how they were eventually overwhelmed. Are there any signs of fire? Because that would have been one of the ways to do it. They could have shot flaming arrows into the homes and set them on fire."

"The stone wouldn't have been affected, but if they had wooden furniture, that would have been an effective method." Kalugal pulled out his phone and shone the flashlight into the hole. "I don't see any scorch marks, and my partner didn't mention it either."

"Would sooty marks have survived over the centuries?"

"Oh, definitely. This outpost was still active in the fourteenth century of the Common Era."

"Then I really can't see how it fell."

"Are you guys coming up?" Jacki said. "If I can't go down there, I want to at least see the artifacts."

Kalugal looked up and smiled at his mate. "You wanted me to take a look."

"Yeah, but since we can't go in, we should move on." She tapped the fingers of her hand over her other arm. "If we had a ladder, though, we could take a look inside. I'm sure we can find one that the excavators used."

When he started shaking his head, Jacki put her hands on her hips. "Stop with that overprotective act of yours. These ruins stood here for hundreds of years, and whatever was supposed to collapse already did. Those homes are like caves that are carved into the rock, so it's not like they have walls that rotted away."

"She has a point." Alena joined Jacki, looking down at them. "This is an archeological site. We should be able to find a ladder lying around somewhere."

Alena

~

As their tour of the ruins progressed, Alena stopped worrying about the lack of phone reception.

It seemed perfectly safe, and the tent with the artifacts was about a hundred feet ahead. The place was completely devoid of vegetation, which was odd since the area received a good amount of precipitation, double what California got annually, but the upside of that was no hidden creepy-crawlies hiding where she couldn't see them but could still hear them.

Having enhanced senses was mostly advantageous, but sometimes she wished her hearing wasn't as good. If she didn't hear the damn bugs, she could pretend that there were none. After all, most were harmless, and even those that were poisonous couldn't kill an immortal. If she was stung by a scorpion, she would be uncomfortable, but she wouldn't die.

"Are you thinking the same thing I'm thinking?" Orion wrapped his arm around her waist.

"That depends. What were you thinking?"

"The area of the lake is covered in lush greenery, but this place is barren as if it was somewhere in the desert. Could the copper in the soil do that?"

"Excess copper is toxic to plants," Kalugal said. "But that's not the only reason."

Alena waited for him to continue his explanation, but he got distracted as Jacki lifted the tent's flap and motioned for them to walk in.

Long worktables were piled with dusty artifacts that Alena didn't find overly exciting. Shards of pottery, some tools, pieces of cloth—very little remained of the people who'd once lived in the outpost. It made her sad to look at those scraps and think that this was all that was left of them.

"What's fascinating about this site," Kalugal said as he walked over to one of the tables and lifted what looked like an arrowhead, "is that older artifacts are found near the surface while more recent ones are buried deep below. What my partner thinks happened was that subsequent inhabitants kept digging deeper to build their abodes, and that's why the deeper we dig, the newer the stuff gets."

"What's that?" Jacki lifted an artifact. It was a mask of a scary-looking face that had huge ears and big slanted holes for eyes. "Oh, wow." She swayed on her feet and leaned against the worktable.

Kalugal was at her side in a flash. "What's wrong?"

She waved him off, but he wouldn't let go. "Talk to me, Jacki. What's going on?"

When he tried to pry the mask from her hands, she held on, clutching it to her chest. "The poor child. She's so scared."

"What child?" Kalugal's tone turned urgent. "Are you having a vision?"

Jacki nodded. "A little girl. This thing scared her. She ran away and hid from it." She turned in a circle and walked over to the tent's eastern side. "It was right here." She backed away and walked toward the entrance. "There are stairs here that lead to a tunnel."

Still holding the scary statue clutched to her chest, Jacki walked out and squeezed herself between the tent's wall and the rock face.

"Wait." Kalugal took hold of her elbow. "You'll tear your skin on that rock."

"It's right here." Jacki crouched next to the boulder. "Can you move it?" Her voice wavered. "She's inside. I hope she's still alive. How did this boulder get here and block the entrance to the tunnel? Did someone trap her on purpose?"

"Who would do a thing like that?" Jin said. "And why?"

Thinking about a child trapped underground had Alena's heart hammering against her ribcage. "The who and why doesn't matter right now. We need to get her out, and once she's safe, then find the ones responsible and bring them to the authorities."

As the males got to work dismantling the tent's eastern wall to make room, Alena wrapped her arm around Jacki's shaking shoulders. "How often do you get visions?"

"Not often, but this was a strong one." She lifted a pair of worried eyes to Alena. "I don't know when this took place. It might have happened a long time ago, and all we will find are bones." She shivered. "But it could have also happened yesterday or a couple of days ago, and we might be able to save the girl."

As the seven males got behind the boulder and pushed, Alena regretted not having the Odus with her. As strong as immortal males were, the Odus were stronger.

"On the count of three!" Kalugal called out.

The males grunted, and slowly, the boulder started moving.

"Again! One, two, three!" The boulder moved another inch.

On Alena's right side, Jin bristled. "If there was any space to put my hands on this rock, I could have helped. I'm strong."

"I'm sure you are." Carol patted her back. "But let the boys do their thing."

"A child's life is at stake," Jin hissed.

"Perhaps." Carol caressed her back as if she was trying to tame a wild mare. "If Jacki's visions are anything like Syssi's, the girl could have run into that tunnel centuries ago, or she might run into it centuries into the future. Visions are tricky that way."

Orion

The damn thing must have weighed a couple of tons if seven immortal males could barely move it. Orion was covered in sweat, and his palms were slick on the boulder's smooth face.

If not for Jacki's panicked insistence that there was a child trapped in the tunnel, he would have given up. But on the slight chance that her vision was true, he couldn't.

Still, he couldn't shake the feeling that the entire scenario didn't make sense. Who rolled the boulder over the entrance and why?

He doubted that anyone had trapped the child on purpose. It was more likely that the workers Kalugal's partner had hired had done that without knowing that the child was there, but even that didn't make sense. First of all, they were human, and there was no way they could have moved the thing without proper equipment. And secondly, why would they do that when it made erecting the tent more difficult?

Perhaps it had been a security issue, and they didn't want anyone falling in?

If not for that massive boulder, they wouldn't have had to put up the tent at an odd angle. Most likely, it had been there when the tent went up, which also meant that the child couldn't have gone into the tunnel recently.

Jacki's vision was probably about a past event.

Hopefully, the girl had made it out before someone had decided to block the entrance, or she'd found another way out. If not, they were going to find either a skeleton or a rotting corpse, which would devastate Jacki and probably the other females as well.

Hell, who was he kidding. It would crush him too. He'd never dealt well with death, not when it was of people he cared about, and not even of strangers, and especially not children.

When they managed to move the rock by a few inches, Kalugal called a halt to their efforts. "Let's see what we got here." He used his phone to shine light through the small opening they'd created.

"Here." Jin handed him a flashlight.

"Thank you." He tucked the phone in his pocket and turned on the strong beam. "Yup, just as I suspected."

"What?" Jacki peered over his shoulder. "What do you see?"

"A long drop and no ladder. There is no way a small child could have jumped down and not injured herself."

"She wasn't that small. She was eleven or twelve, with a dirty face and wild eyes. She went down a flight of stairs, though. I didn't see a drop."

"Could you have mistaken a ladder for stairs?" Carol asked.

"Maybe." Jacki pinched her forehead between her thumb and forefinger. "She was so terrified after seeing that mask, screamed so loudly, and ran so fast that I might not have paid attention to details."

"The mask is a depiction of Cancong," Kalugal said. "The legendary first king of Shu."

"I don't care whose head it is. Can you move the boulder enough for us to go down?"

"We can't go down because there is no ladder."

Jacki lifted a brow. "I could jump twenty feet down as a human, so don't tell me we can't do it."

Turning the flashlight off, he pushed to his feet. "First of all, you are pregnant, and there is no way you are jumping even five feet and risking our baby. And secondly, how do you propose that we get out once we find her or realize that she's not there? Jumping twenty feet up in the air is beyond my capabilities, so it's sure as hell beyond yours."

"We can tie a rope." Jacki turned to Phinas. "You can climb a rope, right? And you can pull us up one at a time."

The poor guy looked to his boss for help. "What do you want me to do?"

"Find a damn rope." Jacki stomped her foot. "Every minute we waste arguing out here, the girl might be dying down there."

Closing his eyes for a moment, Kalugal let out a long-suffering breath. "Find a rope, Phinas." He lifted a finger to shush Jacki. "But you are not coming down. Phinas and I will go, and the rest of the men will stay out here to guard you."

"Like hell." Her hands on her hips, she stared him down. "I'm the one who had the vision, and I saw the girl running through the tunnel. I'll recognize the twists and turns and show you where to go. You'll be lost without me."

"I found a ladder." Phinas dropped a large bundle of ropes and wooden slats at their feet. "That's what the workers use to go down the holes, and it should be sturdy."

Kalugal looked conflicted, but Orion knew how it would end. Jacki would have her way, and if she went, the other ladies wouldn't want to be left behind, and if they went down the tunnel, the other males would go as well to provide them protection.

"Did anyone see a canteen lying around?" Jacki asked. "We should bring water with us. The girl might be dehydrated."

"She might be dead, my love." Kalugal took his mate's hand. "Your vision might be from a long time ago."

"I know. But it's not centuries old. The girl wore pants and a puffer jacket. Those became popular only a few years ago."

Alena shook her head. "They've been popular since the forties, and especially in China."

Alena

Alena felt quite useless as she watched the men push and grunt to get the opening wide enough for them to go down through. Jin and Carol went to look for more flashlights, Jacki was the one with the vision, and Alena was left with nothing better to do than watch Orion's muscles bunch and swell as he strained along with the others.

With a child's life possibly on the line, ogling her guy was just wrong, and so was feeling all warm and fuzzy about the teamwork she was witnessing. Orion was quickly becoming part of the family, cooperating with her cousins, their men and Arwel as if he'd known them for years instead of days.

Kalugal wiped his hands on his slacks and turned to Phinas, who was just as out of breath as the others. "I want that ladder secured to this damn boulder."

"I'm on it, boss." Phinas entered the tent and a moment later returned with a big hammer and a bunch of bolts.

"Stand back," he told everyone as he started hammering the bolts into the rock.

When he was done Kalugal pulled on the rope ladder to test the bolts, and when it didn't budge, he motioned for Phinas to grab the other side and pull along with him to test its strength.

Satisfied with the results, Kalugal dusted off his hands and turned to his wife. "Is there any chance I can convince you not to come down there with us?"

She shook her head. "You need me. If we had functioning phones, I might have been able to guide you from the surface, but we don't, and without me, you will not know where to go."

"I don't like it, but you are right."

"We've got lights for everyone." Jin and Carol came out of the tent holding hardhats with attached lights and several flashlights.

"I'll take a flashlight," Jacki said. "I'm not wearing a hat some sweaty guy had on for days."

After that comment, Alena snatched a flashlight as well, and so did Jin and Carol. The guys had no choice but to use the hardhats.

As Phinas dropped the ladder into the opening, Welgost went down first.

"All clear," he called from the bottom. "Send Shamash down. We will hold the ladder for the ladies."

After Shamash joined Welgost, Jin tucked the flashlight in her waistband and approached the ladder. "Wish me luck."

Arwel went down right after her, then Carol volunteered to go next, and Lokan followed.

"Who's next?" Alena asked.

"You go." Jacki waved her on. "Kalugal and I will be the last."

Orion rubbed his hands, trying to get the dirt off them. "Shouldn't we leave someone on top to guard the opening?"

Kalugal looked conflicted. "No one can move that thing, so I'm not worried about that, but if someone wants to sabotage us, they can cut off the ladder. On the other hand, if Jacki is down there, I want all the men there to protect her. It's a tough call."

"Why would anyone want to sabotage us?" Jacki asked. "Besides, the two limo drivers know to come look for us if we are not out in an hour." She looked at her watch. "We've been here only twenty minutes or so. Do you want to send someone to tell them to wait longer before they come looking for us?"

"I don't know how reliable those drivers are, and I prefer them not knowing that we are going down."

"Why?" Alena asked. "I think someone should know in case we encounter trouble down there. If someone cuts the rope ladder, the drivers wouldn't know where to look for us."

Kalugal arched a brow. "Do we really need the help of two humans? If we can't handle whatever is down there, they for sure can't either, and neither can anyone else they might bring from the village to help."

Alena chuckled. "Since they are probably Chinese government agents in disguise, they might be better trained than you think."

Smiling, Jacki kissed her husband's cheek. "Alena is onto something. If these guys are government agents, they wouldn't allow anyone to come up here and cut the ropes."

"You're putting too much faith in your assumption that those two are indeed agents." Kalugal took her hand. "And as I said, we don't need them. Unless a battalion of Kra-ell purebloods is hiding down there, seven immortal males should be able to handle whatever we encounter."

"Then why are you so worried about me?" Jacki asked.

"What worries me is a cave-in, or some other accident that the so-called agents wouldn't be able to help us out of anyway."

Alena was losing her patience. Did they forget why they were going to all that trouble?

A child's life was at stake. "We don't have time for this." She gripped the ladder and started climbing down.

As someone who was anxious about most things, Alena surprised herself with how confident she felt descending into the semi-dark cavern.

The hardhats and flashlights provided enough light for her to see the interior of the hewn-out chamber, and it was big. This wasn't a family dwelling, or even a shop. It looked more like a chapel, especially given the altar on its far end.

Orion

Where to, lady seer?" Kalugal asked.

The cavern was empty of any artifacts. It was just a roughhewn-out chamber, with a raised platform and a crumbling rock cuboid on top of it that had probably served as an altar.

Orion could see two exits, or rather holes that possibly led into tunnels or other chambers, but Jacki didn't point to either of them.

"It's over there." She walked up to the stone wall and started patting it. "I saw her going through here." She moved a foot to the side and patted the rock there. "Here. This one seems to move." She pulled out a few of the rocks that had been arranged to conceal the opening.

It had been done so well that Orion wouldn't have noticed it, and it confirmed further that Jacki had really seen the girl going in there, and the vision hadn't been a hallucination or something her brain had conjured up.

"Let me." Phinas motioned for her to step aside before gently knocking on the rock wall with the wooden side of his hammer. "It's hollow on the other side." He turned to Kalugal. "Should I break through?"

"Go for it," his boss told him.

Taking a step back, Phinas swung his hammer with all his might, and the rock crumbled under the onslaught, revealing a passage. Phinas swung it a few more times to clear the way, and when he was done, Welgost entered the tunnel first.

It was obvious that the girl hadn't gone through there recently and that Jacki's vision was of either a past or a future event, but by now they were committed, and Orion doubted he could convince anyone to just let it go.

"It reminds me of a video game Mey and I used to play." Jin held on to her flashlight as if it was a weapon. "It was a labyrinth, and there were traps at every turn. It took us weeks to get to the end without getting killed and having to restart the game from the beginning. I wonder if there are any traps in here."

"Indiana Jones," Carol whispered. "Did you see that movie? Talk about traps."

"I'm more worried about spiders and scorpions," Alena said. "Those were in *The Mummy*." She shivered. "I have a love-hate relationship with that movie. I loved Brendan Fraser, and I even thought that the actor playing the Mummy was sexy. But all those bugs gave me the creeps."

"Arnold Vosloo was a major hunk." Carol sighed. "I had a movie crush on him."

"Who is Arnold Vosloo?" Jin asked.

"The Mummy, of course." Carol rolled her eyes. "You were how old when it came out? Two?"

"The tunnel is clear," Welgost poked his head through the opening. "But it gets very narrow and shallow, and I had to crawl part of the way. It opens up to another chamber that has three different tunnels branching off of it."

"Damn it," Alena whispered in Orion's ear. "I hate tight spaces."

He wrapped his arm around her waist. "Would it help if I crawled right behind you and sang praises to your glorious bottom?"

Kalugal stifled a chuckle, and so did Arwel.

Jacki let out a relieved breath. "So far, so good. I was afraid Welgost would find a body." She took her husband's hand. "Let's go."

"Hold on." Jin walked up to her. "In your vision, how far into the tunnels did you follow the girl?"

"What do you mean?"

"Did you see her crawl through a narrow tunnel?"

Jacki shook her head.

"Then perhaps this is not the right one."

"She entered through here." Jacki rubbed her temples. "It's odd. I didn't see her break or move the rock either, and yet I knew that the opening was there. Visions are not movies, they are more like dreams. I get bits and pieces of information, and my brain arranges it into a comprehensive story. The girl might have crawled through the tunnel, but since I didn't see that part of her escape, my brain filled the gap with what I expected to see, which was the girl running through the tunnel system."

Jin groaned. "What is going to happen when we reach a juncture you didn't see in your vision? How will we know where to go?"

"Right." Jacki pinched her forehead between her thumb and forefinger. "I saw her running through the tunnel until she reached a chamber and sat down on the floor. She hugged her knees and cried. I kind of expected to find her in that chamber. But what if that wasn't her final destination?"

"We should mark our way going in," Orion suggested. "If the tunnel system is extensive, we might get lost." He turned to Jacki. "You didn't see the girl going out, so you wouldn't know how to guide us out of here."

"True." She gave him an apologetic smile. "It always looks so easy in the movies, doesn't it? What should we use to mark the juncture points? Should I tear off pieces of my shirt and tuck them into crevices on the way?"

"I have a better idea," Phinas said. "I'll hammer signs, marking each entrance and exit point. No one will be able to erase or remove them."

"Brilliant idea." Orion clapped him on the back. "And a great utilization of what we have on hand, which is plenty of hewn stone walls, a hammer, and brute strength."

Alena

❦

lena was not dressed for crawling over dirt and
rocks. The stretchy black pants would be
ruined, and there was no way her elegant,
form-fitting puffer jacket would survive either. It was
meant to keep her warm, not withstand sharp stones.

She would gladly sacrifice both for a chance of finding
the girl, but she didn't really believe they would. Still, on
the very remote chance that the child was still there, they
had to keep going.

Pulling out the flashlight from her purse, she shone it at
the small opening that looked like a maw with jagged
teeth.

"Are you going in?" Orion asked.

She wasn't sure. The others had already gone in, and only
she and Orion remained in the cavern. It was tempting to
stay behind and let the others handle the situation, but if
there was indeed a scared young girl somewhere in those

tunnels, Alena couldn't in good conscience leave the task of calming her to people who had no experience handling children.

"Yeah." She sighed. "For a moment, I contemplated staying here for all the wrong reasons. If there is a scared child in these damn tunnels, she needs a gentle hand and a patient voice, and I don't know how good the others are at that. None of them are parents."

"True, but one is an empath, and two are compellers. I'm sure that between them, they can handle one scared girl." He turned her to him and planted a soft kiss on her lips. "We could stay here and make out."

"Don't tempt me." She kissed him back before slinging the strap of her purse across her body. "I just need to figure out how to crawl while holding the flashlight."

"I can give you the hat." He took off the hardhat and handed it to her.

"What about you?"

He grinned. "I'll follow your scent."

"Naughty boy." She kissed him and put the hardhat on.

It smelled gross, but given the situation, it was just one more small concession that she had to make.

Crouching, she studied the narrow opening that couldn't be more than three feet in diameter. Orion was tall, and his shoulders were broad. He might have a hard time crawling through it, but since the others had made it to the other side, he should be fine.

Taking in a deep breath, she crawled in. The tunnel was even tighter than she'd imagined, but the hardhat provided plenty of illumination, so at least she could see where her hands were going and that she wasn't touching any creepy-crawlies. If she accidentally put her hand or knee on a scorpion and got stung, she would become more hindrance than help to the rescue mission.

She couldn't have crawled more than five feet when her sleeve snagged on the stone wall, and she heard the fabric tear.

"Damn, there goes a one-thousand-dollar jacket."

Behind her, Orion chuckled. "It's a very nice jacket, but why on earth would you pay that much for a puffer?"

"Amanda. Should I say more?"

"No need. Don't move!"

Suddenly, he was on top of her, and she was squashed beneath his weight.

"Orion! What has gotten into you?"

His arm shot up, and a moment later she heard something land with a squish behind her.

"Sorry about that." He kissed her neck before crawling off her. "There was a spider the size of my hand over your head."

Alena squeaked and redoubled her crawling speed. "Where is it now?"

"It's dead. I squashed it with my hand."

"Are you okay?"

"Except for having spider slime on my hand, yeah, I'm fine."

"Gross. But what if it were poisonous?"

"It wasn't, and normally I wouldn't have killed it, just tossed it aside, but I know how squeamish you are about creepy-crawlies."

Her knight in shining armor, or rather her knight with a slimy hand.

Alena smiled. "Thank you."

As she saw the light at the end of the tunnel, she breathed out. It was only light from the flashlights and hardhats of the others, but right now, it was just as welcome as sunlight.

"I was starting to worry." Arwel offered her a hand, helping her out of the narrow opening. "What took you so long?"

"We had an encounter with a spider." Orion emerged from the small opening.

He looked much worse for wear than she was, with his coat ripped in multiple places but mainly on the shoulders, which was the widest part of him.

"Come take a look." Kalugal beckoned them over. "We found something very interesting."

"What is it?"

"Look at the engraved writing. Jin says this looks like Kra-ell symbols."

"Can you read it?" Alena asked.

Jin shook her head. "Emmett tried to teach us, but it was too difficult, and we decided to focus on understanding spoken language."

"I snapped a photo." Kalugal lifted the device to show her. "When we are back where our phones work, I'll text it to Emmett."

"Check with Kian first," Arwel said. "Or better yet, text it to him, and let him decide if he wants to text it to Emmett or to Vrog."

Alena expected Kalugal to disregard Arwel's suggestion, but to her great surprise, he nodded. "You are right. I don't want to get in the middle of the clan and Kra-ell politics."

"You are part of the clan," Alena said.

"Thank you." He dipped his head. "Nevertheless, I'd rather stay out of its politics."

"People," Jacki said. "Let's find the girl first and investigate the Kra-ell later. We are wasting precious time."

They probably weren't because the girl was no longer there, either because she'd been trapped in the tunnels and died there or because she found a way out. Hopefully, it was the latter and not the former.

Arwel

Arwel wanted it to be over. He wanted Jin and Alena out of the damn tunnels, preferably riding the limousines to the hotel. But it wasn't his show, and no one would listen to him if he suggested abandoning a child to her fate.

Never mind that they were chasing a ghost.

"Which way?" Kalugal asked Jacki.

As she looked between the three openings, Arwel wondered if she'd seen in her vision which one the girl had taken or if she was making things up on the spot.

She was desperate to find the girl, convinced that she was still alive and in need of rescuing, and she might be willing to lie to get them to continue the search.

"This one." Jacki pointed to the opening that was next to the carved words.

As Welgost went ahead once more, Orion examined the carving. "This is not very old." He ran his finger over the grooves. "If you are looking for ancient Kra-ell, that wasn't them."

"How can you be sure?" Kalugal asked. "This is hard rock, not the sandstone that the rest of the structure is carved out from. Sheltered from the elements, it could have been preserved in pristine condition for centuries. And that's a curiosity in itself. How did this stone find its way into these caverns?"

"Could it be a large meteorite?" Carol suggested. "That would explain why this rock is barren while everything in the surrounding area is lush with greenery."

"That's not a bad guess," Kalugal said. "That could also explain why we have no reception. Perhaps the copper has nothing to do with it."

"Haven't you checked?" Arwel asked.

"I didn't have a reason to doubt Jianye's explanation. But perhaps I should bring an expert to investigate the composition of this rock."

"Good idea." Jin turned to Orion. "So, why do you think this was not done by the Kra-ell?"

"I can't read it, but the symbols look familiar. Also, if these were ancient, the edges would have been more rounded. This still looks rough."

"It's not Chinese," Lokan said. "Perhaps it is Tibetan?"

"All clear," Welgost called out from the opening.

This time the tunnel allowed for walking upright, but Arwel and the other males had to bend their heads and hunch their shoulders, or they would have bumped into the tunnel's sides.

"I can't believe that I'm saying this." Alena tapped her hardhat. "But after Orion saved me from a spider in the other tunnel, I'm glad for this stinky headgear protecting my hair from overhead bugs."

"The hero," Jin murmured under her breath.

"He squashed it with his hand," Alena added.

"Ugh, that's gross," Carol said.

Jin shivered. "Yeah, I agree."

Walking behind her, Arwel put his hand on her shoulder in what he'd intended as a reassuring gesture but achieved the opposite.

Uttering a very girly squeak, Jin jumped and bumped her shoulder on the jagged stone wall. "Ouch." She rubbed the spot.

"I'm sorry." Arwel reached for her. "Let me kiss it and make it better."

Turning a pair of angry eyes at him, she batted his hand away. "Why did you do that? You scared the crap out of me. I thought it was a spider."

"I'm sorry," he repeated. "I thought that you weren't scared of them."

"I'm not." She huffed and kept on walking. "That doesn't mean that I like it when one crawls over my body."

The tunnel terminated at a small chamber that was barely big enough to contain all of them.

A pile of firewood in the corner indicated that someone had definitely used it as a shelter, and given the fresh smell, it had been quite recently.

Perhaps a family lived in those tunnels, and the child they were looking for had a father, brothers, and uncles who could pose a threat. Not that a few humans worried him, especially with two powerful compellers in their group, but they could be a nuisance.

"Someone was here recently," Arwel said to Kalugal.

"Evidently."

In addition to the opening they'd come through, there was another opening on the opposite wall, but even though it was dark, Arwel could see the narrow staircase that had been hewn out of the rock. It didn't go down in a straight line but curved a few feet in.

Kalugal took the flashlight from Jacki and aimed it at the shaft. "Did you see the girl going down there?"

Jacki shook her head. "This cavern is where I saw her sitting on the floor, and that's where the vision ended." She turned around and pointed at a niche carved into the stone. "She sat over there, next to the pile of wood. But since there are only two openings in this cavern and we came from that one, she must have used the one going down."

Arwel still thought that they were on a wild goose chase. The people using the tunnels now might have no connection to the girl, and Jacki's vision was about events that hadn't happened recently. The child might have hidden in the cavern, had a good cry, and then gone back the way she'd come.

Kalugal handed Jacki the flashlight back. "Since this is where the vision ended, there is no reason for you to continue. Phinas and I will go down to investigate, while the rest of you head back. You can wait for us in the comfort of the limousines."

His tone brooked no argument, and not because he'd used compulsion. As charming and as easygoing as Kalugal appeared most of the time, he had no problem letting the alpha in him emerge when needed.

Arwel agreed with Kalugal. He wanted Alena and Jin out of the underground, and although he would have preferred to be with them, he knew that Kalugal and Lokan could offer them better protection. Compulsion was a very effective, nonlethal weapon against humans.

Jacki didn't look happy, but she must have realized that arguing with her mate would be futile, or maybe she just feared discovering a body instead of a live girl. "Take Welgost with you as well. Shamash will keep me company, and so will Lokan, Orion, and Arwel. You're not the only one who is worried about your mate's safety." She took his hand and brought it to her cheek. "I worry about you too."

Orion

⌒⌒⌒

Orion cast a sidelong glance at Alena. Should he go back with her? Or should he volunteer to go with Kalugal?

Perhaps he should replace the guy. After all, Kalugal's mate was pregnant, and he probably wanted to stay by her side. As the leader of their group, he'd felt that he needed to lead the search for the girl, but was he the best-suited male for the task?

From the little Orion had learned about the guy from Geraldine and Alena, he'd been a warrior earlier in his life, but many decades had passed since then, and during that time the only battleground Kalugal had seen was on Wall Street.

"I should go." Orion turned to Arwel. "You're a trained Guardian, and you have experience dealing with trauma-tized girls. I think you should come with me, and Kalugal should go back with Jacki."

When Alena put a hand on his bicep, he thought that she was going to object to his proposal, but she smiled and nodded, approving and encouraging.

He could fall in love with her just for that.

Hell, who was he kidding? He was already in love with her, and the twinge of guilt that rushed through him at the realization wasn't as bad as he'd expected.

Miriam would have approved of Alena.

Jin huffed. "If you macho guys are all done flexing your muscles and thumping your chests, I suggest that we start moving." She shone her flashlight at the opening and started down the stairs.

"Hold on." Arwel rushed after her. "Let's talk it over."

"There is nothing to discuss. Orion is right. Kalugal should go with Jacki, and you should search for the girl because you are the best-trained member of our group." She cast Welgost an apologetic smile. "I know that you were a soldier, but that was a long time ago. Arwel is an active Guardian."

"Orion, Phinas, and I will go." Arwel took hold of her arm. "You should go with Jacki, Carol, and Alena. I want you to watch their backs."

As they looked into each other's eyes, a silent exchange passed between them, and at the end of it, Jin nodded. "Fine." She looked at Kalugal. "Are you okay with this plan?"

Smiling, he wrapped his arm around Jacki's waist. "I'd rather stay by my mate's side, so yes, I find this plan acceptable."

Orion wondered what Arwel's comment and Jin's subsequent acquiescence was about. What had Arwel meant when he'd told Jin to watch the ladies' backs? Didn't he trust Kalugal and Lokan? They were Alena's cousins. Maybe he was worried about Welgost and Shamash?

Or perhaps it had just been an excuse to convince Jin to head back with the others, but Orion doubted she would have fallen for that if she didn't believe that she was needed. But for what? She looked like a fierce female, but she wasn't a Guardian.

"Let's move out, gentlemen." Arwel picked up a stick from the pile and cast one last glance at his mate before heading down the tunnel.

"Be safe." Alena took off the hardhat, put it on top of his head, and kissed his cheek before turning around and following Lokan and Carol into the tunnel they'd come through.

Orion watched her until she disappeared inside and then followed Phinas down the steps.

The stairwell was narrow and its ceiling low, forcing them to bend and hunch, but thanks to their hardhats, the shaft was well lit.

The going was slow, with Arwel carefully assessing the stairs and tapping with his stick before putting his foot on the next one. "I think we are below the waterline," he said. "I wonder if this is an escape route for the outpost."

"Could be." Orion looked behind him at Phinas. "It seemed odd to me that the place had just one gate. Typically, even a settlement as small as this one would have two or three exit points. Strategically, it's not wise to have just one entrance."

"I'm surprised that we didn't encounter any traps." Arwel kept his routine of tapping each stair before placing his foot on it.

"Why would there be traps on an escape route?" Phinas asked.

"To slow down anyone chasing those escaping." Arwel stopped. "Can you smell that?"

Orion sniffed the air. "Smell what?"

"Fresh water. There must be an underground reservoir nearby."

"Oh, that. Yeah, I smelled the water, but I thought it was the river above us. What makes you think that there is a subterranean source?"

"It smells different than the aboveground running water," Arwel said.

Orion sniffed the air again, noting the subtle difference. "Yeah, I can smell the difference. Now that you've brought it to my attention, I can smell both sources of water."

Alena

As their group emerged at the second cavern, Alena didn't relish the prospect of crawling back through the narrow tunnel into the first big chamber, especially without Orion watching her back.

This time it was Shamash behind her, and she was very conscious of him watching her butt as she slowly crawled ahead of him.

Welgost got to the other side first, and the vile curse she heard him utter didn't bode well. When a few seconds later his sentiment was repeated by Jacki, just in less flowery language, Alena knew that they were in trouble.

"We are trapped," Jin said. "How did they move that damned boulder back?"

As Lokan offered Alena a hand to help her out of the narrow opening, the darkness that greeted her confirmed what her friends had said. The opening they'd created by moving the boulder aside was closed, and the ladder was gone.

"What the hell?" Carol dusted her pants off. "Who could have done that?"

"And why?" Lokan asked.

"Maybe the Chinese government wants us dead." Carol sat on the ground and leaned against the stone wall. "What do we do now?"

Kalugal looked up at where the opening was. "I don't think that they moved the boulder back because that would have been impossible for humans to do without proper equipment. They probably covered the opening with something lighter. The problem is that it doesn't matter what's up there because none of us can jump that high, and even if someone could, he couldn't jump and push whatever is blocking the entrance at the same time."

"We need to build a ramp," Lokan said. "Phinas took the hammer, though. I can turn around and catch up to them, have them come here and help us. Between the seven of us, we could take turns hammering at the walls and chipping rocks to build the ramp from."

Kalugal shook his head. "That would take days."

"Do you have a better idea?" his brother asked.

"Yeah. We need to find another exit. Those stairs back there probably lead out of the outpost."

Kalugal tried to sound unconcerned, but Alena could hear the worry in his tone. Heck, she was worried too.

Would her Odus come to look for her if she didn't return to the hotel by nightfall? Would they even know where to look for her?

"There is no need to panic," Kalugal said. "Even if we don't find another exit, our drivers will eventually come looking for us, and we can shout to them that we are trapped down here."

"What if the drivers were the ones who did it?" Carol asked. "They looked fishy."

"If not them, then my partner and his crew will come back on Monday and find us. It's not like we can die down here." He cast a worried look at Jacki. "As long as we find water, we should be fine until we are found."

With a sigh, Alena walked over to where Carol was sitting on the ground and joined her. "I should have listened to my intuition and stayed on the riverbank when we found out that our cellphones don't work here."

"Let's get back to where Arwel, Orion, and Phinas went," Jacki said. "I don't want to just sit here and wait."

Kalugal nodded. "I want Jacki to rest for a few minutes, and then we will turn around and join the others."

"Someone needs to stay here," Lokan said. "In case anyone comes looking for us."

"They wouldn't know to look down here." Kalugal rubbed a hand over the back of his neck. "If not for Jacki's vision, we wouldn't have known that there is anything down here."

Alena pulled out her phone, but it still had no reception. "What if we play music? I have some songs stored on my phone. If I put it on full volume, whoever is on top might hear it."

"I have music too." Carol pulled her phone out of her purse. "When yours dies, I will play mine."

"My phone is fully charged." Alena looked at Kalugal. "When we go back, I can leave it here playing as loud as it can go."

Jin, who'd been pacing the entire time, stopped and turned to Kalugal. "Whoever did that wants us dead. I'm afraid for Arwel and the others. What if there is another entrance and the enemy is waiting on the other side to finish us off?"

Alena jumped to her feet. "We need to warn them."

"I'll catch up to them," Lokan looked at Carol. "You can follow at a slower pace."

"We go together," Kalugal said. "It was a mistake to split up."

Arwel

꩜

"Don't you think that we can go a little faster?" Orion said as Arwel prodded the next stair with the tip of his staff. "We've traversed at least a hundred stairs, and none of them were rigged. I think it's safe to assume that there are no hidden traps in here."

"I prefer to err on the side of caution." Arwel went down another step and prodded the next two.

The smell of water was getting stronger. By now, they were so deep in the ground that the river was probably flowing overhead, and he was smelling both the river and an underground reservoir that was massive.

Another two stairs down, another tap, and then a faint click that he'd almost missed. The split second it had taken the sound to register in Arwel's mind might have cost him his life if he were human. Only his fast reflexes saved him from getting skewered as he hurled himself back and slammed into Orion, who slammed into

Phinas, and what saved them from tumbling down head over heels was the narrowness of the passage. They were wedged between the two walls.

Orion groaned. "Remind me never to doubt you again."

Arwel chuckled. "You can bet on it." He pushed himself off the guy and looked at the rusted bolt that was embedded in the stone wall right where his neck had been a moment ago.

As he examined the rigging mechanism, Arwel was impressed by its simplicity and effectiveness. A piece of rebar, a couple of strings, and a well-hidden plate on the stair that had been camouflaged with dirt.

"This is all done with modern materials." He showed the others. "Someone is using these tunnels, and he or she has enemies they fear."

"What makes you think that?" Orion asked. "Maybe there is a hidden treasure down here, and whoever is guarding it wants to eliminate anyone who gets close."

"Perhaps." Arwel looked down the stairs to where his staff had fallen. "We will need to be extra careful from here on out. If there was one trap, there will be others. We go slow."

"We haven't been going fast," Phinas grumbled. "Do you want to use my hammer?"

"Keep it. It's not long enough."

"That's what she said." Orion laughed. "I'm sorry, but I just couldn't help myself. You two were asking for it."

Arwel rolled his eyes but smiled nonetheless. The joke defused some of the tension.

Without his staff, Arwel had to resort to brushing over each step with the tip of his shoe, moving the dirt to check for hidden plates.

Thankfully, no more traps were sprung until he reached his stick. Clutching it, he'd never been more grateful for a piece of wood.

Five steps down, another click sounded, and this time, Arwel immediately jumped back, but instead of a bolt firing at him from the side of the stairwell, an avalanche of rocks fell, pelting the three of them, but mostly Arwel, who was closest.

"Damn it." He brushed the rocks off him. "I didn't expect that."

"Are you okay?" Orion asked. "I smell blood."

"It's nothing." Arwel wiped his bloody forehead with the sleeve of his jacket. "It will heal in a moment."

The next fifteen steps didn't trigger any new traps, and as Arwel had suspected, at the bottom of the staircase was an underground water basin, housed in an enormous natural cavern.

Shafts of pale light shone from holes high above, which meant that they'd cleared the river and were well on the other side of it.

"An entire village could hide here," Orion said. "If there are fish in the water, they could have survived here indefinitely."

"Indeed." Arwel looked around, checking for possible exits, traps, storage bins, fire pits, any signs of habitation, but the place looked like it had never been visited by humans. Except, given the hewn-out stairs leading down to it, people had made use of this hidden gem in the past, and with some digging, Kalugal's team would probably find evidence of that.

"Perhaps the girl is hiding somewhere down here," he said more to himself than his companions.

"She wouldn't have died of thirst here, that's for sure," Phinas said. "And if she knew how to fish, she could have survived on that. But I wonder how she avoided triggering the traps."

"Maybe she wasn't heavy enough," Orion said.

Arwel shook his head. "I doubt that those primitive traps were calibrated for weight. She must have known which steps to avoid."

Aliya

A liya watched the intruders from her perch high above the cavern. They didn't know yet that they were trapped, but they would discover that soon when they made their way back.

With the other entrance blocked, the only way out was through the lake, then a climb up the rock face to where the opening to the staircase was, and then up the stairs to the surface.

It would never occur to them to swim across the nearly freezing water, and even if it did, they wouldn't find the entrance to the staircase.

She still couldn't understand how they'd known to push the boulder aside to get into the large chamber, or how they'd known to break through the barrier she'd so carefully camouflaged and find the other entrance to the tunnel system. It had taken her many days to block that entrance and make it look like the rest of the stone wall, so even if someone got into the large cavern, they wouldn't suspect that it served as an entrance to an extensive system of tunnels.

No one was supposed to know about it, and even the crew searching for artifacts in the ruins had no clue that it was there.

But these men weren't regular humans.

Humans wouldn't have been able to move that boulder without a bulldozer, and other than the rope ladder they'd used to go down into the large cavern, she hadn't found anything that would indicate the use of pulleys or anything else that could have helped them move it. The system of pulleys she'd constructed was still hidden in the same spot she'd left it, safely stowed away in one of the ancient, ruined dwellings.

When she'd discovered that her hiding place had been compromised, Aliya had been certain that the Kra-ell had somehow found her, but looking at these males now, she was no longer sure.

Two of them had dark hair and olive-toned skin, so perhaps they were hybrids, but the third was too fair to be a Kra-ell. As sunlight from one of the shafts hit his hair, it gleamed with golden hues, a color no Kra-ell or a hybrid she'd known ever had.

The question was what she was going to do with them. She couldn't just wait for them to die because it might take months until they starved to death, and what was she supposed to do in the meantime?

Besides, these three couldn't be the only ones who'd entered the tunnels. When she'd returned from her hunt, Aliya had found two limousines parked on the riverbank. The human drivers had been smoking and chatting as they'd waited for their customers to return, completely oblivious to the huntress who could take them down with two well-aimed arrows.

Not that she would.

Humans were not her friends, but they weren't her enemies either, and taking a life without proper cause was an affront to the Mother of All Life.

As Aliya examined the way the males were dressed, they didn't impress her as rich guys who would hire two limousines with drivers for just the three of them.

She'd seen some of the wealthy tourists visiting the Mosuo villages, and they'd been much better dressed.

The three must have split up from a larger group, and the others were probably somewhere else in the labyrinth of tunnels.

It had been a stupid move to block the other entrance.

If she'd thought it through instead of succumbing to the surge of rage and thirst for vengeance that had clouded her mind, she wouldn't have done it. But all she could think about was killing them all, and she hadn't stopped to consider that this was her home, and she didn't want anyone rotting away in it. Not even her enemies.

Now that the rage had subsided and reason returned, Aliya considered unblocking the other entrance. If these intruders didn't find what they were looking for, they would just leave and never come back.

What were they looking for, though?

Had they come for her?

How did they even know that she was here?

She'd been hiding for years, and no one in the Mosuo village should remember her because she'd compelled them to forget her.

Perhaps they'd come for the same reason she and her mother originally had.

Either way, they weren't going to find anything, she'd made sure of that, and if they could, they would eventually leave.

She needed to unlock the entrance now before it was too late and they discovered that the ladder was gone and the boulder was back in place. That would give her away as surely as if she'd walked up to them and flashed her fangs.

For them to remain oblivious to her presence, she had to put everything back the way it was, and hopefully they wouldn't notice that things were not precisely as they'd left them.

But to do that, she needed to wait for these three to get out of the cavern. If these were indeed Kra-ell hybrids, which was the most logical explanation for their ability to move the boulder, they would notice her the moment she moved.

But to get to her, they would have to swim through the lake, and by the time they made it to the other side she would be long gone. Except, that would defy the purpose of the entire operation.

They would know that she'd been hiding in these tunnels, and in order to escape them, she would have to run away and keep running because they would come after her.

Her only option to eliminate the threat was to kill them all, including the limousine drivers. But even though the Mother might forgive her for taking those lives in self-defense, Aliya didn't want the humans' deaths on her conscience.

Orion

"Well, this looks like a dead end." Orion turned in a circle. "The visibility is pretty good thanks to the shafts drilled through the earth, and there are no other openings that I can see. Unless she had a boat here and rowed away, she must have found some other way to get out of here."

"She could have swum," Phinas said. "What I wonder is who made those shafts and why."

"The same people who dug out the tunnels and carved the stairs out of the rock." Crouching next to the small subterranean lake, Arwel put his hand in the water. "If she swam through, she would have suffered from hypothermia and drowned. The water is too cold for a human to survive."

That seemed like an awful way to die, but he reminded himself that the girl might have never existed, and if she had, it had been a long time ago and she'd got out before someone rolled the boulder over the opening to block it.

In fact, he was quite sure that if a child got lost in these tunnels and was later found by her parents, the villagers would have pooled their resources to block the entrance and prevent other children from playing dangerous games.

"Maybe she wasn't human," Phinas said. "Or maybe she was a spirit. Don't forget that we are chasing after a phantom seen in a vision. You all seem to give it a lot of credence and given that the vision was my boss's mate's and it was about a child, I didn't argue or question the wisdom of it. But we've reached the end of the line. We should go back."

"You can't." Lokan walked out of the tunnel opening. "Someone removed the ladder and pushed the boulder back over the hole. We need to find another exit."

"Where are the others?" Arwel asked.

"Making their way over. I convinced Kalugal to let me run ahead to warn you in case the perpetrators were planning an ambush." He looked around the cave. "Did you check the perimeter? There are plenty of hiding places in these rocks, and we are easy targets standing here in the light coming down these shafts. Someone might shoot us from there." He pointed at the stone wall across the water and the many ledges and niches that were visible from where they stood.

There were probably many further down that they couldn't see.

"We can handle ourselves," Arwel said. "You should have stayed behind to protect the ladies."

"With how narrow these passages are, it wouldn't have made a difference, and we feared for you." Lokan smiled at Arwel. "Your mate wanted to be the one to rush over, but I convinced her to stay with the group and let me go ahead." He looked at the hammer in Phinas's hand. "If we don't find another exit, our only option would be to build a ramp, and this hammer might be what saves us."

Arwel shook his head. "Who could have blocked the entrance and why?"

"Beats me." Lokan lifted his eyes to the shafts of light. "It looks like we are only forty feet or so from the surface. Maybe we can climb up and enlarge one of the openings."

As Orion shifted his gaze to where Lokan was pointing, he caught a movement from the corner of his eyes. Quickly turning his head in that direction, he saw a long black braid whipping around a protrusion that was high up on the stone wall across the small lake. It lasted no longer than a split second, and then it was gone.

"There!" He pointed. "I saw her. There must be an exit on the other side."

"Are you sure that it was the girl?"

"All I saw was a long dark braid. It could have been an adult male for all I know."

"We need to follow her." Arwel started removing his clothes.

"What are you doing?" Orion asked.

"Yeah." Jin entered, followed by the others. "Are you nuts?"

Arwel removed his shoes and socks. "I'm going to swim over to the other side, but I don't want my clothes to get wet, so I'm going to make a bundle and tie it to my head. That way I can put them back on when I get there."

"Smart thinking." Orion started undressing as well.

Phinas hesitated for a moment, but then turned to Lokan and handed him the hammer. "This is yours now, in case you'll need to build the ramp after all."

Aliya

⚬⚬⚬

Aliya ran, her long legs taking the narrow stairs four at a time, her arms pumping, her breath leaving her mouth in a mist as it met the cold air.

She'd been up and down these accursed stairs so many times, her leg muscles didn't have to strain as hard as theirs no doubt would, and she could outrun them. Not expecting anyone to get that far, she hadn't rigged them with traps, so there was nothing to slow them down.

How had they evaded the traps she'd set on the other staircase?

What to do now? Where would she go?

When the fourth male entered the cavern and started talking to the other three, Aliya had hoped that they would be distracted enough not to notice her moving around the ledge and ducking into the stairwell. But one of them must have heard her, confirming her suspicion that they were not human.

How many of them were there?

The fourth one said something about the others coming, and Aliya thought that she'd heard a woman's voice, but she wasn't sure. Was it a good or bad sign that they had females with them?

She didn't know and couldn't risk finding out. Her only option was to run as far away from this place as she could and start over somewhere else.

As bitter tears stung the corners of her eyes, she wiped them away with her sleeve and kept racing to the top.

Life had been hard enough for her as it was, and starting from scratch with nothing but the clothes on her back was terrifying.

But maybe it was time.

She'd lived in these ruins for far too long, only venturing into the village when she had no other choice. Maybe someplace else, people would be more accepting of a hybrid freak like her. Maybe she could blend in better and pretend to be human.

The Mother had gifted her with an uncanny ability to learn new languages fast, and Aliya had taught herself English, Japanese, and a little bit of Swedish, the languages spoken by most of the tourists who loved visiting the Mosuo.

There was no way she could blend in among the Japanese, but she might be able to do so among the Americans or the Europeans.

Except, she had no money, nothing she could trade, and she wasn't willing to steal anything that was not necessary for her survival. Food and small tools were okay, and they didn't cause real hardship to those she stole from, but stealing money was on a different level, one she'd hoped never to stoop to.

Today, though, was the day she'd been fearing for years. Her enemies had found her and were either going to kill her or drag her with them to their stronghold. So today was not a day to stick to her morals and principles. Today, she was going to ignore them all to survive.

If she made it out before they caught up to her, she would compel the two human drivers to leave their passengers behind, sending one driving all the way to Lijiang, and the other one to drive her to Shangri-La. She'd heard the tourists talking about it, and it was supposed to be a beautiful place. She didn't know whether it was big or small, but she knew it wasn't too far away.

Or maybe she should compel the driver to take her all the way to Beijing?

Her mother had told her that it was a marvelous city with many millions of people, and Aliya tried to imagine that many people in one place. Supposedly, that was where they came from. Not from the city itself, but somewhere in that area.

She had never left the compound before they'd been forced to leave, and she didn't remember the area or the names of the towns and villages they'd passed through. She had been just a young girl, traumatized, scared, and she remembered very little of their journey across the country.

Perhaps it wouldn't be wise to go to Beijing if it was so close to that place of blood and loss. Perhaps she should ask the driver about another big city where a strange-looking woman could disappear.

Alena

❦

As Orion stripped to his undershorts, Alena shivered, but it wasn't because she was excited to see his magnificent body. It was a sympathetic response. It was so cold in the cavern, and the water was even colder. The subterranean lake wasn't big, it was more of a large pond, and it wouldn't take them long to get to the other side, but if they were human, they probably wouldn't have made it. Hypothermia would have disabled them in minutes.

"How did that person get to the other side?"

"Probably from the outside." Arwel gave Jin a quick hug before wading into the water with his bundle of clothes tied around his head like a strange-looking turban.

How did he expect to keep that from falling into the water?

"Be safe." Alena helped Orion tie his own bundle in a similar fashion.

"Don't worry." He gave her a quick kiss before following Arwel and Phinas, who were already swimming with steady, measured strokes and keeping their heads upright.

"It's all my fault." Jacki let out a breath. "That vision must have been of a past or future event, and I shouldn't have roped everyone into following. Now we are stuck here." She walked to where Lokan was guarding the entrance to the tunnel with Phinas's hammer and lowered herself to the ground. "At least we have water, right? We can survive here for a long time."

"We won't have to." Kalugal sat down next to her. "Arwel, Orion, and Phinas will find the exit, come around, and move the boulder. We will be out of here in time for lunch."

Jin grimaced. "Don't talk about food. I'm hungry."

They'd eaten a big breakfast, so Jin's hunger was probably the result of stress and not a need for food.

Kalugal glanced at his watch. "It's after two in the afternoon. I wonder if our drivers are starting to get worried."

"I just hope that they are still there." Carol joined them on the ground. "And I hope our guys are not rushing into a trap."

While Arwel had been tying up his bundle of clothes, he'd told them about the traps he'd sprung on the stairs coming down. The rest of them had been lucky that there hadn't been more.

As the three men walked out of the water on the other side, their bundles of clothing still on their heads, Alena let out a relieved breath. The three of them were shivering badly, but as they quickly got dressed, the shivering stopped.

Orion waved at her before starting the climb to where he'd seen that dark braid, the other two following him up.

"We found another staircase!" Arwel shouted. "We are going in."

"Be careful!" Lokan yelled back. "Watch out for traps!"

As an answer, Phinas gave him a two-fingered salute and ducked behind the ledge after the others.

Pushing to her feet, Alena started pacing along the pond's shore. "This whole thing doesn't make sense unless there are Kra-ell hiding in these tunnels. They would have been strong enough to push the boulder back. Jacki's vision might have accidentally sent us straight into their lair."

"Perhaps it wasn't accidental," Jacki murmured. "What if the Fates wanted us to find them?"

"There are no Kra-ell in here," Lokan said. "If there were, we would already be dead. I wouldn't be surprised if some local punks decided to play a trick on a bunch of tourists just to amuse themselves. From what I read about the Mosuo, the women do everything, and the men have very little to do, which is not healthy for young males. If they are not kept busy working or training, they are bound to get into trouble. Young bucks have excess energy they need to dispense one way or another."

Alena doubted that was the explanation, but Carol seemed to agree. "Boys can do some really stupid things when they are bored. Stupid, cruel, and sometimes even deadly."

"What about the girl?" Jacki said. "Do you think she might have used the other exit to get out of here?"

Alena nodded. "Maybe in the summer, the water is not as cold, and she could swim over."

"It wasn't summer in my vision." Jacki shifted her weight. "She wore a puffer, remember?"

"Maybe she had a raft or a boat hidden somewhere here," Carol said.

Aliya

As Aliya pushed open the wooden grate at the top of the staircase and peeked out, she cursed. The damn limousines had vanished along with her escape plan.

Her other option was the canoe she'd left on the other side of the ruins, but that meant running across the rope bridge, entering through the gate, and climbing down the rope she'd anchored to the top of the wall.

Except, the canoe could only take her down the river to the lake, and that would not solve her problem of having no home and nowhere to hide. She would have to go into the village and use her hypnotic power to coerce one of the matrons to allow her into her household and give her a place to hide.

It was a shitty plan, but it was better than nothing. Right now, she had to evade the men chasing her and make sure that they didn't know where to find her or that she was even there.

They couldn't have seen much of her on that ledge, not enough to know that she was the one they were looking for, so she might be able to pull it off, but she needed to move fast.

She had a decent head start on them, but they would probably reach the surface before she could make it to her boat, and even if she made it, they would see her rowing down the river.

The good thing was that without a boat of their own, they couldn't follow her unless they swam after her. The bad thing was that they would see her and her canoe and would know where she was headed.

Glancing at the dense greenery behind her, Aliya considered for a moment running into the woods and hiding there until they left. The advantage of that plan was that it would give her time to formulate her next step. The problem with that was that if these men were Kra-ell, they were excellent hunters, and without a large body of water to mask her scent, they would be able to find her and hunt her down.

The river was her only option.

Heaving herself out of the hole, Aliya grabbed the grate and shoved it back in place before sprinting toward the bridge. She wasn't sure that it had been wise to waste that extra second putting it back. If they were strong enough to move the boulder, they would have no problem moving the heavy grate out of the way. Still, it might slow them for a moment.

As she cleared it on the other side, she heard a thud that sounded a lot like the grate hitting the ground and allowed herself one look over her shoulder, gasping when she saw one of the males emerge from the hole.

How in the name of the Mother had they caught up to her so fast? They would have had to swim through the lake and climb up the wall, which should have taken them between five and ten minutes. They shouldn't have been able to close the gap by climbing the stairs faster than she had.

If they were that fast, there was no way she was going to make it to the boat before they caught up to her.

Fear adding power to her tired muscles, she ran even faster, leaping over piles of rocks and dodging the larger ones. The good thing was that she was very familiar with the place and knew where all the obstacles were. The bad thing was that she could hear them gaining on her.

Orion

O rion pushed the grate up, tossed it aside, and heaved himself up the rest of the way to clear the hole. He didn't wait for Arwel and Phinas and sprinted after the woman.

The dark braid flying behind her identified her as the one he'd seen on the ledge in the cavern, but she was definitely not the girl from Jacki's vision.

Given her height and speed, she was not only a fully grown woman, but also immortal, either a descendant of the gods or the Kra-ell. The way she was sprinting and leaping over obstacles could have won her a gold medal in the human Olympics, and even though he was pushing himself to the limit, he was barely gaining on her.

Behind him he could hear his two companions running, and as he hit the bridge, he had to slow down once they jumped on and the whole thing swung and shook. He wasn't afraid of hurting himself in a fall, but he couldn't afford the lost time that would cost him the female.

The thing was, Orion wasn't even sure why he was chasing after her other than the need to get answers. Now that they had found a way out of the tunnel system, they would somehow manage to move the boulder and get the others out of there as well.

Except, the female couldn't have been operating alone. Even an immortal couldn't have moved the boulder and blocked the entrance to the tunnel by herself. She'd either had help or knew who had done that.

Were there more immortals hiding in the area?

Were the tunnels their home?

And why did they want to trap a group of people whom they must have assumed were innocent tourists?

Had they done it before?

Was that what happened to the young girl in Jacki's vision?

Anger over the needless cruelty adding fuel to his leg muscles, Orion ran faster, closing the distance between himself and the fleeing female.

She climbed the steps to the top of the wall with incredible speed, but he was even faster, and when he was almost within reach of her, she leaped over the side of the wall.

Without thinking, he leaped after her, grabbed the back of her jacket and twisted midair, hurling them both back into the hollowed-out ruins.

Their fall wasn't graceful, with him absorbing the brunt of it with his back, her landing on top of him, and the both of them rolling down the steps right into Arwel and Phinas and taking them along for the ride.

As soon as they stopped rolling down, she leaped and started running again.

This time, Arwel chased after her while Orion checked himself for broken bones.

His reprieve didn't last long, though.

Both Arwel and Phinas were getting their asses handed to them by that slim female, probably because they were trying not to hurt her, but she was not only incredibly strong and desperate, she was also terrifying.

If he didn't know about the Kra-ell, he would have thought her a demon.

Red blazing eyes, fangs as long as his, and a crazed expression on her face, she snarled, kicked, bit, and punched whatever part she could reach on the two males trying to apprehend her without hurting her.

Their fangs didn't even elongate.

Orion wondered whether it was physically impossible for an immortal male to respond with aggression to a female even if she was the one attacking, or were Arwel and Phinas just capable of great self-control?

That being said, if he didn't knock her out, she might manage to escape. Besides, she was hurting his friends, and that was unacceptable.

With a groan, Orion grabbed a rock, heaved himself up, and got into the fray. He didn't waste time trying to grab hold of the snarling beast. As soon as the opportunity presented itself, he hit the back of her head with just enough force to knock her out but not kill her.

Her red eyes rolling back in her head, she crumpled to the ground.

Breathing heavily, Arwel bent down, bracing his hands on his thighs. "Thank you." He lifted his head and smiled at Orion. "It has been a long time since someone handed me my ass like that, and never a female. Now I understand how Anandur and Brundar felt after Wonder took both of them down."

"That's a story I want to hear," Phinas said before turning his face sideways and spitting out blood. "We should tie her down before she comes round. I don't think I can last another round with her."

He'd said that with a straight face, but Orion was sure Phinas was exaggerating.

Arwel shook his head. "Do you think ropes would hold her?"

"Do you have a better idea?" Orion crouched next to the unconscious woman and checked her pulse, relieved to find it going nice and steady.

He still didn't know much about immortals and even less about the Kra-ell, who the woman obviously was. Orion had been careful with the force he'd applied, but a blow to the head could cause serious damage even to an immortal, as evidenced by what had happened to Geraldine.

"She's fine." Arwel rubbed a hand over his bruised neck. "I can hear her heartbeat. Did any of you notice that our rides are gone?"

Orion hadn't, and given Phinas's grimace, he hadn't either.

The limousines had been parked on the other side of the ruins, not visible from where they were standing.

"How will we get back to the hotel?" Phinas asked. "And what are we going to do with the hellion?"

Arwel

❧

"We need to get to the others." Arwel bent down, hefted the unconscious woman up, and slung her over his shoulder. "For such a skinny thing, she's surprisingly heavy."

"And strong like two males," Phinas said. "I'm still waiting to hear the story of how Wonder overpowered Anandur and Brundar."

"I'll tell you about it on the plane back home, but the gist of it is that Wonder is also incredibly strong, but unlike this one, she's not a fighter."

"Then how did she overpower two Head Guardians?" Phinas fell in step with him.

"She was pushed into using her strength by the circumstances."

"This lady might have felt the same about us," Orion said. "Are we taking her with us?"

"I don't know. We need to find out where the rest of her tribe is. I didn't hear or feel anyone in the tunnels, but then I didn't feel her either until we started chasing her up the stairs. She emitted very little emotion."

Orion dusted his clothes off as best he could, but he'd taken quite a fall, and even before that, his clothing wasn't in great shape. Arwel could only imagine the reaction of the hotel's concierge when he saw them coming in looking like that.

"Can the three of us move the boulder?" Orion asked.

"Let's check whether it is in fact the boulder that's blocking the entry." Arwel adjusted the woman draped over his shoulder like a sack of potatoes. "If she was working alone, she might have pushed over something lighter to close the opening."

"We need to tie her up," Orion said, "before she starts waking up." He looked at the ground and picked up a round rock. "I have a feeling that I will need this again."

"Aren't you a compeller?" Phinas asked. "Why don't you just compel her to obey you?"

Orion snorted. "In all the commotion, it didn't even occur to me. I could have yelled at her to stop instead of chasing after her." He tossed the stone aside. "Would compelling this woman be sanctioned by the clan, though? I don't want to break any rules."

What had Alena done to the guy to make him so afraid to use his talent?

Arwel hoped that she hadn't invoked some nonexistent clan rules about compulsion to keep him in check because there were none. What applied to thralling also applied to compulsion, restricting its use to concealment of immortals' existence and matters of clan security.

Both of those applied to the situation, and yet Orion seemed hesitant to use compulsion on the woman.

"In my capacity as Head Guardian," Arwel said. "I'm authorized to give you permission to compel this woman to cooperate with us. But even if I wasn't here, this is a very clear case of protecting clan members. The same circumstances that allow thralling also allow compulsion."

"Good to know. So, we don't need to tie her up?"

"It depends on how strong of a compeller you are, and how susceptible she is to compulsion. You might need that rock after all."

Arwel's empathic ability picked up on the woman's fear a moment before she bucked up and tried to escape his hold.

"Don't move!" Orion said.

The woman stopped her struggles, but Arwel was paralyzed as well, and so was Phinas.

Fates, how Arwel hated the feeling of having his will taken over by another. He still remembered how helpless and desperate he'd felt when Kalugal had captured him.

Unlike Kalugal though, Orion used his compulsion like a sledgehammer instead of a delicate scalpel. It was powerful but unrefined. Perhaps he needed to take lessons from the master.

It took Orion a moment to realize that what he'd done stretched further than he'd intended, and then he said, "Arwel and Phinas, you can move."

"Thank you," Arwel bit out. "Compulsion is a precise art. When you imbue your words with compulsion, you should be very careful with how you phrase things and who you direct them at."

The woman groaned, but the command not to move also prevented her from moving her lips, so she couldn't speak.

"I'll be damned," Arwel said as he saw the boulder covering the entrance. "I need to question the lady." He lowered her to the ground, arranging her body so she was leaning against the boulder.

Her eyes were wild with terror, and her fangs were fully elongated and protruding over her lips. Compulsion didn't work on involuntary body functions, to which the elongating of fangs and venom creation belonged.

"Ask her where the rest of her people are, and command her to tell the truth."

Orion crouched in front of the terrified woman. "We mean you no harm. You have nothing to fear from us. But we need to get our friends out of the tunnels, and one of the women is pregnant, so swimming in near-freezing water is out of the question. We need to move that boulder, and we can't move it alone. We need the help of your tribesmen."

Aliya

The male who'd commanded Aliya's body not to move had kind eyes, and he wasn't Kra-ell. He wasn't human either, though.

What was he?

And did he and his friends really mean her no harm? The way they chased her down had implied otherwise, but given that one of the members of their group was a pregnant female, it was no wonder that they'd been so desperate to find a way out that didn't involve her swimming through the subterranean lake's freezing water.

Still, even though Aliya could understand why they had chased her with such determination, she couldn't tell him that she was alone. The Mother only knew what they would do to her if they found out that no one would come to her rescue.

"Answer me truthfully. Where are the other members of your tribe?" When she didn't answer, he narrowed his eyes at her, and they no longer looked kind. "You are allowed to move your mouth, and you are allowed to speak, but you are not allowed to move your hands or legs, and you are not allowed to bite or head-butt any of us either."

The one with the shoulder-length tawny hair chuckled. "You're learning, Orion. That was a very precise compulsion. But what if she doesn't speak English?"

Orion didn't shift his eyes as he answered the male. "She understood when I commanded her not to move." Staring into her eyes, he asked, "Where is the rest of your tribe?"

"I don't know." Her spoken English was good, but her accent was terrible.

If she didn't make any effort to make it better, maybe they wouldn't be able to understand her. The one named Orion hadn't commanded her to speak clearly. She couldn't keep her mouth shut and refuse to answer him, but she could mumble her responses in her bad accent.

"What's your name?"

She wanted to resist the command, but it was impossible. "Aliya," she blurted.

He smiled. "That's a very nice name. How come you don't know where the rest of your tribe is?"

"Most are dead. Some might have been taken away."

She suspected that the bad Kra-ell hadn't attacked just for the fun of it. They had probably been after the pureblooded females, and maybe even after the hybrid girls. Females were most precious to the Kra-ell, and there weren't enough of them to go around. The males had to share them, and maybe some had thought to fix the situation by abducting the females of another tribe.

Orion frowned, but she didn't know whether it was because he hadn't understood her or because of her answer.

The tawny-haired guy crouched next to Orion. "Were you a member of Jade's tribe?"

Aliya's heart stopped, or at least that was what it felt like. How could he have known about that unless he was one of the attackers? But they had been Kra-ell. Or maybe not?

It wasn't like she'd seen them.

She'd escaped along with all the other humans that had been told to leave and forget that they'd ever lived in a Kra-ell compound. The command to forget had worked on the humans, but not on her, and yet the male in front of her was holding her imprisoned in her own body with hardly any effort.

Then again, neither he nor his companions looked like they had even a drop of Kra-ell blood in them. Orion's eyes were the kind of purple blue no Kra-ell or hybrid she'd ever seen had. The other one's were turquoise, a color that the Kra-ell eyes sometimes turned, but the rest of him didn't match. The third one had brown eyes, olive-toned skin and dark brown hair, so he could potentially be a hybrid, but he also looked too human to be one.

What if not all Kra-ell looked the same, though? What if there were others who looked like these men?

"Answer my question," he commanded.

"Yes." She spat on the ground between his legs. "Were you one of the murderers who killed my father?"

His eyes softened. "Neither my friends nor I had anything to do with that."

The tawny-headed male smiled, revealing two rows of teeth that looked very human. "As you can see, we are not Kra-ell. We are a different breed of immortals. Fate brought two members of your tribe to us, and they told us about Jade and about the attack. We came here because of the Mosuo. Their tradition and lifestyle so closely resemble that of the Kra-ell that we suspected it was influenced by them."

"If there are no others," the third male said, "how the hell did you move that boulder by yourself?"

Aliya could answer that without being compelled to. Baring her fangs, she smiled at him. "As you've experienced, I'm very strong."

"You're not that strong." He turned to the compeller. "Make her tell us how she did that. Jacki, Kalugal and the others are waiting to hear from us, and I want to get them out of those damn tunnels. We need to somehow move that rock."

Orion nodded. "Tell me how you moved the boulder, Aliya."

"With the help of pulleys and a lot of muscle."

"Where can we find these pulleys?"

"I hid them in the ruins. If you let me move, I'll take you to them. It's too difficult to explain where they are hidden."

Apparently, Orion's compulsion left her some maneuvering space. All she had to do was not disobey his commands completely but rather dance around them like she had just done.

Maybe she could get free after all?

Orion smiled, but it wasn't a friendly smile. "You must think me a fool, but I assure you that I'm not. I will let you move, but only on my command. You'll be like a marionette with me as your puppet master."

She didn't know what that French-sounding word meant, but it was easy enough to guess what Orion had in mind.

Orion

❦

Orion was beyond impressed. If Aliya had made the traps and also constructed a pulley mechanism herself, then she was very smart, resourceful, and cunning.

He was curious to hear the rest of her story, which was no doubt going to be fascinating. She must have been a small girl during the attack and had somehow managed to escape, but how had she gotten from a small village near Beijing all the way to Lugu Lake, and why?

"I need to get down there." She pointed to a flight of stairs leading to one of the underground dwellings.

The carved-out staircase was barely wide enough for one person, and he didn't want her to go alone. It might lead to another tunnel through which she could escape.

But he was a compeller, and he should be able to direct her with precise phrasing to go down, get the pulleys, and come back up. But what if there were no pulleys down there?

If he told her to come back with the pulleys, she could use it as a loophole to disobey his command. The girl was damn smart.

"You can go, but you have to come back in less than ten minutes with or without the pulleys."

That should do it.

She was back in less than five.

"Give them to Phinas," Orion commanded. "When we get to the boulder, show us how to use them."

After she'd shown them how to tie the ropes and what to do, Arwel cast her an appreciative glance. "That's ingenious. Where did you learn how to do that?"

She shrugged. "I used the tools I could find, and I modified what I've seen others use to drag heavy rocks."

"Show me how to pull," Arwel told her.

"You will not be able to do it. I'm very strong."

"So am I," Arwel smiled. "But I experienced first-hand how strong you are, so I might need your help."

The satisfied expression on her face indicated that Arwel had said the right thing.

Having empathic abilities sure helped boost one's emotional intelligence.

"This is only going to work if we are equally matched," Aliya said. "Two of you need to pull on that side while I pull on this one."

As Phinas grabbed the ropes on Arwel's side, Orion expected the Guardian to make a macho comment about how he was strong enough, but Arwel only grumbled, "I'm glad Richard had those sleeping potion vials on him, or he would have never been able to overpower Vrog."

The rope on Aliya's side slackened for a split second, and Orion jumped in to catch it, but she renewed her grip. "Vrog is alive?"

"Do you know him?" Arwel grunted as he and Phinas pulled the ropes on their side. "Or do you just know of him?"

Aliya gave the rope a mighty tug, and the boulder moved a few inches. "I was too little for him to notice me, but I know who he is. Was he away during the attack? Or was he left for dead?"

"He was in Singapore." Arwel and Phinas kept the pressure on their side while Aliya pulled on hers, and after the initial drag had been surpassed, the boulder inched off the opening at a steady pace.

"That's big enough." Arwel signaled for her to stop pulling. "We can squeeze through."

Wiping her hands on her pants, she tried to hide her heavy breathing. "Well, now that you can get your friends out, you don't need me anymore. See you later." She turned to leave.

"Stop," Orion commanded. "You are not going anywhere."

"Why not? You said that you and your people mean me no harm and that you only want to get your friends out."

"We need to talk," Arwel said. "Besides, I'm not going to make the same mistake twice and leave this rock unguarded. You and Orion are coming with me. Phinas, you stay here and guard the opening."

"I need a new hammer," Phinas said. "And you need a ladder. Where did you stash the other one?" he asked Aliyah.

"It's in my canoe on the other side of the ruins."

She was lying. Orion was sure of that.

"Tell us the truth, Aliya." He pushed compulsion into his tone. "Where is the rope ladder that we used to go down into the cavern?"

"I am telling the truth." She huffed out a breath. "I thought that I could use it in the lake cavern instead of climbing the wall every time. But there are more ladders around here. I can find you a proper one made of aluminum."

Arwel seemed as doubtful as Orion. "Phinas, check the tent for another ladder and a new hammer."

"Yes, sir."

"Why don't you have a small boat to cross the subterranean pool instead of swimming through it?" Orion asked. "You seem to take what you need without a problem, so why not another boat?"

"I tried. The staircase is too narrow to carry a boat down, so my only option was to build one. I was planning to do that one day, but I never got around to it. There were always more important things to do."

"Like what?" Arwel asked.

"Hunting for food, guarding against intruders, building traps. You know, staying alive."

"Who was after you?"

"Everyone."

Arwel rolled his eyes. "How old are you, Aliya?"

"I'm thirty years old."

"That explains it. You are still a teenager in immortal terms, and you think that it's you against the world. Not everyone is bad, and many people are kind and willing to help."

"Not in my experience." Her eyes flashed red, and her fangs elongated. "Not when I look like this, and not when I'm stronger than twenty human males."

Arwel laughed. "My mate is one-quarter Kra-ell, and I think that her fangs and her assertiveness only make her sexier to me."

The red in Aliya's eyes flickered and turned into deep brown. "Is she the other Kra-ell hybrid that you encountered?"

"No, that was Emmett. He left your tribe a long time before you were born. We didn't even know that the Kra-ell existed, so naturally, we didn't know that Jin had Kra-ell in her until we found Emmett. We believe that she was one of the children who were fathered by the hybrids and given up for adoption."

Aliya didn't seem surprised by that, so she must have known about the practice. "Is she here with you?"

"She is, and you are about to meet her in a few minutes. A word of warning, though. She might punch you in the face first and ask questions later."

Alena

Alena had been silently praying to the Fates, pleading, imploring, and making promises just to see the three males return unharmed and for all of them to find a way out.

So far, no one was perishing from hunger or thirst or going into stasis to preserve their resources, but Jacki was pregnant, and she didn't have the option to go into stasis.

Alena shook her head. Talk about overreacting.

No one was going into stasis, but they would most likely have to swim through that lake unless Orion and the others found a way out and brought back an inflatable boat.

For Jacki, of course. But if they already had a boat, then no one else needed to swim in the near-freezing water.

Except, what if the men didn't find a way out and had been led by that braid into more tunnels? What if there were more traps that Arwel couldn't detect?

What if they were—

She shouldn't allow herself to think such thoughts. She had to believe that they'd found a way out and were coming back for the rest of them.

"I'm worried." Alena rubbed her hands over her arms. "They've been gone for a long time."

"It only seems like that," Kalugal said. "It has been less than an hour."

She didn't know whether he was really unconcerned or was just putting on an act for Jacki's sake. The two love-birds had been sitting on the ground with their backs propped against the stone wall, kissing and whispering things in each other's ears as if they were in the comfort of their bedroom and not stuck in a subterranean cave.

"An hour is a long time." Alena pushed to her feet and walked over to the natural pool's edge. "Do you think it's safe to drink this water?"

Kalugal sniffed. "I don't smell anything funky but take only a couple of sips first. If you start convulsing, the rest of us will know not to touch the water."

"Very funny." Jacki slapped his arm. "We should have swum after them. The water is cold, but it's a very short distance to swim through, and I could have made it easily. I hate all this waiting and not knowing what's going on."

Kalugal squeezed her shoulder. "You're pregnant, my love. The cold water might not harm you, but we don't know how it will affect the baby who is still human."

They all had been thinking that, but not wanting to worry Jacki, no one had said anything.

Jacki put her hands protectively over her small belly. "You're right. How can I keep forgetting that I'm responsible for another life now?"

"I'm sure it would have occurred to you as soon as your little toe touched the freezing water." He kissed the top of her head.

"I hear noises." Lokan lifted the hammer over his head. "Everyone, get ready."

While waiting, Lokan had insisted that they collect rocks and keep them within reach. Other than the hammer, the only other weapons they had were the switchblades and throwing knives that Shamash and Welgost carried. Weapons in hand, the two men got in position next to the opening, while the rest of them grabbed a rock in each hand. It wasn't likely that anyone could get past Lokan and the two fighters, but if anyone came from the lake's side, the rocks could be useful.

"It's us," Arwel called from the tunnel. "Don't attack."

A weight lifted off Alena's chest.

They were back, and they'd either found another entrance to the underground labyrinth or had managed to move the boulder.

When Orion stepped out of the opening, his hand gripping the arms of a very tall female, Alena's joy took a nosedive.

Kalugal walked over to the two. "I see that you've caught your prey, oh mighty hunter. And who is your lovely prisoner?"

"My name is Aliya, and he said that I wasn't a prisoner. But I see that he is a liar." She hissed at Orion, who didn't seem impressed by her posturing.

There were advantages to being a compeller.

"You are not a prisoner. You are our guest." Orion winked at Alena.

Only days ago, he'd been told the same thing by Onegus and Kian.

"Yeah, and I'm Shenlong, the rain dragon."

Her English was heavily accented but fluent, and she was clearly of Kra-ell descent. Tall, thin, nearly flat-chested, with eyes that blazed red in the cavern's dim interior and fangs that protruded over her lower red lip.

"Aliya is from Vrog and Emmett's tribe," Arwel said. "But that's all we know for now. I suggest that we vacate these tunnels first and then hear all about Aliya's troubles."

"What happened to you?" Jin looked Arwel over.

His clothing hung in tatters, and he was covered in mostly healed bruises and scrapes—the crusted blood serving as evidence of the beating he'd taken.

"I was attacked by a wild cat."

"Really?" Jin's eyes widened.

"Yeah, of the Kra-ell kind. But don't punch her. She was scared."

"That's not a valid excuse." Jin bared her own fangs and hissed at Aliya.

The Kra-ell female responded as any predator would, crouching and readying to pounce.

"Ladies." Alena walked in between them. "Please. Let's get to know each other first, and if after that you still want to brawl, that can be arranged."

The two backed away from each other, but Alena had a feeling that this wasn't the end of it. The problem was that Jin was outmatched, and she hadn't realized it yet, or she had and was just posturing.

"The good news is that we can get out of here," Arwel said. "Aliya helped us move the boulder with a cleverly constructed pulley system she'd invented. The bad news is that our drivers have ditched us. We will have to walk until we reach a place with reception so we can call for pick-up."

"What about the girl?" Jacki asked.

"I think this is her." Orion turned to Aliya. "When you were much younger, did you get scared by a nasty-looking mask and run down into the tunnels?"

Her eyes widened. "How did you know that?"

Jacki lifted her hand. "From me. Sometimes I get visions, and I got one when I touched that mask. I saw a young girl scream and run into the tunnels. That's how we knew that the boulder was blocking the entrance and where to go from there."

Aliya dropped to her knees in front of Jacki. "You are a seer. You are blessed by the Mother."

"Please, get up." Jacki looked uncomfortable. "It's nothing special."

"I disagree." Kalugal wrapped his arm around his wife's shoulders. "My mate is very special, and she deserves to be worshiped, but we are in a bit of a rush to get out of here, so let's reserve the worshiping for later."

Orion

6∾9

"Hello! Is anybody in there?" A familiar voice called from high above the staircase.

"Jianye? Is that you?" Kalugal called back.

"It is I. Is everyone alright? I brought help, and we are coming down."

"No need. We are fine, and we are coming up. Wait for us to come to you. Better yet, go back all the way to the first chamber."

"Are you sure no one needs help? We brought ropes and a stretcher."

"No one is hurt, Jianye. Go back."

"Yes, sir."

Orion could feel Aliya tense like a coil ready to spring.

"Are you afraid of Jianye?" he asked.

"Afraid of him?" She snorted. "He's nothing. But I don't want anyone to see me. I'm too excited to thrall, and I don't want the humans to see me."

He raised a brow. "Excited?"

She let out an irritated groan. "My English is so-so. I don't know the right word."

"Your English is very good, and the word you are probably looking for is agitated."

"Yes, that's the one." She gripped his arm. "You have to hide me."

"I'll take care of that," Phinas said from behind her. "Orion is needed by his mate."

"Is she the one who is pregnant?"

"No, that's me," Jacki said. "Don't worry about Jianye and his men. Just hunch your shoulders to make yourself look smaller and don't look anyone in the eyes."

"That's not going to work," Kalugal said. "Jianye knows who came here with me, and he will notice one extra female, but that's not a problem. I'll keep him busy."

After climbing the endless stairs and once again crawling through the narrow tunnel, they were greeted by Kalugal's partner and his crew.

"Thank God." Jianye put a hand over his heart. "I was afraid that something happened to you and your friends, and that you were trapped in the ruins. I brought the crew to help dig you out."

"Thank you." Kalugal clapped him on the back and then wrapped his arm around the man's shoulders. "How did you know to come look for us?"

"When you didn't return, your limousine drivers started to worry and came to look for you. When they couldn't find even a trace, they panicked and came looking for me." He looked up at the opening. "I had no idea that there were hidden tunnels under the ruins. How did you know to move that boulder?"

"Intuition." Kalugal tapped his temple. "The boulder looked out of place, and I had a hunch that it was blocking an entrance to a secret chamber. My men and I constructed a clever pulley contraption to move that thing, and we went exploring."

As Jianye glanced at Arwel and Phinas's haggard appearance, Kalugal continued. "We encountered some problems on the way. One of the passages was so narrow that my men had to dig through it, and they got a little banged up while doing that." He smiled at the guy. "We could all use a warm shower and a good meal."

Aliya stayed hidden behind Phinas's broad back, and so far, Jianye hadn't noticed her, but once they started climbing up the ladder one by one, there was no way to hide her.

"Who's she?" Jianye asked.

"A wildlife explorer from Beijing," Kalugal said with a straight face. "Her specialty is wild cats—tigers and leopards of all kinds." He leaned closer to whisper in the guy's ear, "Don't mind her. She's a bit strange. Living for months in the wild as she tracks the migration of the wild cats makes her somewhat antisocial."

"Yes, I can see that."

Orion choked on a laugh, and Alena coughed to hide hers.

Kalugal could have easily shrouded Aliya, but he seemed to be having fun making up stories to cover for her instead, or maybe he wanted to show her that it was all a matter of attitude, and that she shouldn't fear being seen in public just because she looked different.

As they reached the limousines, Kalugal let go of his partner to shake hands with the drivers and thank them for their initiative. He then thanked each of Jianye's men and promised them a hefty bonus for coming out on the weekend to save him.

While he'd been at it, Orion and Phinas escorted Aliya to one of the limousines, and a few moments later, their group was on its way back to the hotel.

"Where are you taking me?" Aliya asked.

"To our hotel," Orion said. "When was the last time you slept in a proper bed?"

Her eyes blazed red. "I'm not sharing any of your beds."

He lifted his hands in the universal sign for peace. "Trust me, none of us are on the menu even if you were interested, so you can relax."

That seemed to be the wrong thing to say.

"Why? Am I not pretty enough for you?"

Leaning over, Alena patted her arm. "You're beautiful, but there are only three single guys in our group, and they are all gentlemen. You don't have to worry about unwanted advances."

Aliya tilted her head. "What does that mean? Unwanted advances?"

"It means that unless you show interest in them, they are not going to bother you."

Aliya

❧

Alena was nice, more like a human than a Kra-ell, but then these long-lived people who called themselves immortals were very different from the Kra-ell.

Other than Arwel's mate, the females were kind of docile, not subservient like many of the human females outside of the Mosuo culture, but not aggressive at all. Still, the males seemed just as devoted to them as the Kra-ell males had been to the Kra-ell females, but it looked like they did that out of love rather than duty or honor, and that was nice.

One of the things that had bothered Aliya the most while living in the Kra-ell compound was the lack of love between the purebloods and even between the hybrids and their purebloaded fathers. The only ones who'd been capable of love had been the human mothers and their children, either human or hybrid.

Her best friend growing up was a human girl.

Chyou had been her only friend ever. Aliya often wondered about what had happened to her. She was probably married, and since the government no longer put restrictions on how many kids a couple could have, Chyou could have several.

"Would you like to talk to Vrog?" Alena asked. "Now that we have reception, I can call him, and you can have a video call with him."

"What's that?"

Alena regarded her as if she was some wild woman who didn't know anything. "Do you know what a cell phone is?"

"Of course." Aliya shifted in her seat. "I never had one, but I've seen people use them, especially the tourists."

"I wonder," Arwel said. "How did you get from the Beijing area to here?"

"We walked, we used the train, the bus, and then we walked some more."

"We?" Orion asked. "I thought that you were alone."

Should she feel flattered? Did he think her so formidable that she could have traveled across the country by herself as a child?

She gave him an incredulous look. "I was eight years old. I traveled with my mother."

"What happened to her?" Alena asked.

"She died." Aliya looked down at her mud-covered shoes. "She got sick and died and left me alone."

"I'm so sorry." Alena leaned forward and put her hand on her knee. "It must have been awful."

"It was."

It could have been much worse if they had been anywhere else.

Aliya had been thanking the Mother daily for whispering in her ear to seek the Mosuo territory.

She'd thought that she would find friendly Kra-ell there, but all she'd found were the Mosuo, who'd adopted many of the Kra-ell good customs and none of the cruelty. The matriarch who had taken them in was a tough, unforgiving female who'd run her multigenerational household with an iron fist, but she'd also been kind to accept a single mother and her strange child in exchange for labor.

In a way, nothing had changed for Aliya's mother after they'd escaped the slaughter. She'd been a slave in the Kra-ell compound, and she'd continued slaving away in the Mosuo village until she died.

"You must tell us all about it when we get to the hotel," the leader of their group said. "After you shower and eat, of course." He smiled. "You look like you could use a good meal. What are your nutritional needs?"

She didn't know what that word meant, but she could guess the meaning. "Are you asking what I like to eat?"

"Yes. The two hybrid Kra-ell we know have different preferences or rather needs. Emmett needs fresh blood to supplement his diet, but Vrog doesn't, and they both prefer their meat barely cooked."

"To eat meat when fresh blood is available is an offense to the Mother. Why kill the animal when drinking a little of its blood can fill the hunger?"

"Blood is not on the menu in most restaurants," the leader said.

Aliya had heard someone call him by his name, but she'd forgotten what it was and didn't want to ask. Someone would say it soon enough.

"I don't eat in restaurants," she said. "I hunt for my food."

He looked as if he was losing patience with her. "Let me put it simply. What can you eat that is not blood? Can you eat meat, rice, bread, noodles, vegetables, fruits, etc.?"

"I can eat all of that, but rice and noodles upset my stomach."

"She is probably gluten intolerant," Alena said. "What about milk? Can you have milk and cheese?"

Aliya nodded. "I like cheese." Her mouth watered as she thought of the ru-shan cheese she'd once tasted but never got a chance to eat again. The delicacy was made from cow's milk, and it was toasted, browned, and slathered in rose petal jam. It was made for the tourists who could pay for it, and not for stray dogs like her. She could have used her mental powers to coerce one of the vendors to give it to her, but Aliya never stole things she could survive without, and she could definitely survive without the delicious cheese.

The question was whether she could survive these people.

What did they want from her?

They'd said that they wanted to ask her some questions, but so far, they hadn't asked much. She could lull them into believing that she was cooperating and pretend that she was grateful to them for offering her a meal and a shower.

If they bought her act, Orion wouldn't use his powers on her.

She'd noticed that he was reluctant to use them and had to be coached by the one named Arwel.

Arwel couldn't compel her but knew how to use compulsion better than Orion, probably because he had experience compelling humans. It was the same as the pureblooded Kra-ell who could hypnotically coerce humans as well as hybrids, and the hybrids who could only do that to humans. Maybe Orion was a pureblood of his kind, and Arwel was a hybrid. It was hard to tell with these immortals. They didn't have distinguishing features like the Kra-ell and looked like humans. Did the males even have fangs?

The only fangs she'd seen so far belonged to Jin, Arwel's mate, and she was one-quarter Kra-ell.

They claimed to have only met two other hybrid Kra-ells beside her. Vrog, whose name she recognized, and Emmett, who she'd never heard of. What if they'd lied about it, though? What if their plan was to sell her to those other Kra-ell who'd attacked her tribe?

It seemed unlikely, especially with the female named Alena being so kind to her, but she didn't know these immortals, and they could be master deceivers.

Her best course of action was to flee as soon as she could.

There was no going back to her subterranean haven.

It had been compromised not only by the immortals but also by the humans. On Monday it would be crawling with the archeological crew digging there for artifacts.

She needed a new home, and the idea from before was still valid. If those human limo drivers were staying overnight in the hotel, and if she managed to get away from her captors, she could hypnotically coerce one of them to drive her somewhere far away.

Hopefully, the immortals had lots of money lying around because she needed some to start a new life somewhere else. She would have never stolen from innocents, but these people owed her for taking away the only home she had.

Alena

"Aliya, you come with Jacki and me," Kalugal said when they arrived at the hotel. "We have the presidential suite, which has two bathrooms. You can shower in there."

Alena detected the slight compulsion in his tone, which explained why the girl did as he'd commanded, and followed him and Jacki into the lobby.

Once everyone had gathered inside, Kalugal said, "Dinner tonight at our suite. I'll call the concierge and have them set it up. Does five o'clock work for everyone?"

They all needed to shower and change, but they were hungry as well, and Alena doubted they could wait nearly two hours until dinner.

But then that's what room service was for.

"Aliya needs new clothes." Jin walked up to Kalugal. "Jacki's won't fit her, so I guess they would have to be mine."

"That would be greatly appreciated, thank you." Kalugal put a hand on her arm. "Naturally, I'll reimburse you for the expense."

"I'm not a beggar," Aliya grumbled. "I don't want anything from her."

"Well, tough." Jin got in her face. "You're dirty, and you stink, and your clothes are rags. A normal person would have said thank you."

Aliya didn't back down. "Who said I was normal?" And to prove it, her eyes flashed red, and her fangs elongated.

Just as before, Alena got between them, only this time she had to push on both of their middles to get them to step back.

"I thought that you didn't want to attract attention to yourself," she said quietly to Aliya. "If the dirt and the rags don't have everyone looking at you, the red eyes and fangs will surely do."

"*Feihua*," Aliya cursed under her breath as she hunched her shoulders and dipped her head.

Jin snickered. "Crap indeed. I'll see you later."

Aliya was taller and slimmer than Jin, but even if baggy, Jin's clothes would be a vast improvement on the rags she was wearing.

As someone with thralling ability, the girl could've gotten herself new clothes with very little effort, and Alena wondered why she hadn't. Perhaps she would ask her over dinner.

She hadn't seen Jacki and Kalugal's suite, but it had to be big to accommodate twelve people for a sit-down dinner.

"I'm looking forward to a long shower." Orion wrapped his arm around her waist as they took the stairs instead of the elevator to the second floor. "Care to share?"

"Sounds lovely, but I'm hungry. Perhaps we can order room service and have them leave the cart outside the door. When we get out of the shower, the meal will be waiting for us."

"An excellent idea." He leaned and kissed her cheek. "I'm so glad that Kalugal is also a compeller and that he took Aliya off my hands. I was afraid that they would foist her on us."

"You were very kind to her." Alena waited for Orion to fish the card key out of his pocket and open the door. "In fact, I was impressed." She walked inside.

"It was nothing." He closed the door behind them and then briefly kissed her lips before heading to the bathroom while unbuttoning his shirt on the way.

Alena stared transfixed, waiting for the shirt to drop so she could admire his muscular back, but he entered the bathroom before dropping the shirt, depriving her of the treat.

Oh well, she would soon have her hands all over his magnificent body in the shower, and there was a lot they could do with the nearly two hours until dinner.

Perhaps she should let him get washed up first, though. He'd been covered in dirt even before catching Aliya, and her capture had left him in an even worse state.

Alena wondered why he hadn't used compulsion to prevent the girl from hurting Arwel and Phinas. Had he been too aggravated to summon his ability?

Orion didn't possess Kalugal's finesse, and he didn't enjoy using compulsion, but compelling Aliya to behave had been unavoidable.

He'd been so patient with her, treating her like a skittish kitten, keeping his voice and his eyes soft. Although given Arwel and Phinas's state after trying to subdue her, Aliya was more of a tigress than a kitten.

If the Fates ever blessed Orion with a child, he would make a wonderful father. Blessed the two of them, because Alena was not giving him up.

The trip and the trying events of the day had solidified her conviction that he was the one for her. If he felt the same, she would implore the Fates to give her one more child with Orion, preferably a boy because she wanted to see Orion do all the things that fathers did with their sons.

Alena had raised her thirteen children with the help of her mother and the Odus, but it was not the same as raising a child with a partner. It would be a new and wonderful experience, one she fiercely yearned for.

"Are you calling room service, or should I?" Orion called out from the bathroom.

"I'll call them. Anything special you want me to order for you?"

"Whatever you're ordering for yourself is fine for me."

Orion was so easy to be with. He didn't make a big deal out of anything, didn't complain, didn't grumble, and was always attentive and patient. She couldn't have asked for a better mate.

There was just one more thing Alena needed to do to make her decision official.

She needed to tell Orion that she loved him.

Aliya

◠◠◠

Aliya's hair had never smelled so good. She'd spent over an hour in the bathroom, first in the shower and then in the bathtub. Washing in hot water was a luxury she hadn't enjoyed in years, and she'd made good use of all those little shampoos and conditioners. She'd even slathered her face and body with the lotion. All those containers were empty now, but just in case she hadn't been supposed to use them, she filled them with water and put them back where she'd found them.

A towel wrapped around her head and another one around her body, she stared at her reflection in the mirror and grimaced. She was clean, really clean, for the first time in years. She'd washed in the river or in the subterranean lake every other day or so, but she was lucky if she had a crude bar of soap, and she hadn't had one in months. To get a new bar, she would have to row her canoe all the way to the village, compel every person she encountered to forget her, and then she had to steal what she needed because she didn't have any money.

Aliya hated stealing, especially from people who didn't have much to start with.

She had one change of clothes back in the ruins' subterranean system, which were not in a much better shape than what she'd taken off, but at least they were clean, or as clean as she could get them by washing them in cold water and no soap.

What she'd had on this morning had gotten dirty and sweaty and even more tattered than they had been before, and she really didn't want to put them on. But unless she wanted to come out dressed in a towel, she would have to put on the clothes that Arwel's mate had brought over.

During Aliya's hour-long cleansing, Jacki had knocked on the door and put the items on the vanity. The problem was that they didn't include new underwear or shoes, and Aliya had no intentions of putting her old ones on.

She would go without.

For now, she could walk barefoot and put her shoes on later when it was time for her to escape.

Shifting her eyes to the bathroom window, Aliya felt guilty and stupid for not using it to escape right now. It was small and high up, but she was slim enough to fit through and strong enough to hoist herself up to it.

Except, it had felt so good to shower and bathe, and her stomach was growling with hunger. The prospect of a full belly was holding her back more securely than any chains they could have put on her.

The problem was that they didn't need to use physical chains. The leader of the immortals was just as powerful as Orion, and he'd told her not to leave the hotel without his permission. Aliya hadn't tried to defy his command yet, but she was pretty sure that her body would refuse to reach for the small window if her intention was to escape.

A knock on the door startled her, and as she turned around, Jacki opened the door. "Are you almost done? The meal will be served shortly."

"I'll be out in a moment." She waited for the door to close before dropping the towel.

When she was done putting on the borrowed clothes, she took off the towel that was wrapped around her head and let her long black hair tumble down her back. She was so used to combing it with her fingers that she'd started on it before realizing that there was a brand-new comb on the vanity top that she could use.

It had been such a long time since she'd enjoyed such luxuries, and she could easily get used to having them again, but at what cost?

Orion

"Hello, beautiful." Orion pulled Alena into his arms. "Do you want me to shampoo your hair?"

He loved her hair. It was thick and wavy and had every shade of blond in it. When the sun hit it, it shone with platinum and gold highlights, and when it was dark, it took on a copper hue.

Before joining him in the shower, she'd released it from the braid, and the long, lush strands parted over her generous breasts, framing the pink erect nipples in copper and gold.

"Have you ever done it before?" she asked.

"I shampoo mine every day."

She smiled. "You know what I mean." Tilting her head back, she let the spray soak her hair.

"No, I never have." When he'd been married, bathing hadn't happened every day. There had been no running water and filling a tub with water that had been heated over a stove had taken a long time, a task he'd gladly performed for his wife twice a week. But Miriam had never invited him to share the bath with her. Back then, it hadn't even occurred to either of them that it was an option.

Why hadn't it, though?

They'd been deeply in love and passionate about each other, so it hadn't been about avoiding intimacy. Or maybe it was?

As she'd gotten older, Miriam had started hiding her nudity from him. She'd stopped undressing in front of him, and their lovemaking had been done in the dark.

"Why are you frowning?" Alena asked.

She probably wondered about his deflated erection, but she voiced her concern in a more polite way.

He shook his head. "It's nothing. Just old memories that have no place here with us."

She cupped his cheek. "You can tell me anything, Orion. Anytime." She smiled. "I have lived for a very long time, and I know that life is not a walk in a rose garden, nor do I expect it to be. I love you just as much when you are sad as when you are happy."

For a long moment, too long, Orion found himself speechless.

Had Alena just told him that she loved him, or had it been just a figure of speech? The same way people said they loved oranges as much as they loved apples? Or they loved the color blue as much as they loved the color red?

"Nothing to say, mate of mine?"

And now she called him her mate as well?

What was going on?

Had they walked through a time warp, and this was weeks in the future?

Alena chuckled. "I've never seen you so dumbfounded before. Is it so difficult to accept that you are my mate?" Wrapping her arms around his neck, she pulled him down and kissed him lightly. "I'll make it easy for you and walk you through it step by step. First, you will tell me that I am your mate, and then you'll say that you love me and that you want to spend the rest of your eternal life with me. You are free to change the order of these statements, but they all have to be there."

"I'm your mate." His throat turning suddenly dry, he swallowed to bring some moisture to his vocal cords. "And you are mine. I've been in love with you from the moment I heard you sing."

It was the truth, and surprisingly, he didn't feel guilty for vocalizing what he'd felt for days. Miriam would have approved of Alena, and she would have been happy for him. And if not, he would just have to beg her spirit's forgiveness.

Throwing her head back, Alena laughed. "I don't know if I should take that as a compliment or an insult. I've been told that I have a good voice, but it's not that good. Besides, I hoped that you were more impressed with my winning personality and my knockout body than with my amateur rendition of 'Let it Go.'"

Her teasing melted away the tension that had crept into his shoulder muscles. Cupping her cheeks, he smiled. "I'm impressed with everything about you, from your kindness to your wisdom, from your selflessness to your assertiveness, and from the beauty of your little toes to the top of your gorgeous hair and everything in between. But I knew all of that before I ever met you. I heard it all in your song. There was power and beauty in it, emotion and determination, a yearning that called to me, was meant for me alone. I knew that the woman whom the voice belonged to would be extraordinary, but you've exceeded all of my expectations."

ALENA & ORION'S STORY CULMINATES
THE CHILDREN OF THE GODS BOOK 58
DARK HUNTER'S BOON

TURN THE PAGE TO READ THE EXCERPT—>

JOIN THE VIP CLUB

To find out what's included in your free membership,
flip to the last page.

Dark Hunter's Boon

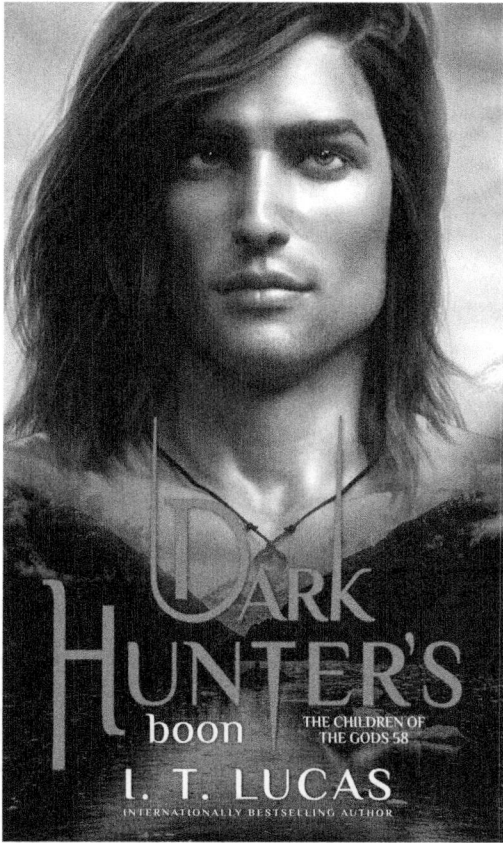

As Orion and Alena's relationship blooms and solidifies, the two investigative teams combine their recent discoveries to piece together more of the Kra-ell mystery. Attacking the puzzle from another angle, Eleanor works on gaining access to Echelon's powerful AI spy network.

Together, they are getting dangerously close to finding the elusive Kra-ell.

Alena

Alena, eldest daughter of the goddess Annani, mother of thirteen, grandmother of seventeen, great-grandmother of twenty-three, and a great many times over grandmother of nearly every member of Annani's clan, sat in front of the vanity and gazed at her lover's reflection in the mirror.

It had been one of those days that would forever remain etched in her memory, and it wasn't over yet.

In the span of twelve hours, their team had been trapped under the ruins of an ancient outpost, had found a hybrid Kra-ell female who'd been hiding there for years, and after they'd returned to the hotel, Alena had finally admitted to Orion that she'd fallen in love with him and proclaimed him her mate.

Her heart was full to bursting with happiness and gratitude to the Fates for the wonderful male they'd chosen for her. They had given her a boon—a gorgeous, kind, smart male who loved her as much as she loved him.

Orion had fallen in love with her voice first, but the rest had soon followed. Somehow, hearing her pouring her suppressed emotions into that song had given him a glimpse into her soul before ever meeting her, and he'd liked what he'd seen.

As he caught her looking at him, Orion grinned and flexed his muscles. Alena smiled back and picked up the brush. She could never get enough of ogling her mate's impeccable physique, but she was supposed to get ready for dinner.

They'd made love in the shower, then on the bed, and then again in the shower, so she should be beyond satisfied and content. But as the saying went, her appetite had just gotten sharpened by the first tasty bites, and she hungered for more.

Right now, the male she loved was giving her an eyeful as he got dressed for dinner at Kalugal and Jacki's. It was a shame to cover all that gorgeous tan skin and those beautiful muscles in clothing, but she had to admit that he looked quite dashing in the white button-down dress shirt and the navy-blue suit.

"Do you think I should go with the blazer or without?" Orion asked.

"We are not leaving the hotel, so you can go without, but you look so good all dressed up."

"Not nearly as good as you, gorgeous." He leaned down and kissed the top of her head. "I don't want to mess up your lipstick."

"Feel free to mess it up anytime you want." She puckered her lips.

With a groan, he lifted her off the stool and kissed the living daylights out of her.

When he let go, Alena burst out laughing. "Go wash your face. You're covered in red lipstick."

Smiling like a fiend, he turned her around to face the mirror. "I have a feeling that we are going to be late for dinner."

Her makeup was a mess.

With a sigh, Alena sat back down and pulled a tissue out of the box. "I'll just take it off."

She hardly ever bothered with makeup, but tonight was special, and not just because she and Orion were officially in love.

Alena had a feeling that the dinner at Kalugal and Jacki's presidential suite would be one of those events that would affect the future of the clan.

The Kra-ell female they'd captured and brought with them to the hotel was about to tell her story. Probably not willingly, but with Kalugal's compulsion, she wouldn't be able to refuse.

Aliya was like a trapped wild animal, and the only thing preventing her from running away the first chance she got was Kalugal's command to stay put. Hopefully, though, after showering and getting fed, she wouldn't be in such a great hurry to leave.

Aliya wasn't a prisoner, but they needed to keep her from running off just yet for her own good.

The poor woman didn't know who to trust, and she feared everyone. If she didn't allow herself time to get to know them and ran off, Aliya would spend the rest of her life alone and wouldn't get to meet the other survivors of Jade's tribe.

Before allowing her access to Emmett and Vrog, though, they needed to find out how she'd gotten from her tribe's compound near Beijing all the way to the Mosuo village on the shores of Lugo Lake. Her escape from the slaughter of her people and her journey to the remote lake in the Tibetan mountains was no doubt a fascinating tale, but what Alena was even more curious about was why Aliya had shunned society, living hidden in the tunnel system under the ruins of an ancient trading post.

The woman looked half-starved, half-wild, and she was wary of people, whether they were human or other.

A powerful female like her shouldn't have been running scared like that. Physically, Aliya was as strong as or stronger than two well-trained immortal warriors, giving Arwel and Phinas a run for their money. If not for Orion knocking her out with a rock, she might have overpowered them both and run off.

As a hybrid Kra-ell, Aliya could also thrall, and combined with her physical strength, she could have used her gifts to live like a queen. Instead, she'd chosen to live like a pauper.

Why?

Was it grief?

After Aliya's human mother had died, the girl had probably fallen into despair. Depression and anger often contributed to self-destructive behaviors, and in some cases, even suicide. For immortals, ending their own life required such extreme measures that it was nearly impossible, and thankfully, none of Annani's clan had ever gone that far, but over the years there had been some members who'd recklessly endangered their lives in the hopes of ending their emotional misery.

In Aliya's case, her emotional pain might have manifested in withdrawal from society and self-inflicted austerity.

Every motherly instinct she had was telling Alena to take the girl under her protective wing. But Aliya was a grown woman, and it was her choice whether to accept Alena's help or refuse it.

Orion

When all the smeared lipstick was gone, Alena pivoted on the vanity stool to face Orion. "I feel bad about leaving Ovidu and Oridu in their hotel room once again."

"They don't need to eat, do they?"

Alena grimaced. "They eat garbage."

"Really?"

"Did you see *Back to the Future II*?"

"Are you referencing Mr. Fusion? The Home Energy Reactor?"

She nodded. "When I saw that movie, I thought about the Odus. You don't need a garbage disposal with one of them around."

"That would be a very expensive garbage disposal." Orion looped his tie and tied the knot. "I'm surprised that Kian hasn't had one of them reverse-engineered. Imagine a cyborg butler in every house." He chuckled. "The brand name should be Mr. Turbo Clean—the recycling superstar."

He thought it was a very clever name, but Alena didn't seem impressed.

She sighed. "We know how that would end. We should heed the warning of history and not repeat the same mistakes our ancestors made. The Odus were created to be servants, but they were easily converted into killing machines. It got so bad that they were decommissioned and the technology to make them was banned."

"People will always find ways to use things as weapons, but that doesn't mean that new technologies shouldn't be developed just because they have the potential to destroy as well as to build. Computer chips are used in missiles as well as in medical devices." He smiled. "I wish I was more technologically savvy so I could give you better examples, but my point is that with proper safeguards, the amazing technology that created the Odus could revolutionize the way people live and work."

Alena pulled out a calf-long sweater from the closet and shrugged it on. "I get what you're saying. What's interesting is that Syssi's vision linked the Kra-ell with the Odus. Back then, we didn't know that the Kra-ell were real, and we thought that Syssi's vision was influenced by the virtual reality story she'd created for the Perfect Match studios. As it turns out, it was the other way around. Her precognition created the imagery for what she believed was her own creation."

"That's interesting." Orion pushed the door open. "How were the Kra-ell connected to the Odus?"

As Alena stepped out onto the hallway, Ovidu opened the door and dipped his head. "Good evening, mistress. Should I escort you and Master Orion?"

It was unnecessary, but that was what Kian wanted. "We are just going to the third floor. You can escort us there and return to your room."

"Yes, mistress."

She turned back to Orion. "In her vision, Syssi saw a dark alien world, with skies that had a reddish hue and very strong winds. The vision happened in a spaceport, where Odus were being loaded into shuttles by handlers who she described as looking like the Kra-ell. They were tall, slim, and dark-haired, and the only female among all the male handlers was the one running the show. The most interesting detail about her was that she had fangs."

"Did the females in Syssi's imagined world also have them?" Orion looped his arm around Alena's waist as they took the stairs to the third floor.

"They did. Except for the location, everything about her Krall adventure was eerily similar to the Kra-ell."

He would have loved to see the created world, but he wasn't sure about getting hooked up to a virtual reality contraption. Perhaps there was a way to see it as a movie? Then again, going on an adventure with Alena that wasn't actually dangerous could be fun. After their earlier excitement in the tunnels, he wanted to play it safe, and there was nothing safer than enjoying an interesting experience from the comfort of an easy chair.

"Where did Syssi place the Krall?"

"Greenland. The story was that they landed there a thousand years ago, and their spaceship got trapped under the ice. One day, a massive earthquake shattered the ice, the Krall woke up from their stasis, and then took over the entire Arctic Circle."

"Sounds like a great story." Orion cast her a sidelong glance. "You've piqued my curiosity. Would you like to go on a Krall adventure with me?"

She laughed. "There are so many wonderful scenarios we can pick from, why go to freezing Greenland and encounter nasty, bloodthirsty Krall?"

"That's a valid point. Were the Krall bloodthirsty in Syssi's vision as well?"

"She only said that everyone's eyes were glowing, which led her to believe that it wasn't just nighttime over there, but that it was a dark world. It might have been just her impression, though, because the atmosphere in the vision was so somber. The Kra-ell were sending the Odus out to space, and Syssi believed that they were getting rid of them."

Orion stopped in front of the presidential suite's double doors. "So let me get it straight. In Syssi's vision, the Kra-ell were in charge of decommissioning the Odus?"

"Or sending them to war. The problem with Syssi's visions is that they show her just snippets, and she doesn't know if what she sees is in the past or the future, or where it's happening or why. That leaves a lot of room for interpretation, or misinterpretation. For all we know, the Kra-ell might have been saving the Odus and sending them somewhere safe, or they might have hidden them on some distant moon to be used in future warfare, or it could have been none of the above. If the vision was true, though, which I believe it was, then it clearly connects the Kra-ell to the gods. We know that the Odus were created on the gods' home planet, and if the Kra-ell were handling them, they either shared that planet with the gods or were close neighbors."

As Orion knocked on the door, his head was swimming with the implications. The clan already suspected that the gods and the Kra-ell had a shared ancestry and that they came from the same corner of the universe, but the vision of them being involved with the Odus opened up a whole new can of worms.

Shamash, Kalugal's personal assistant, opened the door. "Good evening. Please, come in."

Ovidu bowed. "Should you require my services, please call for me."

"Thank you." Alena dismissed him.

Kalugal and Jacki's suite was about five times the size of Orion and Alena's hotel room. It had a living room, a dining room, a kitchenette, a bathroom, and a separate bedroom suite.

The dining room was probably designed to host board meetings because the table could comfortably seat the eleven people in their party and Aliya with room to spare. If needed, they could easily squeeze in four additional guests.

Everyone was already there, and two waiters were waiting by their carts to start serving the meal.

Alena glanced at her watch. "I didn't realize that we were late. My apologies."

"You're just in time," Jacki said. "Aliya insisted on saving the seat next to her for you."

When Orion shifted his eyes in the direction Jacki waved her hand, he was taken aback. The female looked like a different person.

With her skin and hair washed clean, her beauty shone through, but her attitude hadn't improved. She looked agitated, and he had a good idea why.

Even from where he was standing, which was at least twenty feet away from her, he could hear her stomach grumbling.

Aliya was hungry and waiting impatiently for the meal to start.

Hadn't Kalugal fed her?

If she'd been placed in Orion's care, that would have been the first thing he would have done. Perhaps the Odus could be moved to another room so they could invite Aliya to stay with him and Alena. The two of them would take much better care of her than Kalugal and Jacki seemed to be doing. Kian wouldn't be happy about that, though. The Odus were there to protect Alena and therefore needed to stay close to her.

"We'd better sit down quickly." He took Alena's elbow and led her to their seats. "Everyone is hungry." He cast a quick smile at Aliya, but she didn't return it.

Alena

Alena's heart went out to the young woman devouring food as if she'd gone hungry for days, which she probably had. Even Jin's animosity toward Aliya subsided as she watched her pile yet another serving on her plate and then eat it as fast as was possible in polite company.

Aliya was trying to measure her pace, but she couldn't hide the slight tremor of her hands as she reached for the platters. Casting quick looks around, she checked if anyone else wanted to finish what was left over, and when she was satisfied that there were no other takers, she scooped every last morsel onto her plate.

"I don't know what happened to the portion sizes," Kalugal complained loudly. "They are entirely inadequate." He grabbed the phone and called to order more food to be delivered.

Alena could have kissed him for it. The portions were just as generous as they had been the night before, but with all of them pretending to be full so Aliya could eat her fill, Kalugal had wisely decided to order more.

It had been incredibly sweet of him to do so in a way that allowed her to save face.

Once all the platters were empty, including the additional dishes Kalugal had ordered, the waiters cleared the table and served tea, coffee, and dessert.

Aliya looked catatonic from food overdose, but she still had to make good on her promise to tell them her story.

"Would you like some tea?" Kalugal asked her. "It will help wash the food down so you can tell us what we've been waiting patiently to hear."

"Thank you." She straightened in her chair. "I would love some tea."

He lifted the teapot and actually got to his feet to pour tea into her cup instead of passing it to Alena. "Are you ready to tell us your story?"

Aliya hesitated. "I don't know who you are and if I can trust you, but I know that you can force me to talk like you forced me to help you and to come here. I'm at your sorrow."

"The correct phrase is at my mercy." Kalugal pulled out his phone. "Would talking to Vrog assuage your fears?"

She shrugged. "He could be a traitor. Maybe it was him who betrayed us to our enemies and brought the killers to slaughter our people."

With a sigh, Kalugal put the phone back in his pocket. "I would much prefer it if you told us your story without being forced. But you are a very suspicious young lady, and you leave me no choice. Tell me everything that you remember about the attack, Aliya. Tell me how you managed to escape when all the other Kra-ell and hybrids were either killed or taken. I also want you to tell us what has happened to you since then and why you've been living alone in the ruins."

Alena could see the defiance in Aliya's eyes, and for a long moment, the young woman kept her lips tightly pressed together, trying to fight the compulsion. It was a valiant effort and proof of a strong will, but Kalugal was a powerful compeller, and Aliya wasn't immune.

She stood no chance against him.

"I was eight years old," she spat and lifted her hands to press her palms to her temples. "I still looked human. That's how I managed to escape."

"Go on," Kalugal prompted.

Letting out a groan that sounded like a growl, Aliya surrendered to the compulsion. "When the bad Kra-ell attacked, they let the humans go. They hypnotically coerced them to forget where they lived and put lies in their heads."

"We call it thralling," Kalugal said. "To thrall means to enslave through enchantment. We can do more to humans than just hypnotically coerce them to forget things. We can also plant fake memories in their minds."

"I know that." Aliya glared at him. "That can also be called hypnotic coercion, but thralling is shorter, so I'll use that."

"Thank you." Kalugal gave her a reassuring smile. "So, what kind of lies did they plant in the humans' heads?"

"My mother believed that she'd been in a work camp for all those years, and she didn't remember who my father was because the bad people told the humans to forget about the Kra-ell. But I was a hybrid, and their thralling didn't work on me. I knew who I was, and I remembered everything, including what I learned from Jade and the other pureblooded females." She looked down at the dessert on her plate but didn't touch it. "I was so scared, and I kept asking my mother what happened to my father, but she didn't know who I was talking about. My father was a pureblooded Kra-ell, but he wasn't as bad as the others. When no one was looking, he was kind to my mother and me. He brought us little gifts from time to time, and he gave me money for my birthdays."

Alena wondered if Aliya's father was also Vrog's. She hadn't had a chance to talk to Vrog when they'd been boarding the planes, but she'd heard that he'd spoken with affection about his pureblooded father. There hadn't been many pureblooded Kra-ell in the compound, and most had been described as either cruel or indifferent to humans and hybrids alike. What were the chances that there had been two kind males in that small group?

Was it possible that most of them had been decent males, but given their societal rules they had to keep up the pretense?

Alena knew all about social expectations and how they affected one's behavior. Not that it was a bad thing, at least not as a rule. Usually, people behaved better when they knew others were watching. In small, close-knit communities, spousal and child abuse were rare, and so were theft and vandalism. People wanted to be judged positively by others.

"Did your mother have family here?" Jacki asked. "Is that why she brought you to the lake?"

Aliya shook her head. "I knew about the Mosuo people, and I told my mother that we would be safe here. It was far away from where we lived before, and the people here respected women. We were alone, and I'd heard stories about human men mistreating females, so I was scared for my mother and a little for myself too. My mother was too terrified to think, but she didn't remember why she was so scared, so she listened to me. We had very little money. The humans in the compound didn't get paid. But I had never spent the money my father gave me for my birthdays because I never left the compound, so it was all still there, and my mother used it to buy train tickets for us. Back then, there wasn't even a paved road leading to the lake, and the train could get us only part of the way. We walked a lot, and we asked kind farmers to give us rides, and finally, we arrived at the Mosuo village. One of the matriarchs took pity on us and let us join her household in exchange for my mother's work. My mother was a hard worker, and she could sew clothes, a skill that was badly needed at the time. The tourism to the lake was growing, and the villagers were looking for more ways to make money off the tourists. They made traditional outfits for sale, but they sewed them by hand. My mother knew how to operate a sewing machine."

"How did you know about the Mosuo?" Orion asked.

"From Jade." Aliya smiled. "I was a rare female hybrid, so unlike the boys who were treated just slightly better than the human children, Jade was nice to me. She liked to keep me around when I was done with my schoolwork and my chores. I was a quiet little girl, and sometimes she forgot that I was there when she talked with the other females, or maybe she thought that I couldn't under-stand Kra-ell well enough to follow what they were talking about. But I was always good with languages, and if she had bothered to actually talk to me, she would have known that I spoke fluent Kra-ell. One day, she was talking with Kagra about how they were betrayed, and their ship was broken on purpose."

"You mean sabotaged," Orion offered.

"Yes, thank you. Sometimes I don't know the correct words in English."

"Your English is excellent," Jin said. "How did you learn to speak it so well?"

Aliya shrugged. "I have a good ear, and I learned from shows on television, songs on the radio, and from the tourists."

"Television?" Jacki arched a brow. "Did the lake area have reception back then?"

Aliya shook her head. "We had television in the Kra-ell compound. I didn't need as much sleep as the humans, so I snuck out at night and went to the common room to watch TV."

"I didn't know they had English-speaking films on Chinese television," Carol said.

"It was mostly American movies on video cassettes. I think Jade brought them with her from her trips to the US."

That was a piece of information they hadn't heard yet. "Did Jade and the other purebloods leave the compound often?" Alena asked.

"Jade traveled a lot, and she usually took one or two males with her."

"That's interesting," Kalugal said. "But let's get back to what you heard Jade say about the ship's sabotage."

Aliya

Aliya lifted the teacup and took a small sip to moisten her dry throat. It was difficult to talk about the past, but it was also liberating.

She'd had no one to tell her story to, not even her mother while she had still been alive. Sometimes, she wasn't sure that any of it had really happened and that it hadn't been a dream, or rather a nightmare.

She'd wished it hadn't been true and that she was just a little odd-looking human girl, but she had the fangs and red glowing eyes to prove that she wasn't human and that what had happened in the compound had been real. She belonged to an alien race of people whose customs and beliefs had influenced the Mosuo people, and who'd slaughtered each other for no good reason.

Why had those other Kra-ell attacked her tribe? They couldn't have retaliated for some wrongdoing committed by Jade or the other tribe members because no one had even known that they existed. The attack had been unprovoked, and to this day, Aliya still wondered why.

Then again, the purebloods must have known about the others because they must have arrived on the same ship that had been sabotaged, but perhaps they hadn't known who had survived. Maybe they'd evacuated the ships in small vessels that were like the escape pods she'd seen in science fiction movies, and those vessels had landed in different parts of the world.

Perhaps it had been a territorial thing?

Now that she was older and understood a little more about how the world worked, she knew all about eliminating competition for resources. Even in the wild, one kind of predator killed another's cubs to ensure their own cubs' survival.

Except, even that couldn't explain the attack. Earth was a big place, so big that the two Kra-ell groups had been oblivious to each other's existence until something or someone had betrayed Aliya's tribe to those other murderous Kra-ell.

"Whenever you're ready," Kalugal said gently.

"It was a long time ago, and I don't remember all the details." She looked at him. "Sometimes I think that I imagined it all, but the proof is right here." She pointed to her fangs. "And if that's real, so is the rest of it."

He nodded, his eyes soft and full of understanding. "You were just a little girl, and you suffered a horrible trauma. It's okay if you confuse some details. Just tell us what you remember, and we will try to piece it together to make sense of it."

That would be helpful.

Perhaps these people could finally fill in the missing pieces for her.

"I heard Jade say something about a scouting crew who were supposed to arrive first and prepare things for her. She told Kagra that she suspected the scouts had sabotaged their ship, so their landing was delayed by thousands of years. I thought that I must have misunderstood because the Kra-ell couldn't live that long. But I knew the Kra-ell word for thousands, and that was what she said. Then I thought that maybe the ship was like a huge village and that the Kra-ell who boarded the ship were not the ones who landed on Earth, but their grandchildren or even great-grandchildren did."

"They could have traveled in stasis," Arwel said. "We don't know anything about their interstellar travel technology, but if it obeys the same laws of physics we are familiar with, then the only way to traverse the enormous distances of space is in stasis, which is a sort of very long hibernation."

That made sense. If the Kra-ell had the technology to travel through space, they probably also had the technology to put themselves to sleep for thousands of years.

"What must have happened was that the scouting team woke up first," Kalugal said. "Their pods were probably programmed to open ahead of the others, and when they did, they decided to give themselves a longer head start on the others and reprogrammed their fellow travelers' pods to stay closed for much longer."

"You are jumping to conclusions," Arwel said. "It might have been a malfunction. If the scouting team had nefarious intentions, they would have killed the others instead of reprogramming their pods."

"Killing with no provocation is an affront to the Mother," Aliya said. "But it didn't stop the killers who attacked my tribe, so maybe they were heretics."

"Or they might have perceived something as a provocation," Kalugal said. "You don't know what Jade did on these frequent trips abroad."

"True, but she never mentioned any other Kra-ell except for that scouting team, and she said that the joke was on them because Earth females were not compatible. They couldn't produce long-lived children for them, so they died out long before Jade and her people woke up."

Jade's exact words had been that the children born to Kra-ell fathers and human mothers were inferior and defective, that they were a diluted breed who couldn't have long-lived children of their own, but she didn't want to repeat those offensive remarks that had made her feel like a failure all those years ago.

When Arwel looked at her with his piercing blue eyes, there was so much compassion in them that she suspected he knew what she'd said only in her head. Was he a mind reader?

"Did Jade think that the scouting team influenced the Mosuo social structure?" he asked.

Relieved at the change of subject, Aliya had no problem answering that. "Jade knew about the Mosuo, visited their villages, and even brought back souvenirs, or what I thought were souvenirs. I think she found some artifacts that caught her interest. She said it was obvious that the scouting crew had lived in the area and influenced the Mosuo society."

"I wonder whether the Kra-ell were put in stasis with venom or with technology." Lokan turned to Kalugal. "If it was done with venom, they would have been skeletal when they landed. But if they were on life support in some sort of pods, they would have probably awakened just fine. Did our father tell you anything about how the gods first arrived on Earth? Or maybe our mother mentioned something?"

Gods? Had she heard him right? Could gods have more than one meaning in English?

Kalugal shook his head. "Frankly, I don't remember either of them mentioning that, but I always assumed that the gods were asleep during the long journey to Earth, so maybe one of them said something to me when I was very young, and it sank into my subconscious. But it's also possible that I was influenced by science fiction movies."

"Does god mean like God Almighty, or does it have another meaning in English?" Aliya asked.

Alena smiled. "Our ancestors weren't deities. They were a divergent species of humanoids, probably from the same place as yours, but they were so advanced compared to humans and had such power over them that humans believed they were gods. Naturally, our ancestors reinforced those beliefs and created a whole mythology around a kernel of truth, aggrandizing everything they did, including their sexual shenanigans. Other mythologies copied from the first one, and that's how most of the world came to believe that they were gods. There is much more to the story, but let's save it for later, or you will never get to finish yours. What happened after you and your mother arrived at the Mosuo village?"

Aliya would have loved to hear more about the ancestors of these immortals, but if she insisted, Kalugal would just force her to go back to her story, and she hated how that felt. She'd rather keep talking and avoid it.

"The people were kind to us, and for a while, things were good. But then I matured, and my fangs started showing when I got excited or agitated, and I became so tall that I was the tallest person in the village. Most of the time, I managed to hide the fangs, never smiling and keeping my head down. But I couldn't hide my height, and people made fun of me, calling me a freak. And then my mother died when I was fifteen, and things got really bad."

"In what way?" Kalugal asked.

"The humans started to fear me. When I got angry, which happened a lot, my eyes turned red, and my fangs elongated. Some people noticed, and I heard them whispering behind my back that I must be possessed by a demon. I didn't want to wait and see what they planned to do about it. And since I knew that I couldn't thrall the entire village to forget me, I didn't feel safe to stay. I gathered my things, left in the middle of the night in a borrowed canoe, and rowed all the way to the ruins. I knew that I could survive there on my own. By then, I'd already been hunting for several years, and I was familiar with the area."

ORDER DARK HUNTER'S BOON TODAY!

JOIN THE VIP CLUB

To find out what's included in your free membership,
flip to the last page.

The Children of the Gods Series

Reading Order

THE CHILDREN OF THE GODS ORIGINS

1: GODDESS'S CHOICE

When gods and immortals still ruled the ancient world, one young goddess risked everything for love.

2: GODDESS'S HOPE

Hungry for power and infatuated with the beautiful Areana, Navuh plots his father's demise. After all, by getting rid of the insane god he would be doing the world a favor. Except, when gods and immortals conspire against each other, humanity pays the price.

But things are not what they seem, and prophecies should not to be trusted...

THE CHILDREN OF THE GODS

DARK STRANGER

DARK ENEMY

Dark God

Unaware of the time bomb ticking inside her, Mia had lived the perfect life until it all came to a screeching halt, but despite the difficulties she faces, she doggedly pursues her dreams.

Once known as the god of knowledge and wisdom, Toven has grown cold and indifferent. Disillusioned with humanity, he travels the world and pens novels about the love he can no longer feel.

Seeking to escape his ever-present ennui, Toven gives a cutting-edge virtual experience a try. When his avatar meets Mia's, their sizzling virtual romance unexpectedly turns into something deeper and more meaningful.

Will it endure in the real world?

Toven might have failed in his attempts to improve humanity's condition, but he isn't going to fail to improve Mia's life, making it the best it can be despite her fragile health, and he can do that not as a god, but as a man who possesses the means, the smarts, and the determination to do it.

No effort is enough to repay Mia for reviving his deadened heart and making him excited for the next day, but the flip side of his reviviscence is the fear of losing its catalyst.

Given Mia's condition, Toven doesn't dare to over excite her. His venom is a powerful aphrodisiac, euphoric, and an all-around health booster, but it's also extremely potent. It might kill her instead of making her better.

61: Dark God Destinies Converge

Destinies converge, and secrets are revealed in part three of Mia and Toven's story.

Dark Whispers

62: Dark Whispers From The Past

A brilliant scientist and programmer, William lives for his work, but when he recruits a young bioinformatician to help him decipher the gods' genetic blueprints, he find himself smitten with more than just her brain.

A Ph.d at nineteen, Kaia is considered a prodigy and expects a bright future in academia. But when William invites her to join his secret research team, she accepts for reasons that have nothing to do with her career objectives. Wiliam's promise to look into her best friend's disappearance is an offer she just can't refuse.

63: Dark Whispers From Afar

William knows that his budding relationship with the nineteen-year-old Kaia will be frowned upon, but he's unprepared for her family's vehement opposition.

Family means everything to Kaia, so when she finds herself in the impossible position of having to choose between them and William, she resorts to unconventional means to resolve the conflict.

64: Dark Whispers From Beyond

The sacrifices Kaia and her family have to make for a chance of gaining immortality might tear them apart, and success is not guaranteed.

Is the dubious promise of eternal life worth the risk of losing everything?

DARK GAMBIT

65: DARK GAMBIT THE PAWN

Temporarily assigned to supervise a team of bioinformaticians, Marcel expects to spend a couple of weeks in the peaceful retreat of Safe Haven, enjoying Oregon Coast's cool weather and rugged beauty.

Things quickly turn chaotic when the retreat's director receives an email with an encoded message about a potential new threat to the clan.

While those in charge of security debate what to do next, Safe Haven's first ever paranormal retreat is about to begin, and one of the attendees is a mysterious woman who makes Marcel's heart beat faster whenever she's near.

Is the beautiful mortal his one truelove?

Or is she the harbinger of more bad news?

66: DARK GAMBIT THE PLAY

To get to Safe Haven's inner circle, the Kra-ell leader sacrifices a pawn. He does not expect her to reach the final rank and promote to a queen.

67: DARK GAMBIT RELIANCE

Marcel takes a big risk by telling Sofia his greatest sin. Can he trust her to keep it a secret? Or maybe it's time to confess his crime and submit to whatever punishment Edna deems appropriate?

Three miserable centuries of living with guilt and remorse are long enough.

Once the dust settles on the Kra-ell crisis, he will gather the courage to put himself at the court's mercy.

Dark Alliance

68: Dark Alliance Kindred Souls

69: Dark Alliance Turbulent Waters

70: Dark Alliance Perfect Storm

Dark Healing

71: Dark Healing Blind Justice

72: Dark Healing Blind Trust

73: Dark healing Blind Curve

Dark Encounters

74: Dark Encounters of the Close Kind

75: Dark Encounters of the Unexpected Kind

76: Dark Encounters of the Fated Kind

The Children of the Gods Series Sets

Books 1-3: Dark Stranger trilogy—Includes a bonus short story: The Fates take a Vacation

Books 4-6: Dark Enemy Trilogy —Includes a bonus short story—The Fates' Post-Wedding Celebration

MEGA SETS

INCLUDE CHARACTER LISTS

The Children of the Gods: Books 1-6

The Children of the Gods: Books 6.5-10

TRY THE SERIES ON

<u>AUDIBLE</u>

2 FREE audiobooks with your new Audible subscription!

PERFECT MATCH SERIES

Vampire's Consort

When Gabriel's company is ready to start beta testing, he invites his old crush to inspect its medical safety protocol.

Curious about the revolutionary technology of the *Perfect Match Virtual Fantasy-Fulfillment studios*, Brenna agrees.

Neither expects to end up partnering for its first fully immersive test run.

King's Chosen

When Lisa's nutty friends get her a gift certificate to *Perfect Match Virtual Fantasy Studios*, she has no intentions of using it. But since the only way to get a refund is if no partner can be found for her, she makes sure to request a fantasy so girly and over the top that no sane guy will pick it up.

Except, someone does.

> **Warning:** This fantasy contains a hot, domineering crown prince, sweet insta-love, steamy love scenes painted with light shades of gray, a wedding, and a HEA in both the virtual and real worlds.

> Intended for mature audience.

Captain's Conquest

Working as a Starbucks barista, Alicia fends off flirting all day long, but none of the guys are as charming and sexy as Gregg. His frequent visits are the highlight of her day, but since he's never asked her out, she assumes he's taken. Besides, between a day job and a budding music career, she has no time to start a new relationship.

That is until Gregg makes her an offer she can't refuse—a gift certificate to the virtual fantasy fulfillment service everyone is talking about. As a huge Star Trek fan, Alicia has a perfect match in mind—the captain of the Starship Enterprise.

The Thief Who Loved Me

When Marian splurges on a Perfect Match Virtual adventure as a world infamous jewel thief, she expects highwire fun with a hot partner who she will never have to see again in real life.

A virtual encounter seems like the perfect answer to Marcus's string of dating disasters. No strings attached, no drama, and definitely no love. As a die-hard James Bond fan, he chooses as his avatar a dashing MI6 operative, and to complement his adventure, a dangerously seductive partner.

Neither expects to find their forever Perfect Match.

My Merman Prince

The beautiful architect working late on the twelfth floor of my building thinks that I'm just the maintenance guy. She's also under the impression that I'm not interested.

Nothing could be further from the truth.

I want her like I've never wanted a woman before, but I don't play where I work.

I don't need the complications.

When she tells me about living out her mermaid fantasy with a stranger in a Perfect Match virtual adventure, I decide to do everything possible to ensure that the stranger is me.

THE DRAGON KING

To save his beloved kingdom from a devastating war, the Crown Prince of Trieste makes a deal with a witch that costs him half of his humanity and dooms him to an eternity of loneliness.

Now king, he's a fearsome cobalt-winged dragon by day and a short-tempered monarch by night. Not many are brave enough to serve in the palace of the brooding and volatile ruler, but Charlotte ignores the rumors and accepts a scribe position in court.

As the young scribe reawakens Bruce's frozen heart, all that stands in the way of their happiness is the witch's bargain. Outsmarting the evil hag will take cunning and courage, and Charlotte is just the right woman for the job.

My Werewolf Romeo

The father of my star student is a big-shot screenwriter and the patron of the drama department who thinks he can dictate what production I should put on. The principal makes it very clear that I need to cooperate with the opinionated asshat or walk away from my dream job at the exclusive private high school.

It doesn't help matters that the guy is single, hot, charming, creative, and seems to like me despite my thinly-veiled hostility.

When he invites me to a custom-tailored Perfect Match virtual adventure to prove that his screenplay is perfect for my production, I accept, intending to have fun while proving that messing with the classics is a foolish idea.

I don't expect to be wowed by his werewolf adaptation of Red Riding Hood mesh-up with Romeo and Juliet, and I certainly don't expect to fall in love with the virtual fantasy's leading man.

The Channeler's Companion

A treat for fans of *The Wheel of Time*.

When Erika hires Rand to assist in her pediatric clinic, she does so despite his good looks and irresistible charm, not because of them.

He's empathic, adores children, and has the patience of a saint.

He's also all she can think about, but he's off limits.

What's a doctor to do to scratch that irresistible itch without risking workplace complications?

A shared adventure in the Perfect Match Virtual Studios seems like the solution, but instead of letting the algorithm choose a partner for her, Erika can try to influence it to select the one she wants. Awarding Rand a gift certificate to the service will get him into their database, but unless Erika can tip the odds in her favor, getting paired with him is a long shot.

Hopefully, a virtual adventure based on her and Rand's favorite series will do the trick.

Note

Dear reader,

I hope my stories have added a little joy to your day. If you have a moment to add some to mine, you can help spread the word about the Children Of The Gods series by telling your friends and penning a review. Your recommendations are the most powerful way to inspire new readers to explore the series.

Thank you,

Isabell

FOR EXCLUSIVE PEEKS AT UPCOMING RELEASES & A FREE COMPANION BOOK

JOIN MY *VIP CLUB* AND GAIN ACCESS TO THE VIP PORTAL AT ITLUCAS.COM
TO JOIN, GO TO:
http://eepurl.com/blMTpD

INCLUDED IN YOUR FREE MEMBERSHIP:

YOUR VIP PORTAL

- READ PREVIEW CHAPTERS OF UPCOMING RELEASES.
- LISTEN TO GODDESS'S CHOICE NARRATION BY CHARLES LAWRENCE
- EXCLUSIVE CONTENT OFFERED ONLY TO MY VIPs.

FREE I.T. LUCAS COMPANION INCLUDES:

- GODDESS'S CHOICE PART I
- PERFECT MATCH: VAMPIRE'S CONSORT (A STANDALONE NOVELLA)
- INTERVIEW Q & A
- CHARACTER CHARTS

IF YOU'RE ALREADY A SUBSCRIBER, AND YOU ARE NOT GETTING MY EMAILS, YOUR PROVIDER IS

SENDING THEM TO YOUR JUNK FOLDER, AND YOU ARE MISSING OUT ON **IMPORTANT UPDATES, SIDE CHARACTERS' PORTRAITS, ADDITIONAL CONTENT, AND OTHER GOODIES.** TO FIX THAT, ADD isabell@itlucas.com TO YOUR EMAIL CONTACTS OR YOUR EMAIL VIP LIST.

Check out the specials at
https://www.itlucas.com/specials

Printed in Great Britain
by Amazon